CW01507165

# THE SALZBURG
# EXECUTIONER

# THE SALZBURG EXECUTIONER

## L.A. FATZINGER

CopertinaPezzi Publishing

Copyright © 2024 L.A. Fatzinger
A CopertinaPezzi Publishing Book
All Rights Reserved.

First Printing, 2024

**CopertinaPezzi Publishing**
An Evodince GmbH Imprint
Salzburg · Minneapolis

ISBN: 9798218456719
ISBN: 9798218456702
ISBN: BoD7MVLGJB

Excerpt from Rainer Maria Rilke, *Duino Elegies*, trans. Stephen Mitchell (New
York: Vintage International, 2009), 21

All rights reserved. No part of this book may be reproduced in any manner
whatsoever without written permission except in the case of brief quotations
embodied in critical articles and reviews.

# Copyright Notice

In accordance with the U.S. Copyright Act of 1976 and the European Union Directive on Copyright in the Digital Single Market (Directive (EU) 2019/790), the scanning, uploading, and electronic sharing of any part of this book without the permission of the publisher constitutes unlawful piracy and theft of the author's intellectual property. If you would like to use material from the book (other than for review purposes), prior written permission must be obtained by contacting the publisher at info@copertinapezzi.com. Thank you for supporting the author's rights.

\*\*\*

Gemäß dem US-amerikanischen Urheberrechtsgesetz von 1976 und der Richtlinie der Europäischen Union über das Urheberrecht im digitalen Binnenmarkt (Richtlinie (EU) 2019/790) stellt das Scannen, Hochladen und elektronische Teilen von Teilen dieses Buches ohne Genehmigung des Herausgebers eine rechtswidrige Piraterie und einen Diebstahl des geistigen Eigentums des Autors dar. Wenn Sie Material aus dem Buch verwenden möchten (außer zu Rezensionszwecken), müssen Sie eine vorherige schriftliche Genehmigung einholen, indem Sie den Verlag unter info@copertinapezzi.com kontaktieren. Vielen Dank, dass Sie die Rechte des Autors unterstützten.

\*\*\*

Conformément à la loi américaine sur le droit d'auteur de 1976 et à la directive de l'Union européenne sur le droit d'auteur dans le marché unique numérique (directive (UE) 2019/790), la numérisation, le téléchargement et le partage électronique de toute partie de ce livre sans l'autorisation de l'éditeur constituent un piratage illégal et un vol de la propriété intellectuelle de l'auteur. Si vous souhaitez utiliser des éléments de ce livre (autrement qu'à des fins de révision), vous devez obtenir une autorisation écrite préalable en contactant l'éditeur à l'adresse info@copertinapezzi.com. Merci de soutenir les droits de l'auteur.

# Contents

*Important Disclaimer* xiii

*Preamble* xv

1      1

2      14

3      23

4      32

5      40

6      48

7      54

8      57

9      64

10      70

11      73

12      76

13      81

14      86

15      92

16      98

17            104

18            114

19            119

20            122

21            125

22            129

23            133

24            137

25            143

26            149

27            155

28            159

29            162

30            168

31            170

32            173

33            176

34            180

35            184

36            186

37            194

38            198

39            200

40            205

Contents ~ ix

**41** 212

**42** 222

**43** 224

Mental Health Resources 231
Acknowledgements 235
About the Author 237

For my sons, Joshua and Daniel.
Always my teachers. Always my inspiration.

# Important Disclaimer

*The Salzburg Executioner* explores complex themes concerning technology's influence on human behavior and well-being, the moral and ethical issues of using algorithms to influence and control behavior, and the deep isolation that comes from living in a world that is always connected digitally. It explores the mental health of its characters, some of whom grapple with serious challenges, including depression and psychosis.

Readers should be aware that the book includes depictions of emotional distress, self-harm, and suicide. These elements are critical to the story's themes and are written solely with the intent of building understanding and engaging in conversation about these critical issues.

The author does not endorse or encourage any form of self-harm, unethical behavior, or illegal activities toward oneself or others. The actions and decisions of the characters are fictional representations intended to examine the moral complexities and consequences society must address in the age of rapid technological advancement.

**If you or someone you know is struggling with mental health issues, please seek assistance from a qualified professional immediately. A list of recommended mental health and suicide resources is included at the end of the novel.**

# Preamble

*Between the years 1328 and 1803, the Prince-Archbishopric of Salzburg stood on the European continent as an emblem of divine-right authority. A towering edifice of power built upon unyielding will and requiring unwavering obedience.*

*As a sovereign ruler and spiritual shepherd, the Prince-Archbishop controlled nearly every aspect of life, from baptism to funeral, veiled under layers of ceremony and secrecy. His word was indistinguishable from law, his edicts cloaked in the sanctity of God's will.*

*At this time, in this place, justice was not a light used to illuminate the truth. It was a sharp-edged instrument, impenetrable and cold. Forced confessions and torture were common. Guilt and innocence were rarely determined by reliable evidence or due process. Fear and control were justified as a fair price for maintaining order.*

*Frequent public executions served as entertainment and a less than subtle warning: rebellion shall find no fertile ground in the hearts and minds of the people. Paraded along gravel streets toward the outskirts of town, those condemned were taunted and spat upon as they lived out their final terrifying moments.*

*Upon arriving at the gallows, the final order having been read aloud to the cheering crowd, the execution was almost always carried out by an appointee of the Prince-Archbishop. He was called the Salzburg Executioner.*

*For over six hundred years, life for the people of Salzburg continued like this. Powerless to crack the mortar holding the stones of the Prince-Archbishop's opaque dominion together, fearful of meeting the executioner's blade if they tried.*

That is, until one executioner—the last appointed Executioner of Salzburg —began detailing his gruesome work in his personal diary. A diary that would ultimately shine the light of truth on the darkness of fear and oppression. And deliver Salzburg into an era of progress and enlightenment.

# I

SARA'S FACE APPEARED WHITE AND STILL, lying on the surface of the makeup table. Before fading into black, she carefully positioned her head on her crossed arms, facing the double doors of the bedroom —doors he would walk through later that night.

Until her last breath, she made every effort to keep her cerulean eyes open, illuminated by the overhead lighting in their renovated Queen Anne craftsman home, just north of downtown Seattle. Eyes that were lifeless but somehow still glistening and focused.

Focused the way they were as she squatted into ready position during a co ed softball game near Green Lake, eyeing the batter blithely through his warm-up swings at home plate. James was a tall, slightly lanky, but still muscular left-handed batter. His early contact on the first swing careened the ball down the third-base line. With no time to react, it struck Sara squarely on her ankle.

Instead of running to first base as her body collapsed under the pain, he ran to the woman he didn't know, gushing with apologies and offering aid. His teammates scoffed as he carried her to his SUV, and then to urgent care, instead of staying in the game.

Remaining by her side as X-rays confirmed the broken ankle, James gingerly helped Sara back into his vehicle after her cast and crutches had been fitted. He made sure she was settled in at her apartment until a friend arrived to take over through the night. Before leaving, he asked Sara if six hours of apologies were enough to earn another chance at an introduction. She said she'd decide only when the pain, and the meds, subsided. Two days later, it had. And she gave him another chance.

The courtship between James Wohlmuth and Sara Hauser began on a couch, in sweatpants. Binge-watching Netflix, rotating ice packs, and hours of good conversation. As weeks passed, the pain of her injury receded, and fate took over. The glisten of her eyes returned.

Her eyes glistened again the evening James dropped to one knee and proposed to her on the very spot where the softball had brought her to her knees two years earlier. She laughed out loud at the randomness of the ball's trajectory and where it led them.

"Yes!" she screamed into the overcast early evening sky above Seattle. After a long kiss and a deep stare, they walked, hands interlaced and swinging, to a Thai restaurant nearby. A group of friends eagerly waited for the proposal's outcome and, fingers crossed, to celebrate their engagement.

"Just two years ago I shattered her ankle, and she still said 'yes!'" James declared as they arrived.

Cheers and hugs filled the room. In an era of creepy dating apps and increased isolation, theirs was an example of an in real life meeting and courtship gone right. Platters of basil chicken, red curry, and bottles of Singha lager flowed freely, fueling the party.

Later that evening, glasses rang with the sound of spoons and chopsticks tapping their sides. The music stopped, and the room quieted to murmurs.

Vik Gruber, James's college roommate, co-ed softball teammate, and partner in the tech company they co-founded, stood in front of the group. Visibly intoxicated.

"I'd just like to say, James, where are you, buddy, where are you? Oh, there you are," his impaired voice producing audible auto-correct fails.

"James—never hit a ball that hard before the night he met Sara. And, as we've all seen this season, will probably never hit one that hard again." The attempt at a toast interrupted by laughter, scattered "boos," and one "Sit down, Vik!"

"But with Sara, my friend," he concluded, "you really hit the ball out of the park. I love you both. To James and Sara! Prost!"

The room filled with applause and rolling eyes, as the song "Celebration" by Kool and The Gang distorted through the tinny in-ceiling speakers. In the midst of the noise and laughter, arm in arm, they gazed at each other, her eyes glistening.

The same way they glistened the following year on their wedding day. Her confidence and independence, reinforced by her parents visible in the pews down the steps and to her right. Her two sisters and three best friends falling in behind her in the sanctuary. A heart and soul flowing through her hands into his, and vice versa.

* * *

Looking into her deep, wide eyes, everyone could see a long tunnel of potential and opportunity. Sara excelled in high school, carrying her varsity volleyball team to the state championships senior year. She graduated summa cum laude, securing a generous list of offers from top universities.

Four years later, she graduated from the University of Colorado. A business major with a minor in communications. Balancing her academics with membership in a sorority. Volleyball in the fall and internships in the summer.

At graduation, her father glowed, levitated by pride and confidence in the beautiful young woman he had nurtured and protected. Humbled and grounded by what she had accomplished on her own.

Her mother exuded the same level of pride. But the emotion originated from a different place. More driven. More rigid. Solution-oriented and determined.

Independent, smart, and driven, Sara Hauser emerged into adulthood in an image and likeness her mother had architected and forged since she could walk. Mom was that way with all three of her girls. But with Sara, the youngest, her job was complete.

The Hausers were well-to-do and traditional, living in the upper-middle-class neighborhood of Highland Park, north of Chicago. None of the girls were overly spoiled. Parents paid for college, but with a condition: after graduation, each daughter was given a classic Cartier watch with *"Always my little girl—I love you. Dad,"* inscribed on the back, and enough money for three months' living expenses.

The first, a reminder from a sentimental father that he would always brood over their well-being and never fully let go. The second, a reminder from a driven mother. That independence and self-sufficiency come from determination, resolve—and a hard stop on the calendar.

Prior to graduation, Sara was offered three management training roles within well-respected companies. Accepting an offer from Ascendia, a fast-growing technology consultancy firm. And she declined the 'get on your feet' stipend from her parents. Her signing bonus afforded enough to furnish a small, one-bedroom apartment in the Lake Union district of Seattle, within walking distance of her office.

Just weeks after setting foot on her career path, she cultivated colleagues into friends, bonded by long hours, endless meetings, lunches, and late dinners delivered by bicycle and scooter to the ground-floor reception desk of Ascendia's Seattle offices.

Each year, she and her college sorority sisters would make trips to hip destinations—Napa Valley, Santa Fe, Savannah, and Sun Valley. Every trip was fully documented in social media posts, check-ins, reviews, and photos. Videos were touched up, retouched, clipped, and edited with cinematic precision. Appended with stickers, labels, and gifs before uploading.

Between long hours at the office and milestone trips, Sara continually documented her life online. Her social media posts highlighted overpriced theme meals, concerts in the park, sporting events, work parties, birthday celebrations, and an increasing number of destination weddings. A perpetual online documentary of hard work and ample discretionary income. Validation she sought and earned. Sprinkled in with a tinge of resentment toward her mother—a woman so structured, who held such high expectations.

For everyone to bear witness, Sara's videos, images, words, likes, and comments said, "Look at me. I've done everything right. And I am my own woman."

* * *

There would be no social media post of this moment. The moment Sara's body abruptly jolted in the chair. The last reflex of a human's natural instinct to survive, no matter what the cost. Fighting to emerge from impending lifelessness and carry on living.

Even though the eleven-week-old fetus inside her had not.

Anticipation of parenthood began a few years prior, when Sara and James returned to Seattle one Friday night from separate business trips.

After dinner with a small group of friends over Reuben sandwiches, kettle chips, and tall lagers at the Queen Anne Ale House, the couple walked briskly home. Bursting through the front door, James rushed up the stairs to the bathroom adjacent to their bedroom.

Several minutes later, Sara entered, wearing PJs. She quickly washed her face and applied toothpaste to her sophisticated ultrasonic toothbrush.

While brushing, her eyes met his through the reflection in the mirror.

"Eihem whait."

James peered up from his smartphone, a beer-buzz grin on his face, admiring her beautiful face and incomprehensible words.

"What was that?" he asked.

Sara leaned to the sink, maintaining eye contact through the mirror as she spat.

As she wiped her mouth, she uttered, "I said, 'I'm late.'"

Sunday morning, with James first to the bathroom, Sara again entered. While brushing, she met his eyes through the reflection in the mirror.

"Eihm pfruhrehgnuhnt."

James didn't need her to repeat the words.

That afternoon, the glowing couple video-chatted with Sara's two sisters, already mothers themselves. Followed by calls to her parents and his widowed mother.

At ten weeks, when the initial ultrasound confirmed a fetal heartbeat, Sara posted the first unmistakable image to her social media profiles. In an instant, her extended circle of friends, distant relatives, and ex-boyfriends knew about the pregnancy, resulting in hundreds of likes and comments.

Deep within the computer systems of the most powerful technology companies in the world, Sara's demographic and advertising preferences were updated: educated, high-income, well-traveled woman. Now, first-time expectant mother.

Late one evening, tucked under crisp white sheets and a down comforter, Sara read an article she'd found online related to pregnancy nutrition. Next to her, James responded to work emails. Sara closed her laptop and turned to him. Eyes beaming and her hair glowing.

"It's hard to describe, this feeling of euphoria," she said. "If people could bottle and sell it—"

"Yes. It would be called cocaine," James murmured while smiling, still typing.

"Stop!" she said, lightly slapping his forearm. "I'm being serious!"

The slap was enough to turn his attention.

"I can see it in you, love," he responded, holding his stare just a moment longer than necessary. Enough to let her know he was, in fact, hearing her. "Millions of years of human evolution, thanking you for your hard work. Ensuring continued survival of the human species. That's what you're feeling."

His response coating the dry, practical nature of his personality with an empathetic side she helped him hone over the years.

She rolled her eyes at his response, still euphoric.

Baby's room had been painted a subtle, warm yellow. Named "Golden Cradle" by the small craft paint manufacturer in Vermont. A company Sara found while searching the internet for environmentally friendly interior house paint, safe for babies.

She scoured review sites and discussion forums before selecting a high-end crib, changing table, and rocking chair. The link to their on-line baby registry was shared by email, text message, and on social media profiles with friends and family. Offers appeared in her inbox: stem-cell cryogenic freezing, college savings accounts, and children's life insurance. Catalogs filled their mailbox attached to their house. All visually clamoring for a share of the expectant parent's high-limit credit cards.

And yet, just after the first trimester, Sara suffered a miscarriage. For any one of the million possible reasons, her body rejected the delicate, uncertain process of a new pregnancy.

The news left Sara and James stunned and reeling.

\* \* \*

Several days later, James arranged a quiet weekend at a small inn on Whidbey Island, northwest of Seattle. Free from devices and the sympathetic intrusions of friends and family. It offered Sara a few days to rest and think. And to let her body naturally adjust as the pregnancy hormones ebbed.

Search engines and social media sites, however, continued to assume a newborn baby would arrive in the coming months. Algorithms were still waiting for the order for a fifteen-hundred-dollar stroller and bassinet she'd researched in the weeks prior.

Notifications from forums and blogs continued chirping incessantly on her phone. Reminders of a planned future that had vanished. It left Sara caught between a body beginning to heal and a digital world oblivious to her loss.

\* \* \*

Learning of the second pregnancy, Sara found herself overcome with fear of another miscarriage. She did her best to remain positive. James found himself more pragmatic. More guarded.

A thin layer of translucence formed between them during the early weeks. Playfulness was more subdued. Caution was unconsciously added to conversations, in an attempt to avoid feelings of doubt and fear.

James would smile when asking how she was feeling. She would smile back, fine, you know. They wanted to believe they could read each other's minds. But they weren't quite certain they were.

This time, they waited a few additional weeks to announce the pregnancy to family. And several more still for close friends.

As a precaution, an ultrasound was scheduled at eight weeks. James by her side, alternating glances between the screen, the technician, Sara's face, and her hand. While Sara alternated glances between the screen and the technician, pining to gauge any clues in body language or voice.

With the test concluded, the OB/GYN asked to meet the couple privately. The fetus was measuring small. The heartbeat was weak. There was a chance, though—a reason to have hope.

"Come back next week and we'll run another ultrasound."

When they did, the heartbeat was gone.

\* \* \*

Now the curse had a name: mosaicism. A rare and nearly impossible-to-detect genetic condition when one person has two genetically different types of cells within their body. Which, when passed to a fetus, can cause severe developmental anomalies, and eventually, miscarriage.

Sara's OB/GYN suggested additional tests and resources to help the couple better understand the condition that led to the same outcome, now suffered twice. The nature of their conversations changed. Phrases like "trouble conceiving," "complicated pregnancy," and "I just feel terrible for them" passed through the minds, mouths, and ears of friends and loved ones.

Every term Sara absorbed during a doctor's appointment or from a reputable friend later became an entry in search engines and discussion forums.

Months dragged on as well-meaning friends with their own young children offered personal experiences and perspectives. Some valid. Some bizarre. Some to take the empty space of not knowing what else to say.

While Sara and James remained open to the possibility of natural childbirth—someday, somehow—the baby's room, painted its Golden Cradle yellow, became a place for boxes of bills, bank statements, and tax returns, stacked next to clothes out of season or no longer worn.

* * *

When the pregnancy test showed the "+" sign a third time, Sara and James accepted the news—not in the bathroom with a mouthful of toothpaste, but standing in the kitchen, gazing at the test on the granite countertop.

Muted, cautious enthusiasm, followed by a long hug and a quiet dinner.

Real life had kicked in. Not the one she presented on social media. Their fear of another unsuccessful outcome dampened the celebration, knowing how difficult, frustrating, and rare human procreation actually is.

Only immediate family would be informed this time, they decided. And not until the second trimester.

At eight weeks, their spirits were lifted by a positive initial ultrasound, confirming the size of the fetus and viability of the pregnancy.

In the background, Sara felt different. She couldn't put a finger as to why. Enthusiastic but not elated. Fatigued but not exhausted. Occasionally forlorn, but the flow generally countered the ebbs.

*Maybe it's because this child will finally carry to term?* she thought to herself. *Maybe because something is wrong that the doctors aren't seeing? Or saying?*

To keep distracted, feed her need for answers, and retain the sense of control her mother had instilled, Sara spent an increasing number of hours on the internet, reading and discussing symptoms, outcomes, studies, and clinical trials related to at-risk pregnancies. Searching for videos, posting messages of support, commenting on the validity of snake oil remedies and affirmations.

Wanting to believe the water in Seattle was safe, but wondering if user @DesprMama, claiming she worked for the State of Washington, was actually onto something. The more she scrolled, the more it exposed her to new sources, new sites, and new terms to search.

Even when she had to be up for work in three hours, Sara stayed online. Like everyone else with a green dot next to their username, she scrolled. Consuming one more video, reading one more post. Wanting to believe the answer or remedy was out there, just below the next flick of her thumb.

On video calls and meetings. In airport boarding areas and waiting rooms of medical offices. During evenings at home when James was traveling. Or in hotels when she was alone. She searched and consumed. A near-constant stream of information and visuals continuously filling the screens of her smartphone, tablet, and laptop.

Eight weeks into her pregnancy, Sara sat in the exit row window seat on a flight from Minneapolis to Seattle, using the few minutes before departure to touch base with her mother.

"'Therapy through knowledge.' That's what you said when they found that cyst," Sara whispered forcefully as the flight attendant requested all devices be switched to airplane mode. "How many clinics did you visit before you allowed yourself—and Dad—a good night's sleep? You know I'm not looking for a miracle, Mom. I just want to make sure I'm taking every precaution, researching, asking questions, reading everything I can. It's the only thing I feel like I have control over right now. Wouldn't you do the same if you were me?"

Sara paused as her mother attempted to lower the unusual intensity and agitation her daughter was exhibiting, drawing concerning glances from the other passengers in her row.

"Yes, I know you were pregnant at a different time. Now we have the internet. You didn't go through what I'm going through emotionally.

THE SALZBURG EXECUTIONER ~ 11

It's exhausting. Everything about your pregnancies was easier. No, I'm not making light of Ginny's breach, Mother, you know that. Besides, isn't this what you taught me? As in, drilled into me? 'An ounce of preparation,' was it?"

A passing flight attendant signaled with a hand to her ear that it was time to conclude the call.

"I don't know why you're telling me to take a break, Mother. A break from what? My mind doesn't take breaks. I'll take a break when I'm holding a healthy baby. Like you did, three times. Or maybe when all of this just—stops. I have to go. No, the flight's departing. I'll call you some other time. I don't know when, maybe this weekend. Okay. Bye, Mom. Bye."

The man sitting next to Sara could hear her concerned mother talking, even after the phone pulled away from her ear.

* * *

Five days prior to her passing, James tried to calm his agitated and anxiety-ridden wife. He was late leaving for the airport, flying to his company's annual conference in Orlando. The efforts were futile.

"Just go," she shouted at James from the kitchen as he stood at the front door. "I'm not making this up. It feels like something more than that. Go to your fucking conference. I've been going through this one entirely by myself. No, the doctor didn't say that; he said the likelihood was low. Don't *love* me—you weren't there. I'm not overreacting. I've barely seen you in weeks. Don't manipulate what I heard or how I'm feeling; I get enough of that shit from my mother. Fine. No, I'm not going anywhere this afternoon. Why should it matter? Yes, I heard you. You, too. Bye."

James hesitated at the door, glancing back at Sara. Her face was pale, her arms crossed tightly over her chest. For a moment, he considered canceling the trip. The sound and sight of the car's trunk opening re-focused his attention, and he let the door close behind him.

Later in the day, Sara began to feel cramps. Over the phone, her sisters listened to her vent, cry, and push back any attempt at encouragement.

"Do you want one of us to come out until James gets back?" they asked.

"No, I'm fine. I'll be fine," she responded.

Sara paced between the couch and the kitchen before spending the remainder of the day on the couch, scrolling again. On Netflix. Alternating binge-series episodes with darker films: *Prevenge*, *False Positive*, and *The Hand that Rocks the Cradle*.

Monday morning, she sent a message to her team that she would be working remotely for a few days. She closed the internal chat and email apps and placed her phone on Do Not Disturb.

The elements defining her sense of professional pride, identity, and accomplishment had been fully muted. Her friends and family had been pushed to the side. Her husband's attention directed to his company's conference. Now she could continue the one activity she felt she could fully control: reading, scrolling, researching, and replying. Thousands of posts, videos, and search results enveloping her consciousness, becoming one with the feeling in her belly and her heart.

Falling asleep at nearly four in the morning on top of her bed, she woke hours later to spots of blood in the same sweatpants she wore the previous day. Staring out the kitchen window for an hour, holding a cup of coffee she didn't drink, she called the clinic to report her symptoms. Expecting her OB/GYN or nurse to tell her to drop everything and come in as soon as possible.

"Friday? Friday? Are you fucking kidding me? Why Friday? It's Tuesday!"

She already knew what they wouldn't say over the phone. It was over.

Just as her husband was likely concluding his presentation in a convention hall in Orlando, she walked upstairs, sat on the bench at the foot of their bed, and allowed the blood to soak through her pajamas into the plush fabric. The bed she remained in, along with her mobile phone and her laptop, for the remainder of the day and all day Wednesday. Ignoring the check-in calls and texts from James, her sisters, and her parents.

On Thursday afternoon, she stood in front of their bathroom mirror, closing her persuasive eyes and tilting her head back, a handful of prescription medications stung her throat as it was washed down by a half-full glass of Grey Goose vodka, locked in with a dose of cyclizine she'd taken an hour prior, prescribed before a family cruise taken years ago to prevent motion sickness and vomiting, the whole thing a lethal cocktail she'd researched, honed and perfected while reading morbid, unmoderated online forums, frequented by adolescent girls crying for help after a bad breakup or a cruel stint of body shaming, the perfect mixture, as she walked to her makeup table, sat down and laid her head, ingested and dissolved by the vodka, gastric enzymes and hydrochloric acid in her stomach, held down by the anti-nausea meds, making its way into her bloodstream, gripping, slowing, and finally bringing to a halt an otherwise perfectly healthy human life, as her thirty-four-year-old lungs exhaled, one final time.

A moment later, Sara's smartphone vibrated in double pulses. With each pulse, it moved closer to the nightstand's edge before tumbling onto the cream-colored carpet. A few seconds later, a ting sounded on the device from an incoming text message.

*"Hey babe—tried to call you. Boarding my flight out of Orlando. W/ exception of one minor mishap on my part at the end—conference went really well. We are delayed an hour. Pilot says she'll try to make up time in the air. lol Should be home by 10ish. We're going to figure all this out, okay? Promise. I love you. J."*

# 2

Three days before Sara ended her own life, more than one thousand technology company executives, programmers, and journalists cheered inside the main hall of a convention center in Orlando, as the chief executive officer of EchoWave concluded his opening remarks and walked off the stage.

James took the stage, a sea of anonymous faces illuminated purple by the LED lights and screens behind him. His face, by contrast, was pale under the glare of spotlights. At the same hour, Sara awakened at home to spots in her sweatpants.

"This—this is really incredible," he declared into the microphone, attempting to speak over the raucous applause. "Thank you all for traveling to Orlando for EchoWave's sixth-annual Co-Inference!"

"My name is James Wohlmuth, co-founder and vice president of Advanced Research at EchoWave, and I'm super pumped for what we have in store for you over the next three days."

James was well out of his comfort zone in front of a crowd so large. Though his words sounded extemporaneous, they had been carefully orchestrated and rehearsed dozens of times over the previous two months, each sentence crafted to convey maximum persuasive intonation.

"This year, you've traveled from thirty-five U.S. states and twenty-nine countries," he continued.

He had used the company's public speaking training to deliver his remarks with poise and confidence, but no amount of training could take his mind off his wife and the way he had left her just two days ago.

"That you've traveled from around the globe validates what we already know: EchoWave's *Preferences to Personalization* technology platform is key to delivering the social, search, and video experiences your users have come to expect."

Giant screens behind him transitioned to an animated map of the world, dotted with labels denoting the cities and countries from which attendees hailed. The brief pause gave him a moment to sip water and wipe his sweaty hands and brow with a towel.

When the spotlights returned to him, he continued.

"Before we kick off this year's conference, I want to thank Michael Valeno, EchoWave's Chairman and CEO, for his vision, leadership, and commitment to our success. During his tenure, EchoWave has grown fivefold, to a team of over six hundred professionals serving more than three hundred global partners. This includes social media platforms, search engines, e-commerce sites, governments, and other organizations. And we've raised almost six hundred million dollars in venture capital and private equity. None of this would have been possible, Michael, without you."

The audience's applause thundered like heavy rain on a steel roof. Amidst the noise, James allowed his thoughts to drift back to Seattle. She was struggling, isolated in their empty home. He struggled to maintain composure in front of a sea of strangers.

Michael emerged from the side of the stage, waving to the crowd before turning and walking backward. He stopped abruptly, placing his hands together in a namaste-like gesture toward the crowd, then toward James, silently mouthing, *Thank you. Thank you all.*

The teleprompter facing James read: [JAMES: Pause 30 sec for MICHAEL audience applause]. A timer next to it counted down the remaining seconds allotted for the session.

"As many of you know," James resumed, "Vik Gruber and I began working on the original EchoWave algorithms—what was it, Vik? Twelve years ago?" He gestured toward his longtime friend and Duke University roommate seated in the first row of the audience.

After Vik nodded and waved in agreement, James continued, finally finding tempo in his delivery.

"Our goal is to push the edge of what's possible in personalized online behavior prediction and persuasion. So without further delay—are you ready?"

The audience of t-shirt-wearing engineers and fleece-vested executives began dancing like water on a flame as pulsing electronic beats filled the room.

"This week, we're going to show you the technology, tools, and best practices you need to squeeze every last penny of profit and every last minute of engagement from your users!"

With the last breaths of manufactured enthusiasm James could muster, he projected from his diaphragm as he had been coached.

"I can't hear you! Are you ready?"

The crowd whistled and cheered in a frenzy.

"Welcome to EchoWave Co-Inference!" James shouted into the microphone as music filled the room and lights spun.

Then, like laser-guided missiles, the attendees filed out of the convention room, targeting career advancement, industry influence, stock price increases, media scoops, or perhaps a one-night stand.

* * *

"How long have you been down here?" Vik asked James, who was sitting alone at the breakfast area staged for two hundred VIP guests.

"Since about 5:30, when they started setting up. It was the only place I could smell coffee," James responded.

"Why the hell so early?"

"I wasn't sleeping anyway. I'm getting cryptic responses to texts I send Sara when I check in with her. Then Michael emailed last-minute changes to my product roadmap presentation at one this morning. I was up."

"Sorry to hear about Sara. She'll be fine, I'm sure," Vik said dismissively. "As for the technical details, the legal team in Munich got some negative feedback from European regulators on privacy late last night.

I haven't fully reviewed it, but it could just be an overabundance of caution on Michael's part. He's expecting some key media today, so just play along."

"Got it. So I remove these issues for the conference and the press, only to add them back in next week?" James asked, rubbing his temples in frustration.

"Listen, Michael's taken companies public twice before. We're just the algo-jockeys," Vik laughed, glancing toward the door.

"I'm sure Sara will be thrilled when I tell her I'm just an algo-jockey," James muttered.

Vik grinned but didn't disagree. "Alright, I've got to wrap a few things up before the day gets going. Let me know if you need anything."

"Will do," James acknowledged without looking up.

"My advice to you: Never eat at a Mexican restaurant picked by Chinese customers, especially in a seedy part of Orlando," Vik quipped on his way to the doors.

"Excellent advice," James replied dryly, before calling out, "Vik! Hang on a sec."

"James, I really need to—"

"Loan me your laptop charger, will you? Mine's in the room, and I don't have time to go upstairs before the conference starts."

Vik opened his backpack and tossed a bag of cables and chargers toward James.

"Take the whole thing," Vik said, continuing out the doors. "Just bring it to the office tomorrow. There's no way I'm working on the flight home tonight."

Attendees began taking their seats for the final session of the conference as James stood at the side of the stage. He snapped a selfie with a mock-terrified expression and sent it to Sara with the message: *"Wish me luck! Home stretch! See you soon! Xo."*

A deep breath steadied him as he walked onto the stage to present EchoWave's product roadmap. Glancing at the teleprompter, he dutifully recited, "Everyone knows we save the best for last at these things."

The doors of the large room closed as two massive screens illuminated the title of his presentation:

*One Step Closer*
*The EchoWave Roadmap*
*AI in Algorithmic Personalization and*
*Behavior Modification*

"EchoWave pioneered algorithmic prediction technology almost a decade ago, which is why all the leading social networks, video-sharing sites, and search engines on the planet use our technology to drive real business outcomes for users and stakeholders. The proof is in the results: our partners continually see dramatic increases in user engagement and ad performance year after year," James read from his prepared remarks.

The presentation captivated the audience, flaunting buzz phrases and techie terms that sounded like sweet music in the ears of those in the room, but like static noise to anyone outside the industry.

"The EchoWave value proposition is simple and clear," James continued. "We give our partners the tools to maintain proprietary control over their users while discovering new insights and democratizing combined behavioral data to improve engagement and advertising performance."

The lights dimmed as large video screens displayed an elaborate animation detailing the company's future plans. A pre-recorded audio track of James's voice afforded him a brief reprieve to wipe the perspiration from his hands and check his phone. Still no response from Sara.

"A social media user, let's call him John Smith, is interested in gardening. On John's favorite social network, let's call it Network A, he posts photos of planting tools and seedlings he's starting in his kitchen. He's active on various gardening groups and likes and comments when his friends post pictures and videos of their own gardening activities."

The presentation revealed how EchoWave's artificial intelligence could predict a person's behavior by piecing together fragments of data from other search engines and social media platforms—even if users believed they had declined to share their data.

"The more time users spend on each of your platforms," James explained, "the more ads users see in their feeds or search results. By aligning content recommendations and advertising preferences, we're seeing engagement increases of twenty to thirty percent. For many of you in this room, that translates to hundreds of millions of additional revenue per year. Combined across all EchoWave customers, these advancements could translate into billions of new revenues."

The audience broke into enthusiastic applause. James felt a wave of relief, like a fish released back into water.

"We've been working hard on AI behavior prediction for years, and it's my great privilege to announce that this next generation of EchoWave technology is already operating within our network and will be fully deployed to all our partners by the end of the summer."

As the audience applauded, James scanned the room, spotting reporters and key industry players mingling among EchoWave's executives. The Q&A session began, and several attendees queued up at microphones placed in the aisles.

"Good morning, James. I'm Julie Frager with the Wall Street Chronicle," a confident voice called out.

"Hi, Julie. Glad to see you stayed until the very end," James replied, smiling. "What's your question?"

"Thank you. I'm curious. What exactly do you know about me?"

James hesitated. "I'm sorry? Not much, other than I really respect your work—and, of course, your coverage of EchoWave over the past several years."

The audience laughed quietly at James's lightly patronizing tone, but Julie's expression didn't budge.

"That's not what I meant," she clarified. "Let me rephrase. In EchoWave's computer systems, what information tied directly to my identity are you collecting, processing, and storing—specifically?"

The room grew quieter. Seconds after letting his guard down, James's media training kicked back in. His pulse quickened as he spotted Michael Valeno standing near the back of the room, watching intently.

"Well, Julie," James began, "I wouldn't know. Technically, you're anonymous to us. No offense."

"None taken," Julie replied, her tone sharp. "But many of your partners know exactly who I am. I use my real name on my favorite social media and video sharing sites. And from what I've learned at this conference, much of the data they collect is shared with you—regardless of the privacy settings I've chosen."

James's smile grew tight. "Well, that depends on the EchoWave partner. They all have different agreements with EchoWave. And whatever data is shared with us is clearly outlined in their terms of service agreements. Of course, any user can opt out of sharing data with EchoWave at any time."

"Sure they can," Julie said, her sarcasm apparent. "But your company is still collecting and storing a massive amount of data on all of us. In fact, you probably know me better than my husband does—without even knowing my name, as you say."

James glanced at Michael again, searching for a cue. "I'm sorry, Julie. There are several people behind you waiting to ask questions. Why don't we continue this conversation when the session concludes?"

Julie didn't budge.

"My question, Mr. Wohlmuth, is this: now that EchoWave has access to so much data from so many partners, does the addition of complex AI technology cross the line? Are we still talking about predicting behavior for 'advertising effectiveness,' or are we now talking about manipulating behavior for other purposes—commercial or otherwise?"

Michael strode onto the stage with a measured smile, placing a hand on James's shoulder.

"Julie, I agree with James that your question deserves a detailed answer. I suggest we continue this conversation when the session concludes. I also invite anyone else interested in the important topic of user privacy to join us. EchoWave has nothing to hide regarding how our technology drives positive outcomes for our partners."

"With all due respect, Michael—" Julie continued.

"Next question, please?" Michael interrupted smoothly, gesturing to the next person in line.

With a frustrated shake of her head, Julie returned to her seat.

"Michael and James, hi! I'm Brittney Johnson, and I work in marketing communications at—" the next attendee began.

James nodded and smiled, but his mind was still replaying Julie's pointed questions and the uneasy silence that followed.

James, drained of energy, finally crossed the finish line and could return home.

"This has been the most informative, productive, and innovative Co-Inference we've hosted to date. Please mark your calendars for the seventh annual Co-Inference; to be held in San Diego next year! Thank you, everyone!" James declared, his voice hoarse.

As sterile white lights illuminated the room, attendees began filing out toward taxis, Ubers, and the airport. Crews started folding chairs and rolling carts as the buzz of the conference began to fade.

James stood near the stage with Michael, leaning against the wall with his arms crossed. He waited for Michael to chastise him for letting the script deviate, his nerves still frayed.

"You saved me up there, Michael. I don't know how—" James began.

"Don't worry about that blip on the radar," Michael interrupted. "Everyone in this room knows their users, engagement, and profits will grow once they deploy what you and your team keep developing. You're a machine, James. That's what matters. By the time these people reach the airport, they'll be talking about their own roadmaps—not some busy-bee reporter's questions."

James stared at the floor, wanting to believe Michael's reassurance but still kicking himself over the blip.

"And James," Michael added, giving him a soft slap on the cheek and pat on the shoulder, "just yesterday, the chairman of the Wall Street Chronicle's parent company signed a contract to become an EchoWave strategic investor. I think we're going to be just fine."

James exhaled, a smirk breaking across his face. "You're a genius, Michael."

"I know," Michael said with a grin. "See you tomorrow."

# 3

One week and one day after finding his pregnant wife of seven years lifeless in their bedroom, James sat in the front row of chairs laid out on an expansive lawn overlooking Lake Michigan. The weather was unseasonably warm for early March in Chicago, in the mid-sixties, allowing for Sara Hauser-Wohlmuth's celebration of life to take place outside.

Surrounding him were his mother and brother, Sara's two sisters and their husbands, Sara's mother, Patricia, and father, Dieter, his Echo-Wave co-founder Vik and his wife. Two hundred other family members and friends fell in behind, still in disbelief. James sat, hunched over, his shoulders slumped as if bearing the weight of everyone present.

James glanced down at his black suit jacket, white shirt, and black tie; he couldn't remember the last time he'd worn a tie. Probably a funeral. In his professional and personal world, ties were a noose reserved for the end of life.

He then raised his head slightly to the pedestal, holding the polished urn and a large photo of Sara under a trellis of flowers: lilies, roses, and hydrangeas. Flanking it were pictures of her with him and with her family.

Looking across the grandness of Lake Michigan and up to the sky, massive cumulonimbus clouds seemed to spell out W H Y ? in their white and silver plumes.

Repeating in his head were the clues and cues he could have—must have—missed in the prior weeks and months.

As the minister began the memorial with a prayer and a reading from scripture, James's mind drifted back to that night.

The short, cryptic texts all week. The unanswered call he made when his plane landed. The sound of the Uber door closing in the light Seattle rain, followed by the pleasant but weary "Good night" he uttered as the car pulled away. His footsteps up the short walkway, noticing the lights still on inside. The sound of keys in the front pocket of his backpack. The lock turning, and the door opening with a squeal; a tiny chore he would attend to Saturday. The thud of his carry-on dropping in the entryway.

And his voice, calling out her name.

"Sara?"

The ting sound of the bottle cap on the granite countertop after opening a beer to unwind. Thinking to himself, *what she is going through is normal; the baby is going to be fine.* And the sound of his shoes as he walked up the stairs to greet and comfort her in their bedroom.

*"That flight was just terrible, Sara, I'm sorry I'm home late, Sara, are you alright, Sara, what are you doing at your makeup table, Sara, my God breathe, Sara, where's my phone, Sara, hold on babe I'm calling for help, Sara, yes it's an emergency, Sara, yes the address is, Sara, I don't know what happened I just got home, Sara, no she's not breathing, Sara, please come quickly, Sara, just get here as fast as you can, Sara, I don't know, I don't know, Sara, please no, Sara, no, Sara, no, Sara, no, no, no!"*

James blinked out of his trance and refocused on the tearful eulogies read by her sisters, friends, and colleagues. When they finished, he stood, walked to the black urn, and rested his hand on it briefly before standing at the podium.

He looked at his family and the mass of people behind, trying to make a connection. For him and for them. Most were wearing sunglasses, preventing him from seeing their heartbreak and guilt. Or was it their blame toward him? It felt like he was looking in the dark.

He took a breath.

James had delivered countless presentations in his career. Introverted and reserved, he despised every one of them. As EchoWave grew, speaking in front of groups didn't get easier. He just had more resources to help him prepare.

Sara was the extrovert, the planner. And most importantly, the coach. Talking him down from his frequent bouts of anxiety as his role in the company he co-founded—and the industry—continued to grow.

Here he was standing in front of a large audience again. Not only without Sara by his side or the promise of being with her when he arrived home. Today, his words would enshrine her absence forever.

"Nerdy guys like me aren't supposed to wind up—with women like Sara," he began. The congregation of family and friends smiled and nodded, lowering the tension.

When James concluded his remarks, he returned to the seat between his mother and his father-in-law, both of whom set a hand on each of his knees as he wiped his eyes.

Reaching into his suit coat pocket for sunglasses, he noticed a large Cartier watch on his father-in-law's right wrist—similar to the watches each of his daughters had received after graduating college.

*I had one job in the world when this man offered me his blessing to take his daughter's hand in marriage,* James thought. *And that was to protect her. Through health, sickness, and everything in between. And I failed.*

The minister returned to the podium to speak.

"When one of God's children passes in such a tragic manner, it can be difficult, if not impossible, to comprehend. Each of you undoubtedly will think and pray if there was something you could have done. You may ask why you weren't the person she reached out to for help. Or why you hadn't reached out to her in her greatest moment of need. These feelings of guilt and remorse, our minds and hearts are not trained for. Sara's passing is a stark reminder of the silent struggles that so often go unnoticed, even among those who appear outwardly to be the strongest."

He continued as the audience absorbed the soliloquy.

"Yet we, amidst all our grief, anger, and sorrow, must remember

Sara's life. A tapestry of beautiful moments. A collection of joyful memories we were privileged to share. Her spirit, her dreams, and the love she shared with each of us have touched us all deeply and will carry us forward. Until we meet her again. In Eternity. Let us pray."

A high school friend of Sara's approached a microphone as the sermon concluded. She paused, seeking strength from James, and then turned away, knowing she would never get through "Amazing Grace" in her sublime alto voice if she continued to look at him.

As the final "I was blind, but now I see" filled the air, thirty-four white doves were freed into the air, each symbolizing one year of Sara's life.

When the memorial concluded, family and guests crossed the lawn into the showpiece early-20th-century Tudor mansion owned by a good friend of Dieter Hauser, Sara's father.

Dieter was a senior partner at a Chicago-based family investment office, managing the portfolios of very-high-net-worth families. Over time, through consistently above-average investment returns and plenty of mutually beneficial introductions, Dieter became a tennis and golfing partner, and then a friend, of his client.

Stunned and saddened by the loss of Dieter's daughter, the client offered to host Sara's memorial and the reception afterward at his home.

James had no desire to spend the rest of the afternoon at the reception interacting with friends and family. But he felt obligated. Hearing, like a broken record, "I am so sorry for your loss," "Our thoughts and prayers are with you," and "If you need anything, absolutely anything, don't hesitate to reach out."

The words sounded simultaneously sharp and muddled. Sharp because he never believed he'd be hearing them, in this context, at this time in his life. Muddled because he'd heard identical versions of them countless times over the previous eight days.

He processed his grief while absorbing that of others. One moment he released his own emotions; the next, he offered his shoulder for someone else's tears—often in the same embrace. This was a process more complex than any algorithm or system he'd ever designed.

Twenty or so of James's friends and family who flew to Chicago retreated to the home's stunning glass and copper conservatory. Consuming wine and hors d'oeuvres, served and refilled by catering staff, they watched James sympathetically as he addressed every guest, one by one, spending as much time as they needed to talk, hug, and question.

As it does, gossip ensued.

"Did Patricia fly separately from James?" the wife of one of James's childhood friends asked.

"Yes, she insisted on carrying the ashes herself," someone murmured. "It feels like she's blaming him. Did anyone see this coming?"

Another interjected.

"My best friend from high school is a trauma therapist. Blame is common in situations like these. Parents do not expect to bury their daughters."

"Trauma is a trigger. Obviously, Sara was triggered when she learned their third pregnancy wouldn't carry to term. Her mom is clearly triggered. It's terrible all around. There's no other way to describe this. It's a tragedy and nothing less."

James flushed the toilet in a small bathroom tucked under a staircase. He stared in the mirror, exhausted and wondering when he would be able to return to the quiet of his father- and mother-in-law's house. After washing his hands, he splashed a bit of cold water on his face. As he opened the door and turned the corner, he could hear a small group of women talking in the kitchen.

"I know they'd been arguing more over the last several months—ah, James, there you are."

Sara's mother, Patricia, was speaking to the mother of one of Sara's best friends and two other women from the neighborhood. Their glances scattered in every direction.

"Long day, James, I'm sure," Patricia said with a persuasive, motherly nod, eliminating the possibility for rebuttal.

"It has been a long day, yes."

"How are you holding up?"

James nodded politely. "I'm doing my best, thank you."

Turning his gaze to her hands, he felt nervousness, agitation. One hand held the crystal-stemmed chardonnay glass while the other traced a short crescent moon shape over its rim.

"Patricia, I think I'm going to walk outside and to the edge of the property, if you don't mind. I'd like some fresh air off the lake. I won't be long."

A grown man in his late 30s, still feeling as though he had to ask his mother-in-law's permission for just about anything.

"Of course, James. We'll be here."

He started across the expansive lawn, toward the bluff overlooking Lake Michigan, noticing the alternating rows of commercial-grade mower marks left over from the previous fall.

Above the bluff, clouds morphed into streaks of stratus and contrails from airliners passing overhead. The water on the lake turned a deeper navy, almost blue-black, as the angle of the sun dropped. Little details of the sky he and Sara would notice together on their walks in Queen Anne.

*How could she have done this, had I truly known her?* he thought.

A few minutes later, he made his way back across the lawn and into the house. He looked for the friend of Sara's who'd sung the beautiful rendition of "Amazing Grace."

When he found her in the great room, she tilted her head in sympathy.

"Kate, when was the last time you spoke with Sara?" James asked her.

"Right after the ultrasound, which was strange. I can't remember the last time we went as long without talking. I would text her asking if she had time, but she told me she was overwhelmed with work. And it always took longer for her to respond. I just figured it was the start of the year and she'd been hit with a bunch of projects."

"Yes, she was working a lot of hours, I know. But half the time she was at home, so I didn't think anything was out of the ordinary."

"James, don't—we're all looking back in time with a fine-tooth comb, trying to understand, but you can't—"

Kate paused.

"What, Kate?" James asked softly.

She hesitated, glancing away. "I'm doing the same thing, James. I could see it in your face outside. We're all trying to understand what we missed."

"I know," he sighed. "But I lived with her. She was my wife. I should have known."

"Don't do that to yourself," she whispered, squeezing his hand. "I'll never understand either, James. Other than continually responding to me that she was feeling 'weird', the only thing I found unusual was that she was responding with a bit too much, let's say, manufactured enthusiasm."

"I got that too," he responded, looking down at the intricate pattern of the rug beneath his shoes.

"She always seemed in control, even when I knew she was feeling weird or unusual or exhausted from work," James said. "But lately, you're right. I'd heard her talking more about being busy."

"Exactly. She never did that before," Kate continued. "She just seemed a little less authentic than my Sara. Always responding, but very hard to pin down. And then she tried to change the subject to me, or take blame. That was unlike her. I could always count on her to be the one in control."

"I was so focused on our annual conference and our roadmap launch in Florida. The hours I was putting in. I thought it was just the combination of those things that made it appear like she was backing away from—"

He stopped, trying not to choke up.

"The last time we took a really long walk together, maybe a month ago. It wasn't raining, so we did our circle around Highland Drive to watch the skyline. I was telling her about the roadmap, and she asked, 'Does this even matter?' So I explained why I thought it did, to the company at least, but now I'm wondering if she was really trying to tell me something else."

"James, she was smart and confident. But she was also a bit afraid of opening up. I think that originates closer to home, if you know what I mean. And had nothing to do with you. I hope you believe me."

"Thank you, Kate, I appreciate that."

\* \* \*

James and his father-in-law spent the following morning reviewing estate planning details at the kitchen table, but Patricia had left the house before he had come down. Dieter loaned him a car so he could take his mother, brother, and two other friends to O'Hare airport.

He returned later in the afternoon. Patricia had yet to return home. The two men ate from the trays of leftovers from the memorial the previous day and sat in the family room watching college basketball.

The adrenaline from the previous week had begun to wear off, ever so slightly, and James found himself exhausted and ready for bed at 7:00 in the evening. By 7:10 he was fast asleep. Patricia returned home from her best friend's house up the road just after eight.

\* \* \*

James descended the stairs the next morning, placing his suitcase in the foyer of the Hauser house, waiting for his Uber.

He peered into the family room, where Patricia and Dieter were sitting next to each other on the formal living room couch. Looking out the front window, holding hands, whispering in a way they would not have been if he and Sara were there together.

"I'm headed to the airport shortly," James stated, feeling distant and alone, not knowing what else to say. "Thank you again for allowing me to stay here. I'll call next week."

Sara's parents rose from the couch and approached him in the foyer. Dieter brought his son-in-law in for a hug. A long, deep breath syncopated between them. Dieter released, looked at him eye-to-eye with a squinted smile, his sturdy arms grasping James's shoulders with a confident shrug.

James then turned to Patricia, awkwardly trying to lock in on her thoughts. His desperate eyes filled like water balloons with saline and despair. She sighed and approached him, wrapping her arms underneath his shoulders. They both relented. For her, thirty-four years of proud, disciplined motherhood. For him, two years of courtship, seven years of marriage, and a lifetime yet to experience.

They wept, holding each other as Dieter stood in the hallway, watching. Allowing the moment to run its course. He was thankful Patricia allowed herself to succumb to the moment, and grateful James was able to share in it.

Releasing from the grip on his back, she placed her hands on his jaw and cheeks, his tears running over her skin.

For the last nine days, she had been a loaded cannon of blame and anger, ready to fire. This morning, as much as she needed to point it at someone, something, anything, she simply couldn't light the fuse if it was pointed at him. Feeling his heart pumping thick sorrow. Seeing the lifeless gray of guilt and remorse in his eyes. She realized enough is enough. The furrow of her brow subsided and her mouth relaxed.

"I. Am. So sorry." James said, looking at her. Even though the words weren't necessary.

"I'm sorry, too—son."

# 4

After hours of flight delays, James arrived home from Chicago. Dropping his bags inside the now soulless house, he found a bottle of bourbon in the cabinet above the refrigerator and returned to the couch. He didn't bother to unpack his suitcase or venture upstairs. For the remainder of the evening, he drowned himself in a slideshow of photos and memories he and Sara shared. For the first time in weeks, it seemed, he was able to sit.

The following morning, a ping on his smartphone passed through his hangover to awaken him. Reflex made him reach for the device, normally on its charging cradle next to the bed. Instead, his wrist hit the corner of the glass coffee table next to the couch.

His eyes, simultaneously wincing from pain and squinting from a band of morning sunlight settling into his field of view, slowly focused on the device. The notification box showed an email from Cindy Strauber, a close friend and colleague of Sara's, and the HR Director at Ascendia.

He reached to find his glasses on the floor next to the couch and began to read it, still grumbling from the pain, the light, and the morning.

*SUBJ: Sara's laptop*

James -
I'm deeply sorry for the trivial nature of this request. I know it's a difficult time. However, the IT department has requested the return of the Ascendia-issued MacBook Pro, external monitor, and other accessories used by Sara during her time here.

No rush, but if we could get it this week, I'd greatly appreciate it. I could meet you at Pike St. Roasters if you'd like. Coffee and hugs are on me.

We know most team members often store personal documents, photos, etc. on their laptops. I know Sara did a fair amount of personal research and kept photos on her machine. If you would like to review and move whatever you need to your own computer, we have set up a one-time login and access process.

When ready, please click this link.

After clicking the link, an authentication key will be sent to your mobile number, which we have as 425-748-9865. Please use Sara's company email address and the password sent to you to access her device. This is a one-time access code, so make sure to transfer everything you need prior to shutting down or allowing the machine to go to sleep.

And James, please know we are all grieving with you and offer our deepest condolences. If you need anything at all, please do not hesitate to ask.

Respectfully,


Cindy Stauber, MBA, PHRA
Director of Human Resources
Ascendia – Progress. Accelerated.


For a company this size, he thought, I can't believe they're going to allow me to access her machine outside their closed network, even for a single minute.

*I could copy all her project files and sell them to their competitors. How in the world this company doesn't have every employee's salary and Social Security numbers for sale to the highest bidder on the dark web is beyond me. Maybe they already do.*

As the coffee machine making his double espresso stopped flowing, James was struck by how quiet the house was.

On any Monday he wasn't traveling, the house would have brimmed with life: the cheery chatter of bubbly morning news hosts on TV, the rhythmic breaths and occasional grunts from Sara on the Peloton, the hiss of the shower and hum of the hair dryer, or the staccato clack of her favorite Chelsea boots on the hardwood floors as she hurried out the door.

None of those sounds lived here anymore.

James walked to the entry of the house and pulled a laptop from one of the compartments in her black designer backpack, sitting on a bench near the front door.

The bag hadn't been her first choice. It was a gift from her mother that previous Christmas. A little more 'Ms.' than she was ready to be, even in her early 30s, with the gold zippers and a tasteful letter "S" embroidered on the pocket. But it was spacious and wore well for the office and the occasional business trip.

He set his coffee and the laptop at the head of their dining room table and flipped it open. Behind the box waiting for her username and password credentials was a desktop photo of the two of them snow-shoeing at Suncadia Resort, east of Seattle, the previous year.

On a snowshoe walk across one of the golf courses, the photo perfectly framed blue sky, evergreen trees, rolling hills, and sparkling white snow. And the two of them. Her left arm extended into the air in a proud yet defiant "time of our lives" position, right arm clutching his waist. His right arm also raised, but to deflect a large wet snowball that a friend had thrown in their direction. The exploding snowball and their gasps frozen in time by a camera. Gleeful expressions framing their world at that moment. The pain and perceived inadequacy of their second miscarriage out there, somewhere in the distance.

James sank into the chair, wondering why he hadn't held on more tightly to that weekend, that moment, that woman—the way it had been. The way *she* had been during that wonderful weekend with friends.

He clicked the link in Cindy's email. Moments later, a passcode appeared in his phone's messages. He entered her email address into the top box, followed by the one-time passcode below.

The background image from Suncadia was replaced by an open browser window. Twenty-eight open tabs dotted along the top, each showing different logos and icons of sites she'd visited. One of the tabs contained a lowercase "f". He decided while he was logged into her account, he should "memorialize" her page.

As the page refreshed, a white bell with the number "399+" showed in red. Click. He was directed to the Notifications page, listing hundreds of wall posts, mentions, and comments from friends, family, acquaintances, and colleagues. Each expressing shock, horror, and sadness that someone in their circle of friends had taken her own life at such a young age.

He scanned some of the posts. Sad emojis. Anger emojis. Care emojis. Digital gestures offered to people who aren't quite able to find the right words to write, or whose attention span is limited to reacting through emojis before moving on to the next, more comfortable post about babies, fashion, or celeb gossip. The easier content. The content that keeps production of dopamine in the human brain elevated while scrolling.

Each heartfelt message was not just a gesture of support, but also another input for the algorithms, including those he invented. Fuel to keep users engaged and scrolling. Every second of attention reading and writing condolences was an additional second of opportunity to insert an advertisement into the feed.

After all, this was his life's work: understanding how humans behave online. What makes them scroll more, click more, and share more. Inventing and continually tweaking algorithms that keep people in front of screens. More time online means more time to show advertising. More advertising means more profit for social media apps, video sites, and search engines.

He recalled how EchoWave started with noble intentions—to make these sites more user-friendly and online experiences seamless. Connecting users with relevant content and advertising across platforms seemed beneficial back then.

As the company grew, he became insulated from users' personal experiences. Days were filled with overseeing teams, whiteboards, and collaborating on product launches and presentations—dealing with data trends of millions, not individual people. Staring at Sara's screen, the most personal connection he had, he viewed the endeavor with more than a tinge of skepticism.

Over the years, the amount of personal data search engines, video, and social media sites collected exploded in volume. Not just tracking the content users were scrolling, clicking and commenting on, and sharing, but also through location, microphones, photo albums, and memory storage. They could essentially track the behavior of every smartphone-using, smartwatch-wearing, smart-car-driving, smart-home-living human, twenty-four hours a day, seven days a week, for the rest of their lives.

Companies like EchoWave operated essentially unchecked by consumer advocates and government regulators. Which is why little effort was made to understand the downsides or dangers of the technology. Why would they? Users click '*I Accept*' without hesitation every time they buy a new gadget or install a new app. '*I Accept*' grants permission to follow, listen, watch, and track almost every moment. '*I Accept*' grants permission to have supercomputers guide and predict user behavior, with precision.

*They already know she's gone,* he thought bitterly. *Why make me go through this process? Why didn't they just do it?*

All of the thoughtful and sentimental gestures friends, family, and colleagues had posted on her profile redirected his attention from the administrative task of cleaning out the laptop. Suddenly, it wasn't just a laptop; it was Sara's laptop.

Their words and memories helped the social network complete the picture of who she was, and what had happened. Rarely did someone announce their own passing on social media. That was left for those left behind. People used to send sympathy cards. Now they post on social media. More data collected and used to complete the picture of every user, to better tailor content and ads.

James continued to read, trying to ingest everything, but trying not to allow any of it to sink in. He noticed Patricia's silence amidst the outpouring. Curious, he searched her profile, finding the familiar family photo in front of the Eiffel Tower, years before he and Sara met.

Predictable behavior, he thought. Posting two to three times a week: photos of parties and place settings, flower arrangements and fundraisers, trips in progress, and throwbacks of vacations past. Her most recent post was dated 9:18 a.m. on the day Sara died. A slightly overexposed, softened photo of a long row of elegant table settings, flatware, and crystal stems, taken from inside an ornate conservatory.

*"Patricia Hauser—with Jeanette Smythe and 23 others —at Highlands Park Ladies Club."*
*"Immensely proud to celebrate the work my HPLC sisters have done to support the HP/Deerfield Historical Society! Let's eat!"*

Although Patricia had stopped posting after her daughter's passing, her connections became very active. The wall of her social media profile brimming with condolences, old photos of Sara, screenshots of prayers. Many of the new posts received their own likes and comments, further connecting and enhancing The app's understanding of Patricia's digital relationship grid. Dozens, potentially hundreds of people, through their words and their behavior, now identified as grieving. Ready to be served content recommendations for support groups, videos of how to recognize depression symptoms, or ads for the latest meditation app. Patricia didn't need to post anything to the app to know her daughter was gone. Everyone else in her network offered the data equivalent of *"have you heard the terrible news?"* Like magic, the gap in Patricia's life had been filled.

The same way it knew his wife was grieving after her second miscarriage. Avoiding social media for a while, too distraught to scroll through friends sharing photos of the firsts: ultrasounds, births, fevers, teeth, steps, first steps, first tooth, and so on.

When two billion people digitally share their lives on social media, what they don't scroll and what they don't post becomes just another data point used for recommending content and showing ads. He recalled how the algorithms detected when active users went silent—prompting them with tailored content, new features, or discussion groups to draw them back in. It was all designed to keep users engaged.

*We understand. Take a break from posting for a while. In the meantime, might we recommend these discussion groups to you? You see? You're not alone. Stay logged in, just scroll here instead. Remember: we're your community.*

Sure enough, on the right side of Sara's screen, he noticed notifications from Groups she'd joined. Dozens of responses to comments she'd made on posts, some using her real name, some anonymously. Groups with names like:

*Recurrent Miscarriage Support*
*Pregnancy After Miscarriage*
*Depression and Miscarriage*
*Miscarriage & Pregnancy Loss for Couples*
*Gene Therapy in Plain English*
*Carrying On After Miscarrying*
*Light After Darkness – Overcoming Depression*

"Oh my God," he muttered. "They knew everything—her miscar-riages, her depression."

Each moment she spent in online groups painted a vivid picture of her struggle, spiraling out of control. Her time online wasn't helping her cope or learn; it was feeding her darkness, and ultimately, her demise.

Optimizing it. Amplifying it. Triggering it.

James nearly slammed the laptop closed but hesitated, remembering he had only one chance to download her data. Instead, he ran to the kitchen.

And threw up in the sink

# 5

Cleansing the whiskey-acid taste from his mouth at the kitchen sink, James glanced out the kitchen window, spotting his elderly neighbor depositing bags of trash and recycling into their respective bins. He ducked away from view before she could take notice. Accepting her condolences and gestures would happen at some point. But not today.

James sat back down in front of Sara's laptop, the screen casting its sterile light on his face. He couldn't fathom why these apps hadn't flagged her sudden, desperate scrolling through miscarriage support groups, depression forums, and other glaring red flags—signs of someone teetering on the edge of crisis, fully at risk of self-harm.

*She never mentioned any of these groups or online forums to me. Why?* James thought. *Since I've known her, she always used social media to post about positive experiences—their experiences. Happy experiences. Proud experiences. She never mentioned using it as a source for information and communication about serious topics like pregnancy and conception.*

He shifted gears into his engineer's mindset.

*Why, all of a sudden, did a social network, of all places, become her confidante? Her informer? The expert? And her community?*

He envisioned her sitting in front of this screen, scrolling, reading, and posting. For hours upon hours.

*What was all this activity doing to the mental state of someone already terrified about pregnancy and miscarriage?* he thought. *Someone whose body is already in a state of change, both physically and chemically?*

His eyes drifted above the screen, settling on the front windows overlooking the street outside their house. As he gazed out, memories of her and the house flooded back. They had both worked so hard to save for, find, and buy *this* home. Two blocks off Queen Anne Avenue North, located in a highly desirable neighborhood, just north of downtown Seattle. Far enough off the main road to avoid most traffic noise, but close enough to walk to trendy restaurants, bars, and coffee shops.

Shaking off the distraction, he opened her internet browsing history.

Typing "Pregnancy" in the search field isolated hundreds of pages she'd previously visited.

He opened her calendar app and noticed her activity loosely coincided with OB/GYN appointments, travel, and parties they attended.

Next, he typed "Miscarriage," which returned a similar number of links and a similar ebb and flow of browsing activity to her social life and medical appointments.

He paused and took a deep breath, knowing the next terms in his mind might reveal what he suspected, but didn't want to admit·

"Depression."

Scrolling to the bottom of the list of sites, he discovered the first time she searched the topic. About three weeks after her second miscarriage. Across three or four days, the number of websites she visited on the topic increased, peaked, and then subsided. One month later, the activity emerged again and then dissipated for almost a year.

Three and a half months before her suicide, before learning Sara was pregnant the third time, she again started visiting depression-related sites. And sites focused on anxiety. And inadequacy. And medications to help curb the effects of anxiety and depression. And information around the potential risks and side effects of antidepressant and anxiety medications while attempting to conceive or during pregnancy.

As he randomly clicked through the list, he noticed that she initially visited reputable medical journals and respected hospitals. However, over time, she started clicking on links to less reputable sites. Sites riddled with pop-up ads and snake oil offers, using artificial intelligence text generators to manipulate search engine results and entice users to click on ads. Most of the ads led to spam sites. As the frequency of visits to less reputable sites increased, the frequency of visits to trustworthy sites decreased.

James leaned back in his chair. His mind returned to the implications coming out of his company's conference nearly three weeks earlier. The excitement he and his team shared after weeks of planning, preparation, and approvals. His attention had been directed toward his company and his colleagues—the adrenaline of professional progress and accomplishment—rather than the attention he should have directed to his wife as she was agonizing and suffering, silently.

He thought back to the presentations, breakout sessions, and sidebar conversations. EchoWave's algorithms were helping not just social networks and search engines, but hundreds of other companies in optimizing online shopping, airline ticket pricing, coupon redemption, and more.

Now, with the addition of the cutting-edge artificial intelligence features James presented, EchoWave's partners could instantly update their apps and pages to the preferences of any user. The company envisioned a future driven entirely by individual preferences in a way that had never been done before. Even news sites could slightly change a story in real-time to adapt to the reading style or political preferences of the reader.

His pulse was racing as he took another breath and entered: "Suicide."

When the results appeared, James felt his hands begin to shake.

In the EchoWave offices, a running joke among his research team had been, "Be careful what you search for." His thoughts took him back to a series of meetings his team had two years ago, related to safeguards the company would put in place to detect behavior that could be interpreted as high-risk. He had assigned ten engineers and two product managers to a task force, with a directive to report back in twelve weeks with comprehensive analysis, recommendations, and next steps.

A short time later, the founders, investors, and Board of Directors of EchoWave unanimously approved an employment offer to Michael Valeno to join the company as Chairman and Chief Executive Officer. Michael had previously been the CEO of three other companies funded by EchoWave's largest venture capital investors. Two of them had gone public on the Nasdaq stock exchange.

Due to his consistent, predictable track record of success, the investors continued to court him to join EchoWave. He was the "adult in the room" for growing companies with large amounts of young talent, but no experienced management.

After joining the company, Michael gave the teams a clear directive in all-hands meetings and in more intimate team settings: drive growth.

"Not at any cost," he would tell any willing audience. "But *almost* any."

Two months later, as Michael reviewed programs and budgets in an attempt to streamline the company's operations prior to its initial public offering, he learned about EchoWave's Behavioral Safety Task Force, the amount of resources it was consuming, and the risk it posed for adversely impacting revenue growth.

The task force was disbanded the following week.

James turned on Sara's phone and tapped one of the video-sharing app icons. The first video emerged, titled *"Van Life by the Sea,"* showing a blonde woman with an Australian accent waking up early in the morning and opening the windows and doors to her van. She lit a bushel of sage to remove any negative energy from the small space, then extended a tiny cooking surface out of the back to prepare a kettle of tea and breakfast. The audio described the remainder of her day, filled with naps, reading, and hair braiding.

The second video showed a woman sitting in a corner of her bedroom, sobbing. Her head between her legs, with melancholy music playing in the background. The captions had purposefully misspelled "miscarriage."

The next video centered on the theme of depression.

He clicked on her search history. Scrolling down until the search history ended, he noticed she had only searched more positive topics like #vanlife, #springgardening, #beach, #universe, #rescues, and #babylove.

James continued searching for patterns in how content was being selected for her. He scrolled past positive videos, watching only the negative ones to understand what she was seeing.

To keep track, he grabbed a notebook from his backpack. On a blank page, he wrote "Viral Videos" at the top, drew a line down the middle, and labeled the columns "+" and "−". With each video, he marked whether the topic was positive or negative.

An hour later, he totaled the marks for dark mental health messages —miscarriage, depression, loss, hopelessness—and compared them to the topics she had actually searched for.

Eighty percent of the videos he viewed on her feed were negative. Not because she continued searching negative topics. But because she was stopping to view the negative content *longer*, versus scrolling more quickly past the positive content she originally wanted.

*Sara was initially searching for videos that took her to happy places and made her feel better*, he thought. *But if the goal of the video site is to keep her engaged and scrolling, content related to depression, inadequacy, and miscarriages was what encouraged her. These companies aren't just using us to optimize their advertising. They're informing each other, through us, about the best topics to keep users online, even if it's harmful.*

Fully overwhelmed, James pulled away from the keyboard and buried his head in his hands, holding back every instinct to violently shove the machines off the table with one thrust of his arms.

"This is not how it's supposed to work," he said out loud, slamming his hands on the wood table with each syllable. "It's designed to match ads with people's interests. It was never designed to manipulate users to engage with content that unknowingly makes them feel worse!"

He stood up, paced in front of the window for a moment before deflating into the cushions on the couch.

The moment he turned off Do Not Disturb, notifications appeared. Texts from Vik, Sara's father, and other friends, as well as two actual phone calls from his mother. Each checking in to make sure he made it back to Seattle and was doing alright.

"*I'm fine,*" he responded to his mother. "*Taking the day to get some things done around the house.*"

He then copied the message he'd sent to his mother and pasted it, verbatim, to everyone else.

The repetition of his copy and pasting made him stop and wonder: *If this is how some EchoWave partners are using our tech, how many other people could be at risk of...*

He stood quickly and felt dizzy. Mental and emotional overload, dehydration, and hunger.

*What if Sara was not a fluke?* he thought. *What if there are others who have been, or are, or will be, trapped in this feedback loop of negative content, powered by an algorithm I designed?*

James started the company believing that if social media companies and search engines shared some of their data around the products, services, and places users liked, the experience of using these apps would be better for everyone. And the entire industry would benefit.

*It's one thing for a single social media application or search engine to promote negative content,* he thought. *It's not ideal. People can pull themselves out of quicksand, right? But if a user is seeing negative content across every app? That could be very dangerous.*

He walked back to the kitchen, filled a bottle of water, grabbed an energy drink from the door of a refrigerator in desperate need of being rid of expired dairy and produce items. He pulled a half-eaten bag of potato chips from the pantry and returned to the head of the table.

Pushing Sara's laptop aside for a moment, James opened a browser on his own laptop. Unlike Sara's, his browser was much more secure, with a litany of settings designed to block all the dirty little data collection secrets most people allowed.

James needed to understand if the algorithms he invented were being used by the social media and video apps—not just to match the right ad to the person most interested in that product or service—but to keep people consuming whatever content kept their attention. Even if the content was triggering them into violence or self-harm.

He lifted his phone, wanting to call Vik and explain what he thought he'd found. But he didn't know anything yet. Realizing he needed more evidence; he decided to treat his hypothesis like any other challenge he faced at EchoWave.

A moment of clarity came after blinking his eyes and shifting his mind from its daydream state to one of problem-solving. James began taking screenshots of Sara's social media profiles and her search results. He studied and collected digital samples from the "For You" and "Groups You Might Like" sections, which suggested more ways she could spend time online.

He backed up her entire photo and music library, along with hundreds of screenshots he'd taken of her social media profiles and search results. He changed the passwords on her non-work search and social media accounts so he could access them in the future.

On his own laptop, James created a new user account to replicate her laptop onto his. The account would not be connected to the EchoWave servers or security protocols, allowing him to research and run tests without the additional security his company used to protect their employees from data mining and hackers.

James wrote several questions on the large paper pads he mounted on the easels: *Who is not following the rules? What happens to quality control if a partner is artificially enhancing a user's behavior? Are there combinations of non-triggering search entries or behavior patterns that can ultimately lead to emotional triggers?*

He logged into the EchoWave network and began reading the company's policies around mental health and self-harm. While the company designed filters to deprioritize and flag behavior indicating self-harm, violence, or other illegal activity, he suspected the worst: when social media users entered search terms related to topics other social networks relied on to increase engagement—such as depression, sadness, loneliness—the terms signaled to other partners to increase exposure to similar content, even if users weren't searching for it.

All this data was shared back to EchoWave, in real time, for processing and analysis. Trillions of computations per minute, fine-tuning and predicting the thoughts, preferences, and intents of hundreds of millions of humans.

On the surface, it appeared that, at least in Sara's case, one social media site made an algorithmic assumption that she was less interested in pregnancy and baby showers. She had stopped liking, commenting on, and engaging with happy moments. Her interactions with groups became associated with the struggles of pregnancy and miscarriage. This data, combined with her search behavior, was shared with EchoWave, which, in turn informed every corner of the internet how to gain Sara's attention on other topics that would engage her.

The algorithms were performing precisely the way they were designed to perform. Algorithms James and his team had invented, written patents for, and brought to market.

Mentally drained, James fell into a daze, his thoughts blurring into a vivid memory of Sara sitting next to him on the edge of their neatly made king-size bed. She held a small pillow near her belly and sobbed on his shoulder as he cradled her.

*"Pregnancy seems so easy for everyone else, James. Why? Why is this happening to me?"*

James's head jolted off the dining room table. It was just after midnight. He wiped his eyes and glanced at Sara's laptop. Instead of the browser window he was scrolling through earlier, it showed a username and password window. The temporary account access had expired at midnight.

*I guess they did have some security,* he thought wryly. Accepting the inevitable. Being logged out was just another loss, relived. Another final goodbye.

With access gone, there was no rush. James glanced at her desktop background photo one final time, and slowly closed the laptop.

# 6

Days later, James could see his next-door neighbor—octogenarian and Seattle native, Olive Madelin, using her walker to progress slowly up the short walkway toward his front door. The crossbar held a quilted shopping bag containing fresh-baked bread, a bushel of wildflowers, a bottle of red wine from Walla Walla, and a sympathy card she'd spent an hour writing.

Olive had refused to sell their house when her husband passed away suddenly from a heart attack nineteen years earlier. Once the obituary was published, real estate investors started knocking on her door, clamoring for homes to tear down and rebuild as multi-family units. By the time James and Sara purchased their house six years earlier, investors had become near predators, incessantly knocking on the red front door, taping leaflets, even dropping signed and notarized all-cash, no contingency offers through the mail slot.

\* \* \*

James stood from the table and opened the door before she started up the steps.

"Oh, good morning, Mrs. Madelin. I am terribly sorry that I have not come to see you since—"

"Since when did you stop calling me Olive, young man?"

"You're right. I'm just—I'm just very tired."

"Yes, I noticed the lights on throughout the night. You really need to get some rest."

"Yea, I do. Please, Olive, let me help you up the steps."

"I brought you a few things, James. But first, let me just—"

She lifted her aged, weak arms, connected to a back hunched from years of osteoporosis, raising them as high as she could to James's face and around his neck.

James responded with the *thank you so much* he'd uttered hundreds of times, and gently lay his hands on her brittle back.

"James, I watched from my bedroom window that Thursday night. I don't know why I was up, but I was. I saw you go into the house from the taxi. I thought you might start turning lights off. And then I heard screaming. And then the sirens. It took me right back to that afternoon, nineteen years ago, when I walked upstairs and found my Jack."

James nodded, looking at her receding eyes.

He eased her into a chair at the opposite end of the dining room table. Once seated, he walked into the kitchen, set the items she'd brought on the island, and returned with two cups of coffee, creamer, and sweetener.

"I don't know if I ever told you this—the day I lost Jack. I had been baking that afternoon. Blackberries, into a pie. We drove over to Fort Lawton and parked our car near the chapel. All those tall bushes that line the trails there. For hours. We came home with five huge containers of berries. I did my best to administer CPR when I found him. But every time I pushed on his chest, he just sank into the mattress. It must have sounded like something he'd never dared to try on me in all those forty-five years. That's all there was at the end for him. Screaming and squeaking. Worse ways to go, I suppose?"

James smiled.

"I stood up and dialed 911 from the old beige phone in the bedroom —the kind that had actual buttons to press. From the Bell company. Now I have this flip phone. It works great. Stays with me all the time."

James realized it was probably the first time he'd truly listened to Olive. Her world appeared to him so small. And yet, so filled with real life.

"That pie just kept cooking at 325 degrees as they worked on Jack.

Until finally they decided to stop and pronounce him. On to another, better place. But the smoke from the oven sure got the attention of the fire department. Just as they were helping the paramedics move Jack's body down that old, narrow staircase."

James sat in front of her, one hand cupped under his chin. Although exhausted and wanting to continue his work, he enjoyed hearing her voice and her stories—he'd heard the one about Jack, the pie, and the fire department at least half a dozen times.

James paused. "Olive, did you—"

"Did I what?" she responded quickly, almost as if she wanted him to bring out the elephant in the room. Her near-term mind sharp, even if she'd forgotten a few old stories and how many times she'd told them.

"Did you see or sense anything unusual with Sara that week? That afternoon?"

"No, honey, I didn't."

She tapped her wrinkled, deeply arthritic index finger on the side of the coffee cup.

"In fact, I hadn't seen or heard from her since you left on your business trip. Sunday, was it?" She often pointed out details she'd re-membered, which she believed helped her stay sharp.

"With the exception of the lights turning on and off, which I thought was your travel timer, home robot, or whatever you call it. I thought she was traveling, too."

"She miscarried on Monday, Olive. Maybe Sunday. Third time. She didn't tell me because I was at this fu—this stupid conference. She called her OB/GYN on Monday after she'd had terrible cramps and spotting. They told her to come in Friday. Never told me anything. For three days she sat in this house."

"Sara knew this, but did I ever tell you I also had three?" Olive continued. "Miscarriages, I mean. It just wasn't meant to be. To have a family in that way. But we found joy together in so many other ways. Each time I learned the news, it was devastating. But it also made me feel closer to Jack. And I think him to me, too. We managed. Our families helped. People didn't beat around the bush back then."

She paused and took a contemplative sip out of her mug before continuing.

"We faced it, even as other family members and friends had children of their own. They invited us to be a part of their experience. Part of their families. I wish I'd had children. I think that stays with you forever. I just don't understand why Sara wouldn't come talk to me. So I could tell her, no matter what, there's always a way through, even if we can't see it in the moment."

James stared at the window, listening to her and welling up with sorrow, thinking about the playpen, books, and the chaos that should have been surrounding him. And Sara.

"Of course, we didn't talk about it in the same way you do today," she added.

James blinked back into focus.

"I didn't know that, Olive. About your three miscarriages. I'm very sorry."

"It will always be a part of me, James, but it never owned me. I so wish I would have had the opportunity to tell your Sara that. I do."

"Please. You can't—I think that's part of the difference, Olive. People are conditioned to turn inward now. Even if they have good friends or family or are married."

He shrugged slightly, thinking about the conversation as it related to his work, the algorithms.

"In our isolation, on our smartphones—at that point—we're basically sitting ducks."

"Sitting ducks? What do you mean?" Olive asked.

"I'm sorry, Olive, nothing. Ducks on the water, I think I meant to say. Or something else. I don't know."

Olive looked around the dining room, noticing the laptops, scattered papers, and printers spread around.

"So this is what you do?" she asked.

"Yea, I guess it is," he said, glancing around the room, feeling trivial and petty.

"I could never explain to you what happened to this town. Jack used to say Seattle was built on the backs of *salmon-forty-sevens* and *steel sturgeons*. He meant Boeing. And the Navy."

James's angst was allowed a slight reprieve with her attempt at humor. He allowed another smile and a nod for how different Seattle must have been when she was younger.

"The World's Fair was a dream with no plan. Companies stopped building things here. Then some young man dropped out of Harvard and changed this whole area forever with his computers. Not for the better, if you ask my opinion. Now my property taxes are more than Jack ever made in a year. And the nursery up the road charges eight dollars for a bag of potting soil they used to let us take for free. Progress has done more harm than good to this town, if you ask me."

"That's very funny, Olive. Personally, I blame Starbucks."

\* \* \*

For the next two weeks, James's dining room became a war room. Occasionally interrupted by short visits from friends, brief text exchanges with Vik or other members of his EchoWave team, deliveries of fruit baskets from distant relatives, and the occasional plate of homemade cinnamon rolls from Olive.

James sat at the head of the dining room table, recreating Sara's online activity from the previous three months. Wanting to reverse-engineer the persuasive, manipulative, and ultimately triggering experience Sara had gone through.

It was still early, but he could sense that the dynamics of the entire market had shifted subtly over the last decade. The sheer volume of data being collected was staggering. Industry competition had grown more fierce. Companies that were once freewheeling startups had gone public and were now accountable for continuous growth and profit.

By focusing on the online activity and behavior of one user—his wife—he could view EchoWave and the entire industry through a different lens.

If understanding one person's experience exposed cracks in the foundation, then perhaps the entire structure was compromised. Through his loss, he realized that big problems could be solved by digging into and documenting the most intimate details of a single life.

# 7

The night before returning to work, James printed two copies of the fifty-three-page briefing he intended to present to his co-founder Vik the following morning.

After placing the final touches on a detailed presentation of his findings and proposed changes and their implications, he made sure the backup data was secured on computers inside the company.

The documents, as well as two portable memory drives, sat on the far end of the table as James took photos of his notes. He sorted all the papers placed them in boxes and moved them to the basement.

On his way up the stairs, the doorbell rang.

The sky blazed with hues of fiery orange and deep purple, the sunset casting a funnel-like glow over the Puget Sound. The cool evening air carried the faint scent of saltwater.

Hurrying to open the glass door for his next-door neighbor, the light gave her an angelic glow.

"Olive, I'm so sorry I didn't help you up the steps. I was in the basement storing some boxes. Please, come in."

"Scones. Cranberry. For you. But only if you promise to find your way off this hill within the next twenty-four hours."

"I will, Olive, thank you. I'm headed back to work tomorrow."

"That's good. Did you know the hills of Queen Anne are so steep, over one hundred twenty pedestrian staircases have been built?"

"I did not, in fact, know that."

"Because if you had refused to get out, I was going to make you walk up and down all of them with me."

"You walk them?" he asked in amazement.

"Not anymore. But I figured the threat of doing so might be enough for you to at least escort me to the outdoor sculpture museum."

"Can I make you some tea, Olive?"

"No, I just came to bring the scones. Have you finished whatever it was you were working on?" Olive asked as they walked toward the dining room.

"I have," he said, patting his hand on the documents stacked neatly on the table.

She looked at him, waiting for him to expand on his response.

"I think there are going to be a lot of people who won't like what I wrote."

"But you believe in what you've got in there?"

"I do," he said, nodding and looking down at the documents.

"Let me ask you a question, Olive. Have you ever used social media or spent time searching on the internet?"

Nearly as soon as he enunciated the last syllable, Olive began to laugh in an almost witch-like, albeit joyous, cackle.

"Are you kidding me? I consider myself lucky I'm nearing the departure of a world where all our lives are online and, what is it, *twitterable*?"

"James," she continued, "we used to keep our personal lives—personal. You wouldn't share your private business with strangers. But now I read and watch the news, or whatever is left of the real news, and all I see is how these companies are collecting and selling anything they can about us."

He was now glad she didn't know what he did for a living, fearing she may never smile, look, or talk to him again.

"It's just like all those salespeople," she continued. "Coming up to my front door and following me around the parking lot of the market. Watching everything I do to convince me of the idea of selling my home."

James looked up from the documents. "They followed you in the parking lot of the grocery store?" he asked.

"*In* the grocery store, too, yes. And over the phone."

It caused James to immediately think of the online places he couldn't reach. Places his technology and algorithms couldn't see. The idea that the information EchoWave was sending to partners would be used tactfully and judiciously. But it wasn't. They outsmarted him. And it outsmarted Sara.

"But I keep telling them," she raised her voice in unison with her hands, "I'm not selling until Jack comes home and signs the paperwork with me!"

She smiled, ever in her good spirits.

"Well, James, whatever it is that you keep thumbing through there, I'm glad you wrote it out. Put it on paper, rather than all that damn electronic and email hooey. Your ideas on those pages are a permanent record. Just like that stack of sympathy cards that keep piling up on your hearth. Face-to-face and the written word. That's how you know someone really cares, which is why you really should open them up and read them."

James walked her back to her house and up to her porch. As she entered through the front door, she turned.

"But really, honey. If I knew then what I know now, I would never have published that obituary. I knew Jack was gone. My family knew he was gone. The moment I told the world, everything changed. That's when the snakes arrived. We need to be careful what we share. Anywhere."

"I think I agree with you, Olive."

# 8

At the traffic light outside the entrance to the EchoWave campus, James watched the rain droplets land on his windshield, only to be pulled together into a larger stream of water until they vanished completely when the wiper pushed them aside.

*Each droplet,* he thought. *It's really the same as a human using a search engine or social network. They have no idea about the artificial psychological gravity taking place behind the scenes. Unaware that they are being sliced and diced into groups of unknown peers. Often moved in directions different from their original intention or path. Like raindrops.*

An abrupt horn blast from the vehicle behind vaulted him back into the present moment. He hit the accelerator of his electric car just as the turn signal changed from yellow to red. His five-finger apology wave was answered with a single middle finger from the driver behind him, caught at the light.

With his coffee tumbler, backpack, and keycard, James descended the steps to the walkway. He noticed pillow-like, white clouds passing quickly to the east, just over the tops of the towering evergreens surrounding the metal and glass buildings, indicating a break in the rain.

The revolving door kept the fresh air outside and replaced it with recirculated, filtered air. He took a breath in, recognizing the pleasant, crisp aroma of cedar and citrus produced by a diffuser installed in the ceiling.

Walking up the circular staircase of the rotunda, he kept his head low, hoping to avoid any awkward interactions on his first day back.

After reaching the relative protection of his office, James closed the door, dropped his backpack, and sat in his infinitely configurable executive chair. But it didn't seem to fit him anymore.

He slowly rubbed his hands on the front edge of the desk, thinking about Olive's comment last night on the importance of tangible things. The papers and printed PowerPoints lay exactly as they were the Friday before he left for the conference in Orlando. He glanced to his left at the whiteboard covered top to bottom with blue and red text, equations, and sticky notes.

And then the photograph on his desk.

Frozen in time, an image of him and Sara, standing arm in arm, smiling in front of the Mirabell Gardens in Salzburg, Austria. He managed to crack a smile as he recalled the Japanese tourist who saved them from what would have been a far less interesting selfie, offering to take a proper picture. The man then asked, in Japanese and hand signals, for James to do the same for him. And then the next person in their tour group. And the next. Until Sara faked an incoming phone call. James quickly dropped the camera in the hands of the fifth tourist as they ran through the rose gardens, laughing.

The pang of remorse and regret he felt was short-lived.

"Welcome back, James," the head, shoulder, and hand of his friend and co-founder Vik startled him back into reality.

"The drive in was hell. You, too?"

"Hey, Vik. It's good to be back, thank you. Yes, the drive was hell as always."

"See you at nine in my office?"

"With precision."

The phrase 'with precision' had become EchoWave's moniker as they honed and perfected algorithms and services that helped their partners more effectively target ads to their users.

With every passing minute between 7:38 and 8:57, colleague after colleague passed and stopped, knocked on the door frame of his office, and entered to offer condolences, share a memory, cry, or embrace. The playback phrase, "let me know if you need anything—seriously," began to grate on him. Even more so when an engineer added "bro" to the end of the statement, accompanied by a slightly aggressive double slap on the back of his gray Patagonia zip-up. In an instant, his role had shifted from consolee to consoler.

James stacked his laptop, his two copies of the briefing, and the drives containing supporting data, and walked to Vik's office. A knot tightened in his stomach as he approached.

"Why the drawn shutters?" James asked as he closed the door, trying to appear as though he'd just returned from a coffee break rather than bereavement leave.

"I've seen the attention you're attracting this morning. You already look like you need a break. Closing the blinds allows us to talk free of interruption, although we both know they're out there."

"Good point," James responded with the edge of a grin.

"I don't know why you wanted to meet this early on your first day back," Vik said. "Get settled in. Close your blinds if you want. Put your mind back on track. All of this can wait."

"No, this is important," James said emphatically.

"Okay. What is it?"

James paused for a moment and took a short breath.

"My wife is dead because of me, Vik. I had a role. We had a role in killing her. Our entire company. The entire group working on these algorithms."

"I'm not quite sure I'm following you, James."

"After the funeral, I was given one-time access to Sara's work laptop. Ascendia allowed me to remove her personal files and photos. I saw her search history. Groups she subscribed to. Forums she was reading. I went through all her social media profiles. Viewed the ads targeting her. Watched the videos our partners were recommending on their home pages. Vik, she was being inundated with content around depression, miscarriage, anxiety, inadequacy, voodoo remedies, baby products, genetic testing, thinly veiled end-of-life content—you name it."

"What?" Vik said as he blinked and froze his eyes open.

"Vik. Sara was triggered into taking her own life."

"James, can we—" Vik attempted to interject.

"If someone searches, 'I'm depressed, I need a counselor,' this is straightforward. We have thousands of filters to detect overt behavior related to self-harm, abuse—you name it."

"Of course. I'm aware of this," Vik responded.

"The problem becomes exponentially complex when someone searches 'IVF' one day, and then weeks or months later stops using heart emojis on friends' pregnancy announcements and starts using just a 'like' emoji or scrolls past them altogether. The assumption the platform is making is subtle. Psychological. It's assuming envy and anxiety not from what the user is doing, but what they stopped doing."

James finally took a breath.

"Do you see my point?"

"Okay, so we need to reexamine the filtering process," Vik responded.

"That's not enough—not by a long shot," James said, moving forward in his chair.

"Have you ever heard the saying there are not enough grains of sand on Earth to represent the total number of possible moves in the game of chess?"

"No, I haven't, but—"

"By my estimate," James interrupted, "from every type of originating term or action, in all the languages we support, across all the platforms we're connected to, the number of scenarios that could lead someone to self-harm or the harm of others would equate to about 10,000 Earths' worth of grains of sand."

There was no other sound in the room save the slight hum of fresh air coming through the vents in the ceiling.

"In fact, I ran one test where if someone searched why they seemed to experience a bitter taste in their mouth after eating an orange? The content recommendations they received over the next four weeks could plausibly lead them to contemplate suicide."

"James, hang on. Can we slow down for a second? Oranges?"

"I know. I'm sorry," James exhaled, trying to find composure.

"I've been through the data and the evidence over and over again. I wasn't fully prepared on the delivery. I'm learning our platform works too well when certain combinations of negative inputs are used."

Vik stopped trying to press on James's brakes.

"We fine-tuned it. But the way we have it tuned now? Look at the profits of the social networks and search engines. Their stock prices almost never go down. Their revenues never go down. No matter what happens in the economy. That same thing that defies gravity—I'm telling you; this precision can cause triggers to go off in people's brains. *Is* causing."

Vik interrupted, "James, my friend. You just lost your wife. You have just been through the most terrible experience that any one of us could possibly imagine. You are not being objective."

"You and I fucking wrote this thing, Vik!" James exclaimed.

"Okay, James," Vik said, raising his hand and turning his head toward the door. "Man, I knew it was too early to bring you back. You probably knew it—"

"It wasn't too early, dammit!" James said, slamming his hand on the table. "Don't you understand? I was too LATE!"

"Let's pause for a second and look for objectivity," Vik responded, attempting to remain calm. "You know that any research of this kind always goes through peer review—"

"Then get it reviewed!" James slammed his hand on the small but sturdy round table. He looked down at the carpet, cupped his hands into a ball, and rested them on his forehead, in the same position he'd taken during Sara's memorial and in the wealthy man's house afterward. He took a breath in and exhaled deeply, staring at the floor.

"Vik, the pattern in the fucking carpet in this office was designed to subliminally invoke feelings of satisfaction and ambition in the people who work here," James said softly. "The fucking carpet. You know that. I know that. Because we know the people behind the research that proves it works. The carpet that's installed in every office, hallway, and conference room in this company."

James raised his head and looked, wearily, at Vik.

"So please, don't be naive with me. We are essentially enabling tril-lions of digital cocktail recipes that make violence and self-harm harder to detect and easier to carry out. And now we are on a path, in advance of becoming a public company, where AI becomes a bigger part of our roadmap, and where new kinds of companies—like governments, law enforcement, and even bad actors—want what we have."

"My wife," James continued, squeezing shut the microscopic open-ings of each of the tear ducts in his head with all his mental might, "my wife wasn't showing any signs of being suicidal."

"You were at the office a lot, ma—" Vik started and then abruptly stopped, knowing that his instinct and management training for a solution had no place in this interaction. "I didn't. I didn't mean it that way, James. I'm sorry."

Vik took a quick breath in through his nose, held briefly, and exhaled.

"I'm not telling you you're wrong. I wasn't even fully prepared to have you in the office. Me. My wife. Everyone around here. We can only try to help you."

"Listen," James continued, pinching the bridge of his nose while closing his eyes slowly.

"I understand what this document says. I know what's at stake. Money. Huge sums of money. Going public. Lots of millionaires to be minted in these buildings. But this isn't about that. It's about lives. I think we may have some culpability. And I don't think I can attach my name to it knowing it could be the reason I lost my wife and unborn kid."

Vik glanced back at James, his eyelids slightly weighted, not turn-ing away.

"Give me a day or two to process this," Vik whispered. He lifted the bottom right corner of the softcover-bound document about a third of the way in and let each corner of each page pass over the fingerprints of his thumb as they fell back into place.

"Okay?"

"Alright," James relented. "Just—try to look at this objectively. Will you do that for me?"

# 9

On a rare, cloudless Monday afternoon in March, Code&Craft buzzed with the usual tech crowd. Upstairs, at the end of the long bar, Michael Valeno, the CEO of EchoWave, sat scrolling through messages on his smartphone and nursing an amber ale.

Several minutes later, Vik pulled up a heavy, wrought-iron barstool next to his boss.

"I'll have an Anchor Steam as well, thank you," Vik said to the bartender, Chris Phelps, who also happened to be the owner of Code&Craft.

Michael did not look up from his device or his beer.

"I see James was back on campus today. How's he doing?" Michael asked.

Vik coyly glanced around, trying to spot any colleagues. It was just tech bros and gals in the standard Seattle garb of two-hundred-dollar jeans, fleece vests, shoes made of recycled tires, and smartwatches on their wrists. Each of them was paying for their dinner and drinks with someone else's borrowed money.

"That's actually why I wanted to meet you here. Away from the office," Vik responded.

Michael paused, took a sip of the bronze-colored ale, and set the glass down slowly, with precision, on the marble bar.

"Why? Does he need more time on bereavement? You could have solved that in a text message rather than a meeting. Not that I mind.

Even the nanny is fed up with the constant choir of colic and terrible twos, so my wife has put me on daddy duty tonight."

"He's not doing well. But I'm not sure bereavement is the only issue," Vik replied.

"What is it?"

Chris returned with an Anchor Steam for Vik, set it on a napkin, and politely nodded his head. As Vik took a sip, he turned his back, adding the beer to their bill on an iPad mounted to the bar. He was always curious about his patrons' conversations, but never obvious about eavesdropping.

"Over the last two weeks, James had an epiphany of sorts. I'm not sure. He thinks EchoWave—he thinks *he*—may be responsible for the death of his wife."

Michael's beer glass stopped inches from his lips.

"Explain in a little more detail?"

Vik angled his shoulder and head slightly closer to Michael

"Several months ago, we ran some tests in the platform. They bordered on inconclus—"

"Tests on what, for Christ's sake?" Michael interrupted through his clenched mouth.

"James believes Sara may have been triggered into suicide as a result of content she was exposed to across her search and social channels. Content related to depression associated with her two previous miscarriages."

"She'd been pregnant before?" Michael asked.

"Yeah. This was her third miscarriage. James claims to have done extensive research on how seemingly unrelated, innocuous search terms and social engagement can amplify manipulative content from the partners. He handed me a document—"

"From the *partners*," Michael repeated as he stared into the bar mirror in front of him.

"And these tests—said?"

"Well," Vik continued. "Remember when we deployed that 'Influence Policing' project in the UK? It used EchoWave technology to persuade illegal immigrants who'd made their way to France and Belgium not to try to swim the English Channel to the UK. This wasn't targeted advertising for deodorant. The objective was actual behavior modification through the use of images, text, and video. It worked."

"Yes, that effort actually *saved* lives. And now the British government is using it for a number of different public safety campaigns," Michael said proudly.

"Four thousand two hundred eleven campaigns in the UK alone to date. Correct," Vik confirmed. "Back to the tests—"

"You said he handed you a document?"

"Yes, it's about—"

Michael raised his hand to stop him mid-sentence.

"I assume you know even the perception of a whistleblower will scuttle the entire public offering. Regulators? Press? Do the math. But you're telling me it's inconclusive, so what's the news?"

"I know, but maybe going public isn't what we should—"

"Hear me very carefully, Vik," Michael interrupted softly but quickly, looking straight ahead into the bar.

"You are one of two technical co-founders of this company. I don't have to remind you, or your wife, or your kids in private schools, the amount of money you stand to gain when this company goes public later this year. And don't tell me you haven't calculated the number."

Vik's head was spinning.

"Just answer me this, Michael. Does the senior leadership or the board have an ethical or legal responsibility to at least dig a little deeper into his research? Maybe there is a flaw in the algorithm we are overlooking."

"To say I'm disappointed, Vik, would be an understatement," chided Michael. "You sound like a climate change activist. Recycle an aluminum can. Drive an electric car. Reverse global warming. But if China continues to pollute, what happens?"

Vik pretended to scoff in agreement.

"Exactly. Nothing changes. We can alter an algorithm, sure. To what end? Until our partners and everyone else collecting every second of our online behavior changes their practices, what's the point?"

Vik could only stare, catatonically, straight ahead.

"Listen," Michael said, standing up, wiping his mouth with his napkin, and throwing it on the bar. "James Wohlmuth is grieving. That's bias. He's lost objectivity."

"Michael, I knew Sara."

"I'd met her a few times, too. Beautiful, smart, super ambitious. We could have used her here at EchoWave."

"But I'd known her since before they were married. She was stronger than this."

Michael nodded.

"Then you just made my point. If she was so strong, how could something as simple as social media scrolling and browsing in online groups lead her to suicide? It was something else. Something we don't know. Maybe it was him?"

Vik hoped the seething in his mind was disguised on his face.

"I want to see this document. On my desk. Tomorrow morning," Michael said, emphatically. "Tell him we are looking into his analysis carefully. James needs more bereavement leave. And not here. Send him on vacation. Two weeks."

"Michael," Vik responded, still not unlocked from his stare.

"Two weeks' additional leave. That's my decision."

Vik nodded, reluctantly.

"You said he handed you one copy of his analysis?" Michael asked.

"Yes, it's locked in my office."

"I want it on my desk first thing tomorrow," Michael insisted. "And James needs to be on a plane within forty-eight hours."

Michael left, shaking the hands of two venture capitalists at the other end of the bar before descending the stairs.

"Check, please. I guess." Vik raised his finger to Chris, who walked to the iPad, printed the receipt, and set it on the bar.

"Anything else I can get for you this evening?" Chris asked.

"Yeah, a new boss," Vik whispered loudly as he signed the receipt and handed the folio back.

Vik exited into the early evening air, relishing the breeze hitting his face. He looked up to the clouds, beginning to form a stunning orange and purple sunset against the Olympic Mountains. Two sunsets, actually. The one in the sky and its mirror image, reflecting off the calm surface of Lake Washington.

Walking along the waterfront homes toward the marina, he glanced at the vastly oversized showpiece yachts with narcissistic names like *Eye PO'd*, *You Wish*, and *Que Hesse Será*. Contemplating the virtues of building a company at this level, and what it really meant in the end.

He pulled his phone out of the pocket of his gray sleeveless Patagonia fleece.

"Hey," James answered.

"Hey. I just had a good conversation with Michael. He's going to review the document, assemble a task force to replicate your tests, and come back with some answers. It's going to take a few weeks. He really appreciates the work you've done, considering the circumstances."

"Of course. This is good news. I appreciate it, Vik. I really do."

"James, you have a photo on your desk of you and Sara. With that castle in the background?"

"Yeah, Sara and me in Salzburg, Austria. Our honeymoon. Seven years ago. Why?"

"Michael wants to run these tests like it's a sterile lab. He wants you to extend your bereavement leave. It will be paid time off, of course. I think you should go back there. Clear your mind. EchoWave will buy your airline ticket and cover the accommodation. You'll come back fresh and we'll wrap this up."

"That wasn't really what I had in mind," James responded.

"It's the key requirement, James. I'm sorry. The task force will run their tests independently, and when you return, we will reconcile the results and make recommendations to the board. You know him and his 'with precision' bullshit."

"Alright," said James. "I suppose that makes sense."

"How did your meeting with the therapist go?"

"I didn't go to my meeting with the therapist, Vik."

"James, set work aside. As your friend, I think it's really important that you—"

"Vik, I appreciate you going to bat for me. I really do. But allow me to grieve my way. And the way I would have chosen to grieve, as I've been doing for the last two weeks, would be going back into work, connecting with my team, tracing, and replicating these anomalies. Anomalies that could be impacting others as we speak. That's my therapy. Everything you just conveyed to me is taking me away from managing my grief."

"Let's work out the details tomorrow, okay? I've got to run," said Vik, hanging up before James could interject again.

Vik paused and sat on a park bench near a small grassy hill, gazing at the masts in the marina as they rocked gently in the water, to the left and right. To anyone else, the rocking appeared random, but Vik knew better. The movement of the sails in the breeze wasn't random. It's predictable. And most predictable things can be manipulated.

Like human emotions. Human behavior. Human actions.

# 10

"James is on his way to Europe, I trust?" Michael asked Vik as the young co-founder walked into the CEO's massive office. Michael didn't turn his chair as Vik approached, choosing to remain seated at the conference table, looking out the large glass windows next to a man-made pond.

Vik reminisced about the early days of EchoWave, when he and James worked out of tiny co-working spaces, their monitors propped on plywood slabs, cords and cables strung like spaghetti between them. The smell of coffee and energy drinks saturated the air as they worked tirelessly to bring James's nascent idea—an algorithm for predicting user preferences—to life. Their seed capital, obtained with startling ease thanks to James's master's in Computational Linguistics and Vik's MBA credentials, had allowed them to quit their Google jobs and launch EchoWave with nothing but grit and vision.

Now there was a pond, with no practical purpose, outside the window of the CEO's office.

"I haven't heard from him yet, but I believe so, yes" Vik replied, hiding his resentment at how far they'd come—and how disconnected from their roots he now felt.

"Great," Michael said, his tone clipped. "Let's dive into his briefing."

"First, I confirmed with James before he left that he transferred his supporting data and notes to a secure server only he and I have access to at this point. We can use that data for the testing."

"We'll go through the data later," Michael said, adopting the tone of a highly efficient, bullet-point Pacific Northwest executive.

Michael began flipping through the pages of James's briefing, heavily marked with notes and redactions. Vik glanced at Michael's edits, remembering when their Duke University mentor, Rob Cook, had first encouraged them to pursue starting the company.

"We'll present to the team tomorrow morning. In the meantime, I need you to rewrite this section here. And this section needs to be toned down as well," Michael said, his red pen circling sections detailing code snippets, assumptions, and warnings he wanted to modify or withhold.

"Tone down what, Michael?" Vik returned. "This code is in production. Right now. If the team tests it with the same supporting data, they'll likely arrive at the same conclusions."

"If it's in production today, it's making us money today," Michael said, his gaze unwavering.

"I'm confused, Michael," Vik replied, furrowing his brow. "I agreed with you that James should extend his bereavement to clear his head. I agreed he should step back for an unbiased analysis, but not to altering his work. He spent almost three weeks on this. The three brutal weeks immediately following his wife's suicide, I should add. He's the technical expert. I wouldn't know where to start."

"I don't care what you do, Vik. You said it yourself. There's bias throughout this document that reflects his personal circumstances. Remove enough—like the bias, queries, whatever—to refocus this analysis on advertising persuasion, not behavior modification or mental health triggers. And you have two days. We want to make sure this doesn't disrupt progress on the platform or the upcoming roadshow for our Initial Public Offering."

"I still don't know how we're—"

"You'll present the document to the team tomorrow morning. Your conference room. Eight in the morning. Invite the product and technical vice presidents. Bring Rob Cook. And me."

"Michael—"

"Unless, of course, you want to be the one to tell the team that this study, this distraction, will delay our public offering a year. Maybe more. At which point the economy could tank, and EchoWave might not go public at all. Would you like to be the one to tell them that?"

"No, I wouldn't," Vik said, succumbing to Michael's pressure.

"Listen, tone the thing down. That's all I'm asking. I'm not shelving it. Just convince the team to approach this data like it's 'phase one.' When James returns in a couple of weeks, we'll roll out 'phase two' and so on."

Michael had a way of selling bottles of sand to dehydrated people in the desert, and this exchange was no different.

"I understand your point. You're right," Vik said, knowing he'd just become the next customer to buy sand.

"You have the rest of the afternoon and all night to make this right, Vik. Should be plenty of time."

# 11

The sound of church bells permeated the dark hotel room in the old town of Salzburg on the evening of his arrival. James opened one eye and noticed the clock showing just after five. He'd checked in six hours earlier and, not having slept on the flight from Seattle, decided to rest his eyes for a few minutes. Breaking the cardinal rule when traveling from the United States to Europe: on the first day, stay awake as long as possible.

The bed had been prepared in traditional Austrian style—a king mattress created from two twin beds, pushed together. Each side with its own down comforter, turned sideways and folded in half. A large square pillow placed at the head of each mattress.

Switching on his reading lamp, he rolled over and eyed the other half of the bed—the comforter and pillow remained in place, folded and untouched.

During their honeymoon seven years ago, he and Sara would lie in bed each morning, talking, laughing, staring at each other. Their three-year relationship felt new, even though they'd already lived together for almost two.

James tried to place himself in those conversations, under the sheets and in the cafés. They talked about the ceremony, the reception. The generosity of her father, who paid for their honeymoon. The intoxicated aunt who fell backward into the hedge just outside the country club entrance. And the couple who always badmouthed each other, found making out in the back seat of an Uber before it pulled away.

He tried to place himself in the seven years of conversations since their honeymoon. The work, the travel, the parties, company building, and promotions—all the ups and downs. The weddings and a smattering of divorces. The mutual friend who'd died in a car crash—killed by an oncoming drunk driver. The triathlon-obsessed aunt who'd died of cancer, and the chain-smoking uncle who'd survived it.

The nieces and nephews who gave them joy and laughter on holidays and play dates. Who also tested their patience, and their resolve to create a family of their own.

The gut punches of two miscarriages. Three, actually.

James turned on his back and faced the ceiling, wanting to see the memories and anecdotes, good, bad, or indifferent, dancing around in a way he could reach up and grab one, to make him smile or cry. Instead, the ceiling appeared as it was, coagulated into a blur of uniformity. He squinted and blinked, finding it difficult to pin down any one memory of their lives together.

*Jet lag*, he thought.

Planting his feet on the floor, James walked to the window, separated the soft white drapes, and opened the blackout shades to peer out at the late afternoon. The sky was crisp, and the sunset emitted hues of orange and violet. The day had carried on without him.

A hot shower and change of clothes made him feel refreshed and more in control. He sent a few text messages and, before any responses could steal his attention, switched his phone to Do Not Disturb mode. Intent to decompress. To disconnect from work, news, or distractions. To retrace the path of a happier time in his life.

*If I'm going to be here, I might as well be here,* he thought.

James walked down the stone staircase to the lobby of the old hotel, toward the entrance. The bellman stood stoically next to the stalwart, wood-plank doors, wearing shiny black boots connected at the heels. After opening the door, James walked out into the evening air, glancing in both directions, choosing to turn left down the narrow Strasse.

After taking a few steps, he paused and turned around to the bellman.

"Excuse me," James said. "Did I hear the sound of church bells a little while ago?"

"You did, sir. From the Salzburg Carillon. Can I offer you directions?"

"I'm okay," James replied. "I think I'll just walk in that direction—before the sun fully sets."

"Wonderful. You have a crisp, clear evening ahead of you."

"It does appear that way. One more question. Do the bells ring again in the morning?"

The bellman smiled and nodded.

"Yes. Every day at seven o'clock, eleven o'clock, and finally at five o'clock in the evening. With the exception of Good Friday and Holy Saturday."

"Eleven a.m.? I didn't hear the bells this morning after checking in."

"Please tell me you hadn't fallen asleep after your arrival?"

"I'm afraid I did, yes," James responded.

"Well then, sir, I assume we'll be seeing you later this evening—and wide awake in the lobby in the middle of the night," the bellman said, smiling.

# 12

The all-nighter Vik pulled at the office left him resentful and groggy. Each sentence altered and paragraph removed from the briefing seemed to widen the gap in the trust and partnership he and James had built over the last fifteen years. The five thousand miles of distance between them wasn't helping.

Several times during the night, he resisted the urge to call James for guidance. For reassurance that his alterations weren't betraying James's work.

As the subtle, lagging dawn appeared over the towering evergreens to the east of the EchoWave campus, Vik reviewed the document one final time before sending it to Michael.

Anxiety was gnawing at him as he sat at a small table in the cafeteria. His phone leaned against his half-full, mouthpiece-crusted coffee tumbler as he sent a message to his wife, wishing her good morning and asking for a quick video chat with her and their two children before they left for school. It was an attempt to replenish some of the soul he felt had been drained out of his body during the week.

"Do they have beds at your office, Daddy?"

"No, honey, Daddy didn't go to sleep. But I promise I'll sleep really well when I tuck you in tonight, okay?"

"Good, because I had a bad dream last night."

Vik smiled sympathetically, feeling warmth and connection to the child speaking to him, as his wife and their younger child glowed blue in the background, preoccupied with their devices.

"I know what you mean about the bad dream, honey, because Daddy had one, too," he responded.

"So, I guess that means we'll have to protect each other tonight, right, Daddy?"

Vik felt there were enough changes in the analysis to ease the team into the concerns James identified without creating the same level of alarm or disbelief Vik had felt when he first read the document.

But James was the true expert. Vik wasn't sure how the executives would respond. And if they did, what questions they might pose that only James could answer—or how James would react to all the changes made without consulting him first.

A few minutes before eight, the team of twenty executives began filing into the large conference room on the second floor of the engineering and product team's building. Michael entered with his assistant, shaking hands and exchanging pleasantries with team members whose names he neither knew nor cared to learn.

Making his way to the head of the table, he sat and turned toward the presentation screen, his position and body language indicating it was time to start. The seat choice was by design—to have a clear view of facial expressions and responses as the content was presented and discussed.

With everyone seated, the glass doors closed and mechanical shades descended. Michael stood to address the group.

"Good morning. Thank you all for taking time this early on a Friday. I called this meeting to make you aware of and discuss a fairly alarming document James shared with me the day he returned from bereavement leave."

Vik jolted in his seat slightly, wanting to correct the record of the document's initial recipient and Michael's early dismissal of its relevance. The context and facts were shape-shifting before his weary eyes.

"As we all know, James's wife, Sara, took her own life just over three weeks ago. We don't know, and we may never fully understand, all the circumstances around this horrific tragedy."

Michael paused and bowed his head, signaling the room to partake in a moment of silence.

*Without uttering a word, this man sits, and everyone else sits,* Vik thought. *He bows his head, and everyone else bows.*

After a few seconds, Michael raised his head and continued.

"James spent the bulk of his bereavement leave composing an analysis of his wife's online behavior prior to her passing. He analyzed her social media activity, including phrases and terms she searched for and posted in the weeks and months leading up to her passing. He concluded there could be combinations of search terms and activity that lead our partners to deliver dark, unhealthy posts and ads. And by viewing them, over time, some users might develop feelings of anxiety, depression, or self-harm."

The group appeared surprised and alarmed, shifting their bodies and attention more fully toward Michael.

"I take James's analysis very seriously, which is why this week I tasked Vik with reviewing it carefully and coming up with his own set of initial recommendations."

Vik felt dryness in his mouth, realizing he had only a coffee tumbler, but no water.

"Obviously, the safety and well-being of every user across all our partners will always be our highest priority," Michael continued. "We are in the business of helping our partners improve user experience for billions of people around the world, and I shudder to think that anyone could be harmed by what you and your teams have built over the last decade."

Vik realized Michael had sold him yet another bottle of sand; he was now as parched as if he were trekking across the desert.

Fifteen minutes into Vik's halting presentation, Rob Cook raised his voice from the back of the room.

"Good God, this is just another Vance and Belknap fiasco."

"Vance and who?" Vik asked.

"Back in 1985, two guys—Jimmy Vance and Raymond Belknap. Days before Christmas, they grab malt liquor, a boom box, weed, and a shotgun, and head to a park. Somewhere in Nebraska. They're blasting Judas Priest. Stained Class, was the album, I think. After getting drunk and high, one of them shoots himself under the chin. Dies instantly. The other one waits a while, then shoots himself, too. He survives it, and ODs two years later."

The room was stunned and silent, uncertain how this story was connected to James's briefing, EchoWave, or anything at all.

"Anyway, the parents sued the band, claiming subliminal messaging in one of the songs told them to 'do it.' They claimed a song caused their sons to take their own lives."

"And?" one executive ventured cautiously.

"Judge threw the case out almost immediately," Rob replied. "Blaming the band was easier than facing reality. That drug use, bad parenting, and kids making stupid dares were the actual cause. But the case set a precedent. Exposure to content is nearly impossible to prosecute. And is rarely the root cause of someone's demise."

He let the weight of his words hang for a moment.

"I've known James for years. Brilliant engineer, sharp theorist. But this report? It's confirmation bias. It's his grief, plain and simple."

The group was assigned sections of the modified document to research and report. But by the time the meeting adjourned two hours later, Michael felt comfortable the briefing would be but a minor blip on the radar in the coming months.

"Vik, meet me over in my office in twenty minutes," Michael said.

"Of course," Vik responded, not peering up from his screen, scrolling through the company's internal chat app, trying to disguise that he was petrified and shell shocked.

As Michael started toward the stairs, one of James's team members, Angelica Chen, rushed to catch up with him.

"Michael? Do you have thirty seconds?"

"Thirty seconds, sure. What is it?"

"The old man is wrong, Michael. I feel an obligation to tell you that."

"What do you mean?"

"Setting aside the fact that we should always do the right thing, even if we think we're shielded from liability—emotional triggers caused by a song? This isn't even remotely close to what we're dealing with here."

"I'm not following you, Angelica."

"Our algorithms adapt to the person or a group of people. They don't remain static. They evolve with the user's psyche. What if our partners are feeding us data that overly emphasizes 'can't look away' content? The song doesn't remain the same."

Michael said nothing, allowing Angelica's frustration to burn out unchallenged.

"When is James returning from leave?"

"A few more weeks, I believe," Michael responded as he descended the staircase.

# 13

Turning left out of his hotel led James through a small plaza, an arch-covered portal, and into more plazas, dotted with cafés and shops, until he reached the Mozartplatz. Every turn offered a commanding view of the landmark fortress atop the hill overlooking the city.

As he continued, streets and alleys became narrower, plazas smaller, until he finally reached the Salzburg Justice Center and Neue Residenz, where the administrative and residential buildings for Salzburg's historical Prince Archbishop were located.

In this area, tourists began to thin out, leaving only the more curious and adventurous, asking, "What is on the other side of the fortress?"

With nothing but time on his hands, James walked.

An elderly woman on a rickety city bicycle rode past him, wicker baskets filled to the brim with groceries and flowers. James followed, thinking he could keep up with her, his lungs burning from the cool air. Several minutes later, atop the hill behind the fortress, the woman disappeared into the distance, leaving James struggling to breathe.

I have got to get back into shape when I get back to Seattle, he vowed.

He pressed on toward a large, ornate iron gate affixed with the letters "HL." *So this is where this is, he thought.*

Hotel Leopoldskron. Made famous by the movie The Sound of Music.

He continued walking toward a white building along the shores of a pond, noticing a restaurant with a patio. Although spring was just beginning to emerge, guests were seated outside, enjoying the view, their meals, and conversation under warm wool blankets and heaters.

As he approached the host stand, the restaurant proprietor, Valarie Entdeckheim, greeted him in German.

"*Guten Abend. Kann ich Ihnen helfen?*" she asked.

"Uh, *Tisch für eins, bitte?*" James responded, using his best high-school and college German to request a table for one.

"Of course," Valarie responded in English. "Follow me, please."

Maybe he would practice his German another time.

"*Danke,*" he replied in his last linguistic effort, pulling in his chair and absorbing the view of the pond and the famous hotel on its bank.

"*Bitte gerne.* Your server will be right with you."

James gazed at the menu for several minutes. It appeared to be in German, although Valarie handed him the English version.

When the server returned to take his order, he squeezed his eyes closed and blinked twice.

"Jet lag," he responded with a confused smile. "Why don't you just bring me your favorite item on the menu and whatever bottle of wine you'd pair with it?"

"Of course, sir. That would be beef tenderloin in a white pasta cream sauce, along with a bottle of Austrian white wine. The bottle is sixty euros. Will that suit you?"

"Yes, thank you for telling me the price beforehand. And I'll start with a gin and tonic and some bread, please."

Waiting for his meal allowed time to consume the loaf of bread and two cocktails. The surrounding sounds of German-language conversations and flickering candlelight arrived in his brain as if he were submerged in the ocean. At night.

Thirty minutes later, the entrée was placed in front of him. The bottle of wine, uncorked and poured, was set on ice next to the table.

It took some effort for James to resurface into reality. He stared at his meal for a few moments rather than diving in, causing fleeting glances from the staff.

The plate in front of him, elegantly prepared and delivered with polite service. Since Sara's passing, food consumption was for utility rather than enjoyment.

James finally cut into the first bite of meat, swirled it into the sauce, and placed it in his mouth. The perfected combination of flavors forced its way into his dull consciousness as he chewed.

The fork carrying the mouthful of pasta dropped into the bowl, prompting the proprietor to quickly approach James and ask if everything was alright.

"It's wonderful, thank you. I'm sorry, I'm just... is this your restaurant?" James responded, trying to redirect the conversation.

Valarie explained the restaurant's history, now ten years old, and the building which housed it, twenty times older. She operated the front of the restaurant and managed the wine cellar. Her husband, the head chef, was responsible for the kitchen and everything else.

Like many establishments in Austria, the building also served as their home, with views of the fortress, the pond, and the famous hotel directly outside their windows.

"May I ask where you are visiting from?" Valarie asked, having a moment to chat as the restaurant began to clear out.

"I'm from the United State—"

He paused, knowing she was probably aware of his nationality based on his accent and the logo emblazoned on his fleece.

"I mean, I'm from Seattle."

"Ah, Seattle. Beautiful," she said. "I've been once. My husband and I stayed downtown and walked to the Pike Street Market."

"Yes, the Pike Place Market, of course. Very popular."

"Pike Place Market, correct. Those men throw the fish from one side of the counter to the other. So cool. And the gum wall."

"Yes, the gum wall," he responded as he gently set his wine glass on the tablecloth.

"Although I could never understand why we saw so many people sleeping on the streets," she pondered.

"That is a problem, I agree," James responded. "And I'm glad to see that's the message we're sending to the rest of the world."

He just missed catching the condescension in his voice before it escaped.

"I'm sorry for my tone. My, my wife passed away—a month ago today, in fact— and I'm—"

Valarie's hand vaulted immediately to her heart.

"Oh, *es tut mir sehr leid*, sir," she said, not allowing the phrase "I'm sorry" to translate in her mind before it left her mouth.

"Thank you. We spent the first few days of our honeymoon in Salzburg years ago. I came back to clear my mind a bit, I guess."

"Allow me to bring you a dessert and an aperitif. With my compliments, Mr—?"

"Mr. Wohlmuth. James Wohlmuth. I appreciate the gesture, but it's really not necessary."

"But I insist," Valarie said, raising her eyebrow with a somewhat surprised expression on her face.

"Did I say something unusual?"

"Not unusual, Mr. Wohlmuth. It's just not a name I hear often from American visitors. Are you aware you have an Austrian name?" she asked.

"Really? An Austrian name? I was always told it was of German origin. I didn't know it was Austrian."

"Yes. And, well actually, quite a famous, or infamous, name to Salzburg," she continued. "Excuse me. I'll be right back with your dessert and drink."

As he waited, the smartphone in his pocket tugged at his curiosity.

Open a browser and search this name—your name. Infamous Wohlmuths? Do it now! Search now!

But he remained committed to his screen-free evening.

"*Guten Appetit*," Valarie said, as she set the plate and glass on the table. "And again, please accept my deepest sympathies for the loss of your wife."

"Thank you," James responded, looking at her instead of the dessert. "When you said infamous... I mean about my last name. What exactly did you mean?"

"Ah, *schau ma mal*, I was just wondering to myself if I made a mistake even mentioning this to you, as you are here trying to enjoy a quiet meal."

"It's fine, really. Please tell me. I'm curious by nature."

"Well," Valarie started with a sigh of reluctance, twisting the cross around her neck between two fingers and gazing across the pond. "A long time ago. Seventeen hundreds, I believe. A man named Franz Joseph Wohlmuth lived and, well, worked, in a house on the other side of our pond here. Just over a kilometer in that direction."

Pointing in the direction of her gaze, she continued.

"He occupied that house for almost sixty years as the last appointed executioner of Salzburg. He was the man who actually performed the executions ordered by authorities. Most of them were carried out on his property. But what made him infamous was—"

She paused.

"Yes?" James asked. "But what made him infamous?"

"What made him infamous was the detailed diary he kept of every execution he performed on his property."

# 14

Vik was led to the conference table in Michael's office twenty minutes after the team meeting concluded. After taking a leisurely bathroom break and speaking to a couple of other executives, Michael entered.

He sat at the table and looked at Vik with a smile.

"What in the hell happened back there, Michael?" Vik demanded.

"What do you mean? I thought it went well overall."

"You asked me to modify James's analysis and document, and then, you threw me under the bus."

Michael paused for a moment, as if the ignition sequence to a rocket were about to commence.

"Vik, when James gets settled overseas, we're cutting him loose. We're not going to have a crisis like this on our hands so close to the finish line."

"You cannot do that, Michael. He's going to talk. I'm going to talk," Vik responded, his heart pounding so hard he thought it might be shaking the zipper on his pullover.

"Talk about what? That using social media is bad for your mental health? I can have the public relations team generate a report on that for me in about an hour. This is the direction we're going. The Board of Directors is with me. Anything else?"

"No. I mean, yes. There is. He's going to talk about the algorithmic elements that could be steering people to self-harm. And he's going to talk about how our partners could be using the data we collect for purposes we hadn't considered."

A short, condescending burst of air emitted from Michael's nostrils.

"Let me explain to you why he's not going to do that. And, for that matter, why you're not going to do it, either."

Vik's face was motionless, but his body felt like it was taking part in a high-intensity workout.

"Because I will terminate you, right now, if you don't categorically retract the words you just said."

He allowed his statement to ring in Vik's ears for a moment.

"You and James and your early-stage investors wooed me to join EchoWave for months. And if I remember correctly, I think your reasoning was, 'to bring adult supervision into the room and take this thing to the next level.' Am I right?"

Vik blinked slowly but did not acknowledge Michael as he leaned forward.

"Remind me how many employees the company had when I joined?"

"One hundred, I believe," Vik relented.

"And how many does it have now?"

"North of six hundred. Almost seven."

"And how many social networks were partners when I joined?"

"Three."

"And how many are partners now?"

After pausing, Vik relented again, sighing.

"All of them. All the majors, anyway."

"And, again, as we discussed the other day, how many millions of dollars do you and your family stand to gain when this company enters the public markets later this year?"

Vik did not respond.

"This isn't some loose bolt on an airplane, Vik. A bolt that can be physically inspected by some lackey at the FAA. This airplane is invisible. There is no way for anyone outside this organization to conduct safety inspections. There is no quality control."

"And do you know why there is no quality control in companies like these?" Michael continued.

"Why?" Vik asked.

"Because there is no one, in any government, regulatory body, or advocacy organization, anywhere in the world, that has any idea what your millions of lines of code actually do."

Vik didn't move.

"The beauty of what you—you and James—built is that every time you take a prospective partner out to Mexican food and nearly shit your pants afterwards, what happens?"

"They sign the contract," Vik whispered.

"They sign the contract. That's correct. And not only do they sign the contract, but every time a new partner connects into our back-end, the complexity of the data flow between all the partners increases, what, threefold?"

Vik exhaled as if he'd been holding his breath for minutes.

"Remind me, please, as I'm clearly terrible with numbers. How many grains of sand make up that number of algorithmic possibilities?"

"I think I understand your point," Vik conceded.

"No, I actually don't think you do yet, Vik. Because if you and these teams start digging in and some busy bee comes to the conclusion that the algorithm James—and you—invented and perfected, could be, may be, might be, killing people? Starting with the wife of the co-founder?"

Vik knew where he was going, and it showed in his eyes. Vik had no poker face.

"Yea," Michael continued. "Then someone inside the company is going to tell someone outside the company. And if it somehow comes to light in the media that you neglected to—or purposefully withheld —such critical data when you hired me? When you brought in those millions of dollars in venture capital?"

Vik felt as if the entirety of his skeletal composition had suddenly been extracted from his body.

"That's right, you're getting it now. Every single investor you've taken money from. Every single executive you've recruited. Every single customer you've sold to. They're going to come after you. They're going to sue you. And James. Personally. And when that happens, you'll have more judgments against you than a butcher has blades—carving you up piece by piece until there's nothing left."

Vik was speechless. Michael had always been all business with most people in the company. And visceral with anyone who stood in the way of the company's goals. It was fun for the two founders to watch him be the henchman on their behalf. Vik never imagined these traits would be turned toward him. And now against him.

Michael stood from his desk and placed his knuckles on the ebony surface.

"You guys got me into this thing. Practically begged me, even after I told the investors I'd join. Such a joke. That night at Canlis restaurant when you and James tried to woo me over with that 2007 *Domaine des Comtes Lafon Premier Cru*. Twelve hundred dollars for that bottle, right?"

Vik angled his head and squinted, trying to understand where Michael was going with his statement.

"Frank Elatra at Percussion Ventures told you to order that bottle of wine. Right? Do you know why he told you to order that bottle? And why he said he'd approve the expense when he never previously approved an expense like that?"

"No, I don't," Vik succumbed.

"Because a few months earlier, at a wine tasting at his house, just after he'd returned from France with two cases of that exact wine, I told him I thought the wine lacked structure. Even though, honestly, it was marvelous. I just said it to get under his skin. And look what happened? He had you deliver me another bottle. This time with a great view of Lake Union."

Michael began tapping his pen on the desk before continuing.

"You guys sign the employment and stock option agreements your investors tell you to sign. You hire the attorneys we tell you to hire so you can tell your wives that you're fully protected. But what you don't know is that those same lawyers were also at Frank's wine tasting, slurping six-hundred-dollar bottles of Premier Cru, having no idea why it's complex, snorting piles of the finest Colombian coke, and getting blindfold lap dances from the most exotic women you ever imagined could be trafficked through Vancouver."

Vik had previously believed all this underground activity was just rumors geeky venture capitalists spread to make themselves sound cool.

Until now.

"You know, I didn't have to take this gig, Vik. When AxxelX went public ten years ago, the Board of Directors gave me unfettered access to the company jet. But once the company was acquired by IBM, my wife and kids couldn't use it for our trips to Aspen and Cabo."

"I thought your kids were young, Michael," Vik said, trying to recoil his mistake.

"That was my first wife, Vik."

"Right."

"A month later, I'm standing at SeaTac with my, yes, soon-to-be ex-wife and kids. We're about to take a two-week trip to London and Dublin. British Airways. 747 non-stop from Seattle to London."

Vik began to realize reality had departed the meeting.

"Do you know what my kid says to me as we're standing in the boarding area?"

"No, Michael, what did your kid say to you?"

"She said, 'Daddy, I don't understand why we can't take the little plane to London.'"

"The little plane?" Vik asked.

"Yea, the private jet. The one the Board of AxxelX gave me to use. The one IBM took away."

Vik was stunned into speechlessness.

"I've got a thing coming up, Vik. Listen to me. Don't worry about James. This is a good thing for him. You told me the other night. He's not the same. He's lost objectivity. That's what you told me."

"That's not what I—" Vik tried to interject.

"His shares in the company will be fully vested by the time of the public offering. And we will give him a more than adequate severance to stay quiet about this thing. Which, based on the document you presented to the team today, is not a thing, right? Right?"

The double slap of Michael's hand on Vik's back was more physical proof that his spine had evaporated. He was trapped and powerless.

"Vik, I'm protecting you. And your team and your family, okay? And when this one goes public? I get the little plane back. Smooth sailing for you and James for the rest of your lives. Trust me. You keep doing what you're doing. Okay? Good."

# 15

The cool air settled the food and alcohol into James's stomach as he turned toward the dimly lit far side of the Hohensalzburg fortress, the only landmark to guide him back through town and to his hotel.

He walked the path with a slightly different perspective. A deeper connection to the ground, unsure if it was his innate sense of direction or learning the coincidence of his name from the restaurant proprietor.

*How many Wohlmuths outside my family have I known in the United States?* he wondered. *None? Almost none?*

Turning a corner, he walked past a baroque chapel he'd missed earlier in the day. A small copper tube extended from the front façade, water pouring into an ornate tiled basin below.

He allowed his hand to flow under the water, watching as the direction of the splash altered the reflection in the basin. It was icy cold and clung to his skin, creating a fleeting moment of lucidity as it sparkled under the streetlights above.

The voices of two young women walking up the Strasse caused him to pull his hand from the fountain, wipe it on his pants, and continue walking.

One woman stopped at the fountain and removed a stainless steel bottle from her backpack. She placed it under the fountain and filled the container before continuing on.

James paused after the women rounded the corner, wondering why he'd been so timid. He walked back to the fountain, placing his hands under the brutally cold water. This time, he cupped them, splashed his face, and took a drink.

Walking another few minutes, he passed a small café, open late, with free seats scattered among students and couples. On the bar was a high-end espresso machine and bottles of spirits and liquors.

Hoping for a seat at the bar but not knowing how to convey his preference in German, the host led him to a small white table wedged between a couple sitting across from each other on one side, and a group of female university students on the other.

"*Entschuldigen,*" James uttered as he squeezed between the tables. But the couple was preoccupied with their devices, each in their own worlds, not speaking to each other, let alone answering him.

James felt a tinge of remorse. *Damn, my work contributed to that,* he thought, which made him further resolved to keep his own device in his pocket until after he returned to the hotel.

On the other side, college students sipped coffees and long glasses of Stiegl beer. A couple of them smoked. All of them held devices in their hands.

The pattern of their behavior followed exactly what EchoWave's market research teams had predicted. A woman lifted her phone and showed an image or a short video to a friend. Others laughed. Another searched for something relatable. Yet another took a selfie. Then leaned into a friend for an '*us-sie*'. Peace sign. Click. Puckered lips. Click. Tongue extended. Click. Laughter. Click to post. Repeat. Until closing time.

*Insert behaviorally relevant advertisement between every third flick of the thumb,* he thought. *And that's how tech millionaires are made.*

The scene made him feel isolated, even as he sat in the midst of social activity. One of the world's foremost experts in understanding predictable behavior, watching a group of girls in their early twenties scroll through their devices—a half a world away from home.

*Youthful naïveté, no matter what language they are speaking,* he thought.

Confident, but only out of the unknown. Sweaters showing wear from the two or three years of being washed in commercial laundromats.

Well-worn jeans. Scuffed Puma and Adidas shoes. Good bags. Expensive phones. No established image—just youth.

A wave of nausea tightened his stomach. Guilt swelling from the thoughts he'd allowed into his brain—a brain instructed to be on bereavement leave. A brain encouraged to unplug, reset, and relax. A brain cultivating the idea that, with incredible speed and accuracy, content can be manipulated based on human behavior. And human behavior can be manipulated based on electronic content.

A brain that had led him to the company he'd created. The tragedy he'd experienced. To his sitting in this bar alone, as a late thirty-something widower, staring at college girls, rather than sitting across the table from his beautiful, pregnant wife.

James once felt positive about his work, and the briefing he'd written to course-correct the technology he believed could be harmful in certain circumstances. Out of this terrible tragedy—a tragedy that had set his life on a vastly different course than he ever believed he would experience—maybe something good could come from it. He had a capable team, and when he returned to the office, they would address the issues with the algorithm, adjust, with precision, and move forward.

Every few minutes, an eternity in the attention spans of college students, one of the young women would glance in his direction, blink, and again look away. Large brown eyes, set perfectly within the frame of her elegant Parisian face, unnecessarily contrasted with heavy eyeliner.

As she rose from her chair to use the bathroom, a slight smile emerged from her face—or so he imagined—as she navigated behind her friends. Her youthful, athletic proportions distorted his consciousness, seeing her as two feet taller than he, when in reality, she was probably six inches shorter.

James blinked, severing the glance between he and the young woman, turning his eyes down to his drink. The shining wedding ring on his finger caught his attention.

She squeezed between the tables, leaving a drift of a fragrance he'd never encountered before. Youthful. Bright. Carefree. He exhaled and blinked, nervously turning the circle of white gold, noticing its loose-ness from the travel and the stress.

In a matter of weeks, he'd gone from confident and self-aware to vulnerable and insecure. He was a senior executive at a technology company in Seattle that would go public later in the year. He'd invented much of the core technology that made the company so successful. He'd found and married a woman out of his league and tried to make her feel beautiful, safe, and loved. Or at least he thought he had.

Looking up out of his daze, James motioned to the server to pay his check.

As he stood to leave the bar, he glanced toward the far side of the café. A young couple was seated next to the window, gazing into each other's eyes. Potted plants sat on a narrow stone windowsill with small flowers emerging. The window above them partially fogged from hours of exhaled breaths inside.

*Do we listen in on your conversations?* He thought back to Brittney's question from the conference. *Of course they do. We all do.*

But these two weren't speaking. They were gazing at each other. Elbows on the table. Each hand locked in their partner's like they were about to arm wrestle.

The scene was a perfect frame of the last remaining untrackable, untraceable, analog moments. A rarity. He couldn't even see devices on the table.

*Impossible.*

Real, direct human interaction, uninfluenced by anything more than primal attraction.

He left the café, continuing through the old town into the narrow *Judengasse* alley, with its tasteful boutiques labeled with ornate wrought iron signage and strings of soft incandescent bulbs crisscrossing and illuminating the yellow, tan, and light blue buildings.

James was not a disciple of the arbitrary. Nor did he tend to track the intervals of life, save for birthdays and anniversaries. And even then he was known to miss a few. But something in his mind had shifted, causing him to mention the one-month mark since his wife's passing to the restaurant proprietor.

Another memory ascended into his consciousness, and he could see himself and his new wife, seven years prior, slowly walking arm-in-arm up the same alley.

They paused under the lights, gazing at each other for a moment, as newlyweds do.

Sara had said, "This street is amazing at night. Selfie!"

They turned their heads and snapped one photo, and then the next, and the next. James maintained one goofy pose. Sara shifted her eyes, mouth, and hair with every click. And then they continued.

"I could live here, in Salzburg. You?" Sara asked him.

"I'm not sure. It's beautiful, for sure. But the language," James responded.

"You took German in college, right, Mr. Wohlmuth? You'll be fine," she'd said, tugging at his arm while burying her thick brown hair into his shoulder.

"Yes, and in high school as well. And my German barely got us through customs in Munich."

"You're probably right. And our friends. And jobs. And your parents. And mine. Okay, it's not going to work. Let's just pretend we live here for the next three days."

After arriving at the hotel, the front desk receptionist looked at James and asked if he was allergic to Salzburg's spring pollen. His eyes, red and inflamed from alcohol, jet lag, loss and regret.

"Yes, that must be what it is—allergies," James responded, even though he had no allergies.

"Not to worry," she responded. "There's a pharmacy not far from here you can visit in the morning."

James closed the door to his room and removed his shoes, noticing the turndown service housekeeping provided. The two comforters on the bed had been unfolded and turned into place, welcoming him and the presumed second guest back from an evening in Salzburg. Bottles of still water, along with drinking glasses, and squares of dark chocolate had been placed on each nightstand. Small white mats had been set on the floor next to each side of the bed, along with terrycloth slippers.

Still dressed, James lay down on the neatly prepared bed, unwrapping and eating each chocolate as he gazed at the ceiling.

And fell asleep.

# 16

After waking, James needed a minute for his eyes to regain focus, the lights in the room still shining brightly. His head turned toward the sound of Mozart emerging from the TV mounted on the wall.

A welcome screen and the text *"Herzlich Willkommen Herr Wohlmuth"* displayed above his room number, along with options for Room Service, Channels, and Things to Do Around Salzburg. It was just after two in the morning.

He stood up, limped to the bathroom, and changed down to his underwear, leaving everything else on the floor.

For the first time since landing in Europe, he pulled the laptop from his backpack, and sat at the small table next to the window to log in.

He entered his username and password, and a red exclamation point flared in the top right corner of the screen, signaling an urgent email. As dozens of messages populated the inbox, one stayed fixed at the top of the email app window:

*SUBJ: EchoWave Secure Communication*

*James-*
*Please see the attached secure message from EchoWave Human Resources. After accessing, copies will be forwarded to your personal email address listed in your personnel file.*
*Kind Regards,*

*Alisa Hermes*
*Chief People Officer*
*EchoWave, Inc.*

*CLICK HERE TO DOWNLOAD*

A document on EchoWave letterhead opened in the browser window. Under the current date, his name, and address, the letter read:

*RE: Notice of Termination of Employment*

*Dear Mr. James Wohlmuth,*
*This letter is to officially notify you of the termination of your employment with EchoWave, effective immediately. This decision comes after a thorough internal review and is in accordance with our company policies and your employment agreement.*
*Despite the termination of your employment, you remain bound by the confidentiality agreement you entered into at the commencement of your employment with EchoWave, Inc. You are required to maintain the confidentiality of all proprietary information, trade secrets, and other sensitive information of EchoWave, Inc. that you were privy to during your tenure. Violating the confidentiality agreement may result in legal action and claims for damages.*
*We request that you return all company property, including*

*electronic devices, keys, and documents, within 14 days of this corre-*
*spondence. Failure to do so may result in additional legal action.*

*Please review, sign, and return the attached documents, which*
*include the Contingent Severance Agreement, Contingent Stock Op-*
*tions Vesting Agreement, Contingent Benefits Continuation Agree-*
*ment, and Release of Claims Agreement. A secure email containing*
*copies of these documents, as well as instructions for returning com-*
*pany property, has been sent to your personal email address on file,*
*as well as your home address.*

*We wish you success in your future endeavors.*
*Kind regards,*

*Alisa Hermes*
*Chief People Officer*
*EchoWave, Inc.*

James sat, bewildered and in shock, staring at the blinking cursor in front of the email response he planned to type. But couldn't.

He stood up and paced the room. Then sat again, skimming the documents a second time, still in disbelief. Parallel thoughts scattered and collided through his muddled, foggy head.

"There must be some mistake," he said aloud. "This letter didn't come from Michael. It came from Alisa. Michael personally recommended her. Vik would have given me a heads-up. But Michael? We recruited him to be CEO. He can't just fire me. Can he?"

"What time is it in Seattle? I need to call somebody."

"I really should call Sa—"

"Why is my screen blacked out? I barely used my phone today."

"3:25 a.m... What time is it in Seattle? 6:30? 7:30?"

"It's a mistake—a prank. No chance this is a prank. So a mistake. Has to be."

"That *other* famous Harvard dropout did this to *his* co-founder. Twenty years ago."

"No way EchoWave's attorneys—our attorneys—would allow this."

The spinning in the room led him to the opposite side of the bed—the side Sara would have occupied. He lay down, grabbing his phone from the nightstand. The screen was dark. He squeezed the large button on the side, then pressed the volume buttons up and down, attempting to restart the device.

The phone powered up, opening to the home screen but only showing the Settings icon. Apps for email, scheduling, internal communication, watching movies, and reading the news had vanished.

Powering the phone off and on again, his palms shook as if he were losing grip on a rope that kept him from falling into a deep ravine.

His ability to reason, to calmly and confidently work through a problem, had vanished like the apps on his screen. The accrual of nearly twenty years of academics and business-building experience, for now, fully occluded.

James set the device on the nightstand and wiped his nose, noticing a streak of blood on his index finger. He rushed to the bathroom, ran water over a hand towel, and pressed it against his face, tilting his head back toward the ceiling. When he returned to the room, he noticed several drops of blood drying on the crisp white sheets.

He sat at the table, noticing the EchoWave screensaver on his laptop. Running his still-bloody index finger across the trackpad, he brought up a login window requesting his username and password. After entering his credentials with one hand and clicking Enter, the phrase "Invalid User" appeared in bold red type.

James allowed the bloodied towel to fall on the carpet as he re-entered his credentials several times using both hands. With each attempt: the same result. The submission of his identity, a process as natural and predictable as breathing, so ingrained in the depths of his consciousness, was failing.

Staring at the wall in front of him, he slowly closed the laptop. For a moment, he was transported into the courtyard outside the hotel, engaged in a game of *Blinde Kuh*, a version of blind man's bluff the children of Salzburg used to play centuries ago. James, his eyes covered by torn black remnants of a wiry cloth sack, ran aimlessly, his hands extended out, following the echoes of Sara, pages from his briefing, Michael, his unborn child, Vik, his future, and the truth—as all of them, all of it ran, ducked and twisted out of his way.

He kept chasing the voices, trying to close the distance between his fingers and the sounds. Fragments of the call Sara made to the OB/ GYN clinic the day after he left for Orlando. Bits of the meeting finalizing his termination. The look of pure joy and surprise as the birthday cake with ten candles was placed in front of his child.

*I'm a founder of this company,* he thought, barely able to catch his breath. *Vik must have been terminated, too. These fucking money guys do the same thing every time. They give you money to grow the business. Work you to death. Shove cocaine and energy drinks in front of you. Promise you'll be rich. And figure out how to push you out.*

A fresh streak of blood over his lips and chin caused him to blink back into awareness. He picked up the towel from the floor, pressed it against his face, and returned to the bed.

When the nosebleed subsided, he stood and opened the window. Cool air rushed in, providing a fleeting moment of clarity.

*This blood will stop flowing. I will access my accounts from a computer in the business center. I will contact Vik. And my lawyer.*

"Screw this, and screw them," he shouted into the quiet darkness of the old town.

James needed more air. He walked to the closet, donned one of the plush terrycloth robes, and walked to the lobby. No staff or bellman were present, and the stalwart wood-plank doors of the hotel were closed.

A sign was placed on the center of the reception desk. Even with its large text, he needed to squint to read it.

*Die Rezeption ist von 0200 bis 0600 Uhr geschlossen.*
*In dringenden Fällen rufst du bitte 0664 224 68 60 an.*
*Um das Hotel zu betreten, ist ein Zimmerschlüssel erforderlich. Vielen Dank!*

"How the hell am I supposed to translate that?" he said, using too much volume for that time of morning.

*'Geschlossen' means closed. At least I know that. So the reception is closed from two to six.*

"*Wunderbar!*" he shouted. "I'm trapped in this hotel!"

Returning up the stairs, his legs felt like anvils had been attached to his knees. The door to his room, and the room itself felt smaller, more confined. As if he'd grown out of the space in the last few hours.

With the cold having found its way into every square inch of the room, he closed the windows and dropped back into bed. The blood on the sheets had dried a deep brown and burgundy color. It was 4:27 a.m—

# 17

A knock on the hotel room door brought James out of near-unconsciousness.

"*Bitte? Haushaltshilfe,*" the housekeeper said, opening the door slightly.

"Sleeping, still—" James mumbled into his pillow.

"*Tut mir sehr leid, Herr Wohlmuth,*" the housekeeper replied apologetically before closing the door.

An overcast day shone through the windowpanes. The TV and every light remained illuminated as he shifted the pillow from the side of his head. The clock read 9:43 a.m.—almost 1 a.m. in Seattle.

*Or was it two?* he thought.

James reached for his phone, his trembling hands attempting to re-start it. Still blocked. The Settings app illuminated like the North Star against an otherwise black screen.

As James glanced around, trying to orient himself, it appeared as though blind man's bluff had been played within the room's walls. Bed disheveled, towels strewn, blood stains on the sheets and hand towels.

James managed to shower but had no energy to shave off his three days of accumulated stubble. Basic processes of cleaning, grooming, and preparing for each day had ground to near paralysis.

An hour later, he returned to the lobby, bustling with tourists and visiting musicians, guests entering and exiting the hotel's restaurant and entrance.

"I trust you had a restful evening, Mr. Wohlmuth," the manager remarked as James approached the front desk. "Can I give you directions to the pharmacy for your allergies? Or have they improved after a good night's sleep?"

"I'm not quite adjusted to European time," James replied, struggling to process pleasantries, let alone conversation. "I might take the recommendation later. Right now, I'm having issues with my phone. And I need a computer with internet. Is there a business center here?"

"This often happens with visitors from America," she said sympathetically. "Of course, we have a public computer. Take the stairs down one level; you'll see the desk. Use this code along with your room number," she instructed while handing him a small slip of paper. "I'm afraid I'm not very technical, but if you have any issues, please let me know."

"Thank you. I will."

"And, Mr. Wohlmuth?"

"Yes?"

"You do appear rather tired. Perhaps some coffee and a bowl of muesli would help? Breakfast is available in the restaurant until half past ten."

James turned away without expression, passing the restaurant on his way down the stairs.

An outdated computer with a printer/scanner next to it sat on an antique writing desk in the small, dimly lit area. Entering the access code on the mauve-colored keyboard lit the screen like the flick of a switch, causing James to turn his head sharply until his eyes could adjust.

Click the flag of your language: *Deutsch, English, Français, Italiano, Español.*

Below were several options: *Browse the Web. Check Email. Find Flights.*

James clicked "Browse the Web" and typed icloud.com. A pop-up requested his email address and password.

*My password? My password is in my Password App,* he thought. *Which is on my phone. Which I can no longer access.*

He reviewed the process for resetting his password slowly, often having to reread sentences. Resetting his account required uploading his passport or other identification to verify his identity. He reduced the screen brightness, making the screen appear turned off, ran the two flights of stairs to his room, retrieved his passport, and returned to the desk, completely winded.

He scanned his passport and clicked "Submit."

The next screen required his phone number to receive a temporary password via text message once his identity was successfully verified.

*Of course,* he thought. *I need my phone to work first.*

The keyboard bounced as his hand hit the desk in frustration.

James clicked the home button on the browser, needing to exert control over something, anything. The Yahoo! homepage filled the expanse of the screen, waiting for whoever was using the machine to scroll and click so that it might collect more data. Nestled inside Weather, Scoreboard, Horoscopes, and Finance, the "Stories for You" section led with the headline: "Social Media and Search Companies Expected to Announce Record Profits This Earnings Season."

Below it, another headline caught his attention: "How Lead Singer From 90s Mega Act is Coping with Son's Suicide."

James clicked the link.

An entertainment reporter stood outside a sprawling suburban home in Nashville.

"A makeshift memorial has been set up outside the towering gates of this palatial estate, where hundreds of fans have come to pay their respects for the loss of his seventeen-year-old son, Stiller."

The video cut to the singer and the mother of the boy, seated in a lavish living room adorned with enormous bouquets of flowers.

"My beautiful son, Stiller Kings, the very light of my life, decided to end his earthly struggle and is now with God. May he rest in peace, and may no one follow his example. My baby. I love you so much," the singer said tearfully.

The video transitioned to archive footage of the band's stadium performances, as well as clips of the singer and his son walking red carpets at various ages, high-fiving fans.

"My son should not have died," he said, sitting beside the boy's mother.

"Listen, I know social media and all these apps are complicated—I really do. And I think they can do good. But these apps—we're allowing our kids to spend so much time on them. I think we have to look into what's happening. Because whatever we're doing right now—it isn't working."

"My son should be alive," the singer concluded, breaking down into tears.

*No shit, it's not working,* James thought. *You don't know the half of what's going on. Let me tell you why there's nothing for you to do. There's nothing you can do. Because 'what we're doing right now' is actually being done to you.*

Distracted, and not entirely sure where to go or what to do next, James placed the cursor in the search bar and typed "Franz Wohlmuth."

The name he'd learned from the restaurant proprietor the previous evening.

The first search result displayed what appeared to be a medieval painting of an old man. Below it were several sites describing executioners and Salzburg history.

There he is. Franz Wohlmuth. Just like the woman at the restaurant said. How had I never heard of this man?

James clicked on the Wikipedia link, opening a page detailing the Salzburg executioner's life.

Under his breath, James mumbled.

*Franz Wohlmuth—Born 1739, Salzburg—appointed executioner in 1761 by Prince Archbishop Sigismund von Schrattenbach—executed over five-hundred people during his sixty year appointment—was often ordered to carry out brutal tortures and unjust punishments—secretly kept diary of two hundred sixty-two executions he performed on his land—diary exposed injustice and torture ordered—contributed to the end of public executions and torture in Salzburg—no executioners appointed after his death—*

As he read, an elderly man with a thick West London accent interrupted him with a light tap on the shoulder.

"Pardon me, young man. How much longer might you be? I must print these vouchers for our Sound of Music tour this morning."

"Five minutes," James responded curtly.

"Oh, you speak English. Brilliant. Although I've been down here twice already. You've been at it for quite some time."

"Five minutes, alright? Jesus," James snapped, turning back to the screen and muttering.

—*replica of diary and sword on display at the Salzburg Museum—godfather of Joseph Mohr, writer of Christmas carol Silent Night, Holy Night —Wohlmuth died in 1826—Executioner's house still stands in Salzburg at Neukommgasse 26—*

A moment later, an elderly woman joined the man and, in a similar British accent, said gently, "I'm sorry, young man, we're not trying to be rude."

"I said one minute. Alright, lady? One minute. Let me print this. Just let me—"

The couple stood silently behind him, their presence making James feel increasingly claustrophobic and nervous.

After reading the pages detailing Wohlmuth's life, he closed the browser, pushed the chair back abruptly, grabbed the page and rushed up the stairs.

"Someone's already having a day, aren't they?" the woman called out after him.

"Good morning. Again," James said to the receptionist, his breath heaving as if he'd climbed twenty flights of stairs instead of one. "I think I will take you up on the pharmacy recommendation."

"Yes, Mr. Wohlmuth," the receptionist said kindly. "I'll write it down. It's just near the hotel. Turn left. About three hundred meters. Pass the cathedral on your right."

"And I'm having some issues with my phone and computer. Can you recommend a nearby mobile phone or computer store?"

"Yes, but not within walking distance. I'd recommend taking an Uber."

"But without my phone," James said, waving the black-screened device sarcastically in a see-saw motion.

"Mr. Wohlmuth, I will call a taxi for you. Navigating Salzburg will be much easier with your phone issue resolved."

"Call the Uber now. I'll be back in a minute with my jacket and wallet."

James shoved his passport, wallet, phone, and charger into the front pocket of his laptop backpack. Again he started down the stairs to the lobby.

*Shit, I forgot my laptop.*

Darting back into the room, James grabbed the laptop from the table, and tried to force it into the main pocket of his backpack. A copy of his briefing blocked the space, crumpling under the force. The briefing, written too late to save Sara. The briefing that ultimately brought him to Salzburg.

He paused and sat at the edge of the bed to organize the document neatly next to the computer.

*What a mess this is, Sara,* he thought. *Why? I'm sorry this happened to you. I'm sorry I did this to you. I would do anything to bring—*

"*Bitte? Haushaltshilfe,*" the housekeeper said, peering through the opening in the door. "May I come in?"

"Oh, yes. I was just leaving."

The Uber met James outside the hotel, driving him through the narrow, winding streets of the old town, then across the Salzach River near the train station. Ending at the mobile phone store the hotel manager had recommended.

"Excuse me, do you speak English?" James asked after walking into the store, making no attempt to converse in German.

"Of course, almost everyone in Salzburg does," the clerk responded.

"I can't access my phone or any of my apps. Can you help me?"

The clerk tried restarting the phone, but the same blank screen appeared.

"This looks like a device managed by a company. To use it, you'll need to delete everything and start over. Then I can sell you a new SIM card."

James looked at the phone in his hand. It was the device he'd used to message Sara every day. The one filled with her photos, her calls, her voice. If he wiped it, any unsaved memories would be gone forever. But he had no choice.

He handed the phone to the clerk, numb as he watched them wipe the contents and install a new SIM card. When the phone was returned, it felt foreign—empty and disconnected, even though it wasn't.

James walked out of the store, backpack and phone in hand. A kebab restaurant two doors down emitted the warm aroma of grilled chicken, lamb, and sautéed onions.

He hadn't had a meal in over fifteen hours.

As he waited for his döner kebab and fries, a password reset message arrived, allowing him to restore his personal apps, messages, and emails. His call to Vik went to voicemail. His text received no response.

Dozens of emails flooded in: promotions, newsletters, junk. Then a message from his mother:

SUBJ: "Everything okay?"
James you were going to call me after you arrived in Salzburg.
It's been two days. Is your phone working?

James quickly responded,

Hey mom. I'm in Salzburg. Problems with my phone. Call you in the morning your time.

And a message from his attorney, regarding Sara's estate and accounts.

*SUBJ: S Wohlmuth assets*

*James,*

*Responding by email, knowing that you are traveling. I hope you are taking a break from your devices for a few days and enjoying the sights of Salzburg.*

*In response to your email below. Yes, it is certainly within your rights to donate the entirety of Sara's 401(k) proceeds to Mental Health America. It is an incredibly selfless gesture. But I would recommend we discuss in more detail upon your return.*

*I will keep you informed as we hear back on the social security issue. As you correctly assumed, there is no payout on the life insurance.*

*Be well, James.*

*Brian Denning, Esq*


Before ordering the Uber, James opened his backpack to store the SIM card receipt. Seeing the briefing document next to his laptop jarred his memory.

*That first day. I created another account on this laptop for Sara's photos and data. Just because EchoWave shut me out doesn't mean I don't have access to—*

He jumped out of his seat and scrambled from the restaurant.

The hotel room had been cleaned and organized when he returned. James collapsed on the bed, breathless after losing patience waiting for the Uber, deciding instead to run back to the hotel, his backpack jostling with every step.

A few minutes later, he opened the laptop, entering a combination of keystrokes that would theoretically allow him to choose the version of the computer he wanted to use: the EchoWave version, now disabled. Or the version he created after Sara's funeral, to store her photos, internet searches, and browsing history.

The version with Sara's backup opened as expected.

James emptied the mini bar of its small bottles of whiskey, vodka, and schnapps, and spent the next hour scrolling through Sara's photos before returning to the bed and falling asleep.

Vik hadn't responded when James woke several hours later, leading him to believe both had been forced out of the company. A leadership coup, common among fast-growing tech companies financed by venture capitalists.

James typed a quick email to Vik on his phone:

> *In Salzburg. Received termination papers from EchoWave yesterday. What the hell is going on? Who should I call? Are you alright?*
> *EchoWave cut off my phone and laptop. I have a new number. Call me on FaceTime or message me on WhatsApp.*
> *~J*

Before calling his mother, his family lawyer, or anyone at the company, it made sense for him to hear from Vik. Assuming Vik was getting his messages. Assuming Vik was still employed at EchoWave.

His head aching from the alcohol, the panes of the windows again black from the fall of night. James opened the laptop and typed "Franz Joseph Wohlmuth" into the search bar of the browser.

Seeing the name Wohlmuth related to an 18th-century executioner from Salzburg, rather than a 21st-century tech executive, was unnerving.

As James read about the historical executioner through his fuzzy, gummed up vision, he found the diary to be the most bizarre part of the story. A man ordered by the Prince Archbishop of Salzburg to behead and torture hundreds of people on his property. A job terrible enough. But then to keep meticulous personal records over decades? Why?

James began to think of the cold detachment of the executioner's meticulous record-keeping, mirrored by the impersonal nature of what the EchoWave algorithms had become. So far removed from the needs of one human being, silently crying out for help, while James was sitting in an office with an entire team, thinking about how advertising could be improved for millions. Wondering why a man would be compelled to keep a diary of events that were so gruesome.

James gently closed the laptop, stood, and walked to the bed, again collapsing. Intending to rest his eyes for a few minutes while waiting for Vik's response.

Hours later, the see-saw wail of an Austrian police siren jolted him awake. It was early Sunday morning. His phone, now restored from an online backup with his personal apps and emails, showed the preview of an email from Vik.

The blue-white illuminated James's face as he lay on his side, attempting to read the short message.

James -
*Tried to send you a text, but it bounced. It's about the briefing. Working behind the scenes to resolve. It's a mess. Don't contact me. I'll be in touch.*
-V-

# 18

"They were never going to change anything after reading your briefing, were they, Sara?"

James sat up, feeling dizzy. His hands trembled.

"No, they weren't," he continued aloud in the empty room. "They're not going to do anything to make the algorithms safer. Fifty thousand suicides a year in America. They can bury the dangers. Deny that the algorithms do anything bad. Like they did to you, Sara."

He swung his legs over the edge of the bed. A framed black-and-white photograph on the wall next to the window showed a close-in crop of a church arch. An abstraction requiring the viewer to imagine the bigger picture: something James had struggled with for a month.

"Vik was part of this all along. Vik and Michael. They didn't send me here so they could test my theories 'in a sterile lab.' Michael can spin the briefing however he wants—to my team, the company, investors, the media."

James stood too quickly. He paced with one hand on the wall, holding him up. The *shhhhhh* sound both calming and oppressive.

"What if they're going to make the algorithms even more powerful? Pump even more harmful content in front of people? Revenue numbers will look better for the IPO. Michael doesn't care, as long as he gets his new houses, cars, and jets."

He clenched and released his fists, murmuring through his teeth.

"If I leak the document, he'll figure out a way to bury it. To bury me. 'A grieving man with no objectivity,' they'll say. No one cares about you, Sara. Or me. We'll be forgotten in a day."

He stopped pacing and turned to the laptop.

"The problem is the briefing—it was about you, Sara. I wanted to prove that what I invented killed you. But I lost the bigger picture. Why did I do that?"

James dropped into the chair in front of the laptop, deleted Vik's email, and opened a browser window.

"What kept that poor kid scrolling? What was he searching for? What did we force into his mind?" James asked aloud.

He typed "Stiller Kings" into the search bar, wanting to understand how his invention was being used—away from his preconceptions, goals, loss, and expectations. From the outside in.

Seconds later, links to hundreds of sites and articles appeared. Social media and video-sharing sites Stiller used, as well as articles about his death. All of the accounts were public, allowing anyone to view his posts.

"This kid had nothing locked down," James said. "Everything out there for the whole world to see."

He clicked on a link to a video-sharing site and played Stiller's most recent video, published six days prior to his suicide. It opened with Stiller sitting alone on a tour bus, raindrops streaking the windshield before the wipers cleared them away. A second clip showed him on a couch in a different bus, his head leaning against the window as cornfields blurred past. It then cut to an unmade bed with black satin sheets—the camera panning closer and closer to his eye until the frame went black. As it closed, hashtags of self-harm words appeared, written in Slovenian, their meaning undeniable.

"If these people won't change anything after what we did to you, Sara," he said. "Maybe they'll do something if they learn what we did to him. Or anyone else. Or everyone else."

Each time James clicked on a video, a pop-up window appeared on the screen, requesting him to log in or create an account.

*"To obtain the best experience millions of others enjoy every day, please register for an account or sign in!"*

James scoffed.

"This is where it begins with everyone, Sara," he said to the screen. "Missing out if you're not inside the party, instead of people like me, sneaking a peek through the kitchen window."

To create an account on the video-sharing site, he signed up for a dummy email account from an email provider known for keeping the identities of their users anonymous and impossible to track. Similar to how James's team at EchoWave would avoid tracking when they needed to conduct market research.

After creating a fake account using a fake email address, he watched each video Stiller posted. Read each description he wrote. And then read each of the comments, cascading below.

He watched other videos using the same hashtags and searched for content that shared the same themes.

After several hours, the screen began to blur, becoming whiter and whiter, even as he reduced the brightness to its lowest setting.

He stood from the table for the first time in hours and walked to the bathroom, relieving himself without lifting the toilet seat. The chrome fixtures on the bathtub caught James's attention, contrasted against the "Golden Cradle" yellow of the bathroom walls.

"Golden Cradle yellow," he murmured. The color they painted the baby's room at their home in Seattle.

Steam curled around the room as water filled the porcelain tub, its cascading *shhhhhh* sound calming, but no less oppressive than his hand on the wall. James stripped off his clothes and stepped into the water with a slow exhale. The up and down of his breathing the only motion moving the water. He sat, staring at the shiny chrome faucet against the pale yellow walls.

Some time later, he glanced down at his body.

A few drops of blood from his nose had streamed down the side of his face and neck, departing his skin into the water. Like a vivid crimson flower with its tendrils, delicate and wispy, spreading outward before feathering.

Blinking at the sight, James pinched his nose with his thumb and forefinger. It was still bleeding slightly. His motion caused the blood in the water to dissipate and blend even further, into an almost unnoticeable hue of pale pink rose.

Drained of energy but drawn back to the computer, James returned to the table and refreshed the browser pages. The algorithms had already started honing his viewing habits and tailoring recommendations with unsettling precision. The content shifted, becoming darker and more disturbing; a direct reflection of how quickly the social media services were sharing data with EchoWave and adapting to this new, anonymous "user."

AI-generated scenes of apocalyptic, Earth-like planets and wandering zombies. Snippets of videos showing young men glamorizing depression, as if they were being interviewed by deity-like figures on 60 Minutes. Tutorials for off-the-grid survivalists building bunkers stocked for an imminent, self-assured doomsday. Each video felt like a breadcrumb trail leading deeper into isolation, despair, and paranoia.

"Imagine what I would see if I were logged into Stiller's profile," James said aloud, his voice hoarse.

Even without having access to Stiller's account, James noted a disturbing pattern: over just two months, the tone of Stiller's videos had darkened significantly. The more disturbing the content, the more likes, comments, and shares it received. Social validation for spiraling into the void.

"How long have we been in the room, love?" he muttered, his voice drowned out by the hum of the laptop and the clanking of the radiator. Outside, the faint light of the day's rising sun was shrouded by the intense glow of streetlights below.

No species in the animal kingdom can chase its prey or be chased as prey for an infinite amount of time.

Eventually, every body relents. Every mind numbs. Every soul searches. Every day must come to an end.

# 19

Dressed in the clothes he'd discarded on the bathroom floor hours earlier, James hobbled down the stairs and into the lobby.

The space was quiet, save for the early morning kitchen personnel starting to prepare breakfast. A sign informed late-night guests that the manager would return at 0600.

Before walking outside, James raised his hand to wipe sweat off his brow. His index finger rubbed against his forehead's dry skin, with no perspiration to rub off. He looked down at his index finger, free of the blood from his nose.

*Shit,* he thought. *Blood on my forehead now*

He rushed to a mirror at the entryway of the hotel, expecting to see a long streak of blood across his forehead. But it was clean and dry. And pale.

Outside, the early morning air was cold and damp. The kind of cold that can see around corners and in between the seams of jackets and hats.

His head throbbed, his mind fragmented and bouncing without resolution. What once was a meticulous mind capable of solving complex equations now felt like a kaleidoscope of scattered scenes and memories.

He turned onto the same path he had walked two nights prior. Past the fortress and the hotel.

Nothing is open in Salzburg on Sunday, the day of rest.

He stopped in front of the restaurant where he'd dined a few nights prior. The white Renaissance-style two-story building, shuttered and dark, the outdoor heaters and umbrellas stored away.

The restaurant where the proprietor introduced him to his own infamous last name. Wohlmuth. The executioner,. Franz Joseph Wohlmuth.

The Wohlmuth terminated from the company he and Vik built. The Wohlmuth who exposed the dangers of the technology that triggered his wife into suicide, telling all the other companies it was okay to inundate her with content that was dangerous for her state of mind. The Wohlmuth who arrived in Salzburg before the company shut him out, cutting off his connections to everything he had worked for.

*A man named Franz Joseph Wohlmuth lived and worked in a house on the other side of the pond here,* James recalled the restaurant proprietor having said. *Just over a kilometer in that direction.*

James turned toward the pond. He walked the wide gravel path that circled it, his footsteps crunching rhythmically against the gravel. A lone jogger passed him, glancing back briefly to assess whether this man—disheveled, half-tucked shirt, and vacant eyes—posed a threat or was merely coming off a long, regretful night.

The path led to a residential road that crossed a narrow canal before opening into a large, grassy field. In the center stood a weathered house built in traditional Austrian style, an old barn with its dark wooden beams stark against the pale morning sky.

"Wohlmuth's house," James said aloud. "The Salzburg executioner's house."

The large expanse of history pressed against his chest. He felt it in the ground beneath him. And in the breeze that moved the tall grass on the field, swaying back and forth. Predictable, like masts on sailboats.

He closed his eyes and began swaying back and forth, allowing his motion to mimic the movement of the grass. The translucent shrouds of every life brought to an end appeared in front of him on the ground on which he stood. Lives ended not through their natural course, but by decree of the land's sovereign ruler.

"They're not people to us. They're 'users.' On every one of these apps, on every one of these sites," James said. "They weren't people to me. They're just shrouds. Examples to be made of. Pixels filling a column on a PowerPoint slide. Connected masses. Until they stop clicking, scrolling. That's when they're forgotten. Erased."

He opened his eyes and allowed his feet to move over the ground, around the house and on the grass surrounding it.

"There was so much blood spilled here, love," he said, his gaze meandering over the windows, doors, and rotting cornices.

James turned back toward the path, the fresh cool air and the rising sun clearing the gray from his mind, momentarily. The house was just a fragment of the story. The diary, he realized, had power. It was where the truth lived. A view into the mind of an executioner as he methodically recorded his punishments and tortures. The diary brought the truth to light, and spoke truth to power. The diary, written by Franz Joseph Wohlmuth, helped end public executions and torture in Salzburg. It helped restore justice to the people.

Just as James attempted to convey in his briefing about Sara and the overwhelming content she had been exposed to, ultimately resulting in her demise.

"I need to see this thing. I need to see Wohlmuth's diary."

# 20

A distant memory emerged into James's consciousness as he walked across the expansive Residenzplatz in front of the Salzburg Museum. Horse-drawn carriages lined one side, their Lederhosen-clad chariot-eers waiting for tourists to embark on rides through the narrow streets, taking selfies, and capturing videos of churches and monuments.

Sara's allergy to horses kept them at a fair distance.

Instead, she ran ahead, among the tourists, toward the spectacular fountain serving as its centerpiece. Extending her arms, she began to twirl, mimicking the famous *"hills are alive with The Sound of Music"* scene from the movie. After catching up with her, a gust of wind forced a cool spray of water from the fountain onto their faces as they spun together, her head tilting backward, fully trusting James would never let her go.

As James approached the doors to where Franz Joseph Wohlmuth's sword and diary were on display, a sign in black and red letters pulled his attention away from the memory:

*Das Salzburg Museum ist Montags geschlossen.*
*Wir haben ab Dienstag, 9:00 Uhr geöffnet*

The breakfast at his hotel and the walk afterward gave his brain an opening to translate. The museum was closed on Mondays. It would reopen at 9.00 a.m. tomorrow.

In frustration, he gave the locked door to the museum a slight tug. Turning around, he saw another gust of wind send a column of water toward the line of carriages where tourists stood. Everyone ducked and laughed as the cool water hit their faces.

James noticed a line of benches on the other side of the Platz, along the walls of the DomQuartier art museum, absorbing sunlight after each break in the clouds. Before sitting on the only unoccupied bench, he attempted to translate text engraved on a small brass plaque affixed to its backrest. It was written by a gentleman who professed eternal love and devotion to his wife; both of whom had long since passed away. Two souls, vanished from this world, permanently memorialized through text. Witnessed by anyone who paused to relax there.

Cycles of clouds, blue sky, mist from the fountain, and ducking tourists allowed his mind to unwind from the galloping aberrations of the previous days and weeks. A short time later, James noticed a group of teenage schoolchildren walking out of the Salzburg Cathedral after having attended a musical performance. With a few minutes to spare before chaperones herded them into tour buses, the group wandered into the Platz.

Powerful smartphones gripped their young, impressionable hands. Each device pulled its owner in whatever direction it pleased—anywhere but toward the blue sky, the towering fountain, or the line of horses and carriages. Everything they believed they needed—connection, entertainment, information—was in the palms of their hands, rather than the world around them. A group of human beings, standing inches apart, their devices drawing them away from each other, into isolation and loneliness.

In the midst of this centuries-old city, James watched as they played and forwarded memes and videos accumulated during their time inside. The cathedral's towering ceilings, massive organ, ornate frescoes, and shadowed catacombs had only momentarily tugged at their attention, like his hands on the doors of the museum, closed on Mondays. Now, freed from the curated experience paid for by their parents, their attention could return to where it was always drawn.

There were the fruits of his labor for the last decade, right in front of him. In the Platz outside the cathedral. On either side of him in the café. His contribution to the world, in real life. Technology that had taken his wife and their opportunity to build a family. Technology that had been reframed and reformed by his experiences over the last six weeks.

Sitting there, as tufts of thick clouds passed overhead and the temperature dropped, James felt rage. Not the sorrow he felt from losing his wife. Not the anger and betrayal he felt from losing his job.

Rage.

# 21

James awakened to a full moon rising in the eastern sky of Salzburg. As he looked out the window, tiny ice crystals formed in the air of a cloudless, azure sky, glistening like millions of tiny floating diamonds.

The lobby of the hotel was empty and almost completely dark, with the exception of two oil lanterns mounted on the wall near the entrance. The space smelled of soot, beeswax, and cinnamon. He tugged twice on the handles of the stalwart wood-plank front door, as if its resistance were warning him of the elements awaiting on the other side. As the door began to move, its iron hinges rubbed in protest.

When they relented, a blast of frigid air rushed in, cutting like knives across his nose, cheeks, and fingers.

"How could it be so cold after such pleasant weather yesterday?" James asked himself.

He immediately closed and latched the door, allowing the flicker of the lamps to return to steady light guiding him back to the staircase. As the wind's howl dissipated, James could hear the sounds of a woman, moaning with increasing desperation, coming from the second floor.

James walked gingerly up the stairs, the sound growing louder with each step. When he reached the second floor, he noticed the door to his room, slightly ajar. Peering around its edge, he saw a woman lying in the bed, in labor. Sitting at her bedside, there were two other women, attempting to subdue and comfort the expectant mother.

Exhausted and hallucinating, the young woman dripped in sweat despite the cold air pouring through the open window and shivered from fever. One of the women, a midwife, futilely attempted to move her body into a position of comfort; the straw and feather filling in the mattress shifted and clumped in all the wrong places.

"May the grace of Heaven shield thee in thy hour of need, and may thy heart find solace in the divine light that guides thee through the darkest of days," the midwife mumbled, gently stroking the expectant woman's hand while rocking in a chair next to the bed.

After each recital, the midwife motioned her fingertips to the shape of a cross. First forehead, then chest, left shoulder, and right. "May the grace of Heaven shield thee in thy hour of need—"

"Worry not, my dear," the expectant mother's sister whispered as she walked toward the bed. "My Anna Maria has always been the strongest of our three sisters. As sturdy and sure-footed as a chamois on a rocky hillside. I have faith the Good Lord shall bless her with a healthy child today."

Despite the sister's optimism, the midwife continued to murmur her prayer.

For a moment, the contractions subsided into a quiet valley, allowing Anna Maria to doze off, reasonably cradled by the lumped mattress and nestled into the feather and horsehair pillows.

"While we wait for this child to bless us, my dear sister, I shall recite verse from Königsmarck, the Swedish poet."

"Thank you, Eve," Anna Maria whispered through her nearly blue, buckled lips. "Your grace knows no bounds."

Eve lifted the volume from a basket next to the bed, turning to a spot she'd marked with an orange-brown beech tree leaf, collected the previous autumn, and brought herself closer to the lamp on the nightstand.

Clearing her winter-dry throat, hand coiled to her mouth, she began.

"To a Mighty Duchess—"

For the two sisters, poems, parades, and daydreams would be the closest either would come to experiencing a life of comfort and privilege, as the Prince Archbishop of Salzburg demanded penance from the bourgeois, and obedience from the women.

Eve continued reciting aloud:

*"To a Mighty Duchess*
*Your feminine nature, your power,*
*To command, praise, and write about,*
*Can delight the brave-hearted,*
*And dedicate themselves to your fame.*
*As wise as strong, and, above all,*
*In high virtues,*
*Provide protection to the valiant people*
*From the heart of a mother."*

An hour later, the contractions returned, their spacing closer, and the amplitude of pain grew louder with each passing wave. James was frozen in the doorway, feeling powerless to call for aid, or offer.

Alternating between duties of comfort and support, the women would recite a prayer or hum a biblical hymn in unison. One would press warm towels soaked in raspberry leaf against Anna Maria's abdomen, her lower back, and between her legs. One would massage her stretched, undulating womb. One would rest for a moment to regain strength. And they would start again.

Hours later, Anna Maria stood next to her bed, legs shaking, squatting over a pile of yellowed and bloody sheets. Held up by her sister and the midwife, a child emerged, along with a steady stream of afterbirth and feces into the soaked sheets and bedding lying on the floor.

The midwife used a long pair of sterilized shears to clip the infant's umbilical cord. She grabbed its two tiny feet, turned it upside down, and slapped the pinkish-white buttocks of the baby boy.

Soon after the boy let out his first shrill. Up and down wailing, ebbing and flowing with brief pauses, followed by more gurgles and cackles. Laughter and cries of relief from the delighted women commenced.

James could do little more than stand in awe of what he had just witnessed.

Anna Maria was guided to the edge of the bed, exhausted and unable to stand, peering out the window on the new day as the midwife tied the baby's umbilical cord. Her sister lowered her into the rocking chair as she was presented her son. Clean, swaddled, and hungry.

*As he began to nurse, Eve placed her back against the bedroom wall and slid down to the floor, arms resting on her knees.*

*"Thanks be to God," she exhaled to her sister. "Franz Joseph Wohlmuth, born upon this day. Seventeen thirty-nine, the year of our Lord."*

A wailing siren of a police vehicle nearby jolted James from his dream. The clock showing 8:36 a.m. If he wanted to arrive at the museum the minute it opened, he had just twenty-four minutes.

# 22

Paying his entrance fee the moment the security guards removed the locks from the front door, James hurried through the otherwise empty museum to the Information Desk.

"Where is the Salzburg Executioner exhibit?" James asked the volunteer, breathing heavily.

"*Und guten Morgen,* to you as well," the elderly woman chuckled as she drew a line to the exhibit on the museum's floor plan. "I've volunteered in this museum for twenty-two years. You're the first to request directions to this exhibit with so much urgency."

James snatched the piece of paper and, without uttering a word, sprinted up the stairs to the third floor.

As James approached the display housing Franz Joseph Wohlmuth's diary and the blade he used to execute the Prince Archbishop's orders, a profound sense of reverence and awe filled his chest.

The diary had a stiff cover made from pigskin stretched over thin wooden boards. Watercolor caricatures and the texts "*Fiat Justitia*" and "*et pereat mundus*" adorned the front. At the bottom of the cover were the words "*Memento mori,*" a Latin reminder of death's inevitability.

Franz meticulously numbered each of the two hundred sixty-two executions he performed. After each execution, he would sit with his pen and quill to write: the name of the person, the date, any life details he had been given, and a detailed description of the scene as he remembered it.

The executioner wrote with a factual tone, devoid of any empathy or sensitivity. Often, the crimes that led to public executions and torture were petty ones—theft or adultery. Some were more heinous—murder or repeated assault. Still others relied on the discretion of the church—sorcery or witchcraft. Regardless of the crime, the punishments were searingly, bone-crushingly brutal.

Franz was a faithful servant of the Prince Archbishop of Salzburg. When the decree arrived at his door, he carried out the sentence against the condemned without question or hesitation.

The exhibit allowed James to virtually flip through its pages and learn about each of the lives ended at the hands of Franz Wohlmuth. He read about the torturous interrogations that were carried out, including additional penalties before or after the executions, until the practice was abolished in the year 1805.

Franz was also tasked with carrying out other gruesome duties. He was required to collect and bury the bodies of suicide victims, face down in unmarked graves. After carrying out punishments on his own grounds, Franz often received orders from the Prince Archbishop to leave the heads of the condemned on stakes for months, even years. A morbid warning against committing similar crimes, and a tool to keep the population on edge and obedient.

Next to the diary exhibit, James read the account of a handwriting expert, enlisted in the 1980s to assess Franz's state of mind. "A man of extreme control and emotional detachment," the expert wrote. "Characteristics generally only found in murderers."

Lost in contemplation, James was jolted by the sound of laughter echoing through the hall. A boisterous group of children entered the room, dancing around, not paying attention. Some held hands, while a few followed their teacher dutifully.

The disruption caused James to shift his attention from the diary to a painting of Franz, commissioned when he was forty-seven years old. The eyes of the man seemed to follow James, their emerald green depths mirroring any one of the deep lakes in the region. A shiver ran down his spine as the boundaries between past and present, between himself and Franz Joseph, blurred.

*Are we all that different?* James thought.

"You knew what I didn't, Franz. The sword without the pen is just a killing tool. The pen and the sword need each other to make change. My briefing needs a sword, or else they will bury it."

"But what is my sword?" James asked as he turned toward the blade, now encased behind glass.

The long handle, forged of brass and wrapped in cord, showed signs of wear from use. Appearing heavy and burdensome to lift. Transfixed by the sight, James slipped into another time.

He imagined what it felt like to hold the massive blade, waiting for the condemned to travel slowly by horse-drawn cart from the building in which he now stood. Along the rough gravel paths to the executioner's house on the outskirts of town.

What it sounded like, as the Prince Archbishop's final order was read aloud in front of the rambunctious crowd of onlookers.

What it looked like, staring down at the condemned person, covered in a black hood, kneeling in front of him, shaking and crying, knowing the end of their existence was rapidly approaching. But not knowing exactly when.

What it was like to go against every human instinct and his own morality, to allow a blade to swing down from its peak, under the control of gravity, falling toward the earth, severing the cloth hood, the skin, muscles, vertebrae, blood vessels, and airway, separating it cleanly from the body, tumbling down, and landing on the platform with a thud.

James felt himself standing over the lifeless head of the condemned, adrenaline flowing. His ribcage flexing to its breaking point. Wiping the sweat and the blood from his hands and his brow on the front of his shirt.

Watching as the cart began rolling back toward town, carrying only the signed decree of execution, James saw the crowd disperse, numb from witnessing another faceless human life, guilty or not, meet a violent end. They returned to their homes, their trades, and their travels. Resuming their everyday lives.

James imagined himself standing alone on the platform, the blade glinting beside the blood, the head and the body of the lifeless soul before him. To clean up and to bury.

He then approached the head, kneeling down to tear the cloth that shielded spectators from the horrific expressions on the condemned's face in their final moments. His orders were to make the person an example, of course. But to do so with dignity.

Pulling the blood-soaked cloth away, he turned the head toward him to see the condemned person's face—white and still.

—Sara's face.

# 23

Descending the grand staircase into the dining area, James felt as if he was floating within its walls and arches, as white as the massive cumulonimbus clouds that frequently capped the summit of the Untersberg mountain, south of Salzburg. Although the sun had set, the room was brighter than it should have been, illuminated by a few oil lanterns housed in sconces mounted to the walls. Each lantern cast long shadows around the room, causing the arches to appear as if they rose infinitely upwards.

A man sat at the head of one of the large wooden tables in the middle of the space, his head buried in his hands. Next to him sat a woman, leaning toward his face, attempting to console his angst. A child, no more than eleven or twelve years of age, sat at the table with them, devouring a bowl of venison broth, strips of smoked char, and thick clumps of deep brown bread.

James glanced around, but the dining area was empty save for the family and himself. Pulled in by curiosity, but not wanting to intrude on the conversation, James chose a seat near the family. There was a softness in their presence that made James instinctively wipe his eyes.

The boy turned his attention away from his bowl, mother, and father, furrowing his brow at James before returning to scrape the final remnants into his mouth.

"Franz, what are you looking at?" Anna Maria asked. "Can you not see your father is speaking under duress?"

Her voice was impatient and tinged with urgency as she turned back to her husband.

"Continue, Samuel."

"And so, my aim to secure judicial mercy prior to His Holiness the Prince Archbishop issuing the final order of execution has fallen on deaf ears," Samuel uttered, taking another gulp of ale from the stein in front of him.

"I know you have toiled over this outcome for some time," Anna Maria continued.

"Yes. The treatment this young maid had endured since her apprehension had given me great cause for concern. She had been detained in a tiny, moist chamber not far from here for nearly a year. Undernourished and lacking sufficient water, as I witnessed with my own eyes just a fortnight ago."

Samuel raised his head and glanced around the room, attempting to avoid having his son or anyone else hear the details of the condemned young woman's condition. James did the same, noticing no one.

"And after the rigorous interrogation she faced—two hundred sixty-two questions—it is no wonder she offered to confess the witchlike cognitions and deeds of which she was accused."

"Remind me again, Samuel, the name and age of this young maid?" Anna Maria asked, tucking Samuel's hair behind one of his ears to better see his face.

"Pauer. Maria Pauer. From the town of Müldorf. She has yet to reach the age of sixteen years."

"Not yet sixteen years of age. Interrogated under duress," Anna Maria repeated back to her husband in disbelief, disbelief that the church, which had begun moving away from executing accused witches on such frail evidence, would move ahead with publicly beheading a sixteen-year-old girl.

Anna Maria stood from the table and left the room for a moment, returning with Samuel's stein, refilled with ale.

James glanced at Samuel as he stared at the ceiling in disbelief, in a way only a man who had the weight of a human life on his shoulders could. Watching him caused a knot of guilt to tighten in James's stomach, feeling the ache that comes after the grip of control slips from one's hand.

Anna Maria returned to the table and set the full stein of ale in front of Samuel, which he lifted and began to consume.

"Should it not be punishment enough, Anna Maria, that my own father and brothers disavowed me for refusing to continue our Wohlmuth's legacy as executioners? Or that my wife and son would never be permitted to meet my *mother as a result? Should it not be enough that carrying the Wohlmuth name still prohibits us from sitting inside the sanctuary, or among other patrons at a Gasthaus or banquet? Given I have spent my life attempting to ensure even the perception of justice?"*

*"Your work is noble, Samuel," Anna Maria said. "You abandoned every-thing—at a similar age of this maiden—to fight for what you believed in your heart was right. You at least have the ear of His Holiness. And because of that, my husband, we are permitted to live within the boundaries of Salzburg. We are permitted to send Franz Joseph to an acceptable school. Neither your father, nor his, nor his prior, could boast such good fortune as what you have built on your own."*

*He took a sip, glanced at her briefly, then looked up to the heavens.*

*"Did His Holiness offer any other words to you before signing the order?"*

*"Yes, after my futile attempt at resistance, he immediately turned and said, 'Never forget, Herr Wohlmuth, living under a crooked stick is good.'"*

*"A crooked stick?" Anna Maria asked, perplexed.*

*"The phrase he uses when questioning his own judgment. The 'stick' is used to maintain order among the citizenry. 'Crooked' is his admission of ambiguity or contradiction."*

*"A 'crooked stick,'" she replied. "When do you believe she will meet her fate?" Anna Maria asked.*

*"Her day of condemnation is set to be the sixth of October. Young Maria's head will meet Executioner Georg Pinkl's blade at midday on his grounds at Salzburg's edge. She will then be burned on the stick. The crooked stick."*

"Mr. Wohlmuth? Mr. Wohlmuth?" a woman said, gently nudging him on his shoulder.

James shook his head and blinked twice, shaking his arms under the blanket covering his shoulders.

"It's fine, Mr. Wohlmuth. You're fine," the front desk manager assured him. "You just fell asleep here in the Biergarten."

Purple lighting formed a glow around the server and the front desk manager, hovering over him as reflections from a disco ball hanging beneath one of the arches stung his weary eyes. Electronic lounge music pulsed in the background as he glanced above the courtyard into the night sky.

"Not often, but it happens every once in a while, Mr. Wohlmuth. Guests from overseas fall asleep on couches under the heaters. May we help you to your room, sir?"

"No. No, thank you. I'm fine," James said, dropping the blanket on the couch. He stammered through the busy lobby before ascending the grand staircase to his room.

# 24

James murmured to himself as he sat down in front of his laptop, feeling the enormity, the scale, of what was unfolding before him.

"The kid in my dream, Sara," James said aloud. "He grew up to be the Franz Wohlmuth I saw in the museum. His father wasn't an executioner—he worked in the justice system. Noble work, had there been any justice. Innocent people, allowed to be executed, as a warning to the rest of the people."

James should have gone to sleep the moment he entered the room. Instead, he opened and consumed one of the three energy drinks from the minibar.

"One man, powerless at the feet of the all-powerful," he continued. "One briefing, pointless on the desk of the all-powerful. Neither could do anything to help two helpless women."

He popped open a second energy drink and took a sip.

"No one will ever know what I know unless more victims are documented," James murmured to himself.

"Think about it, Sara. A dozen, twenty, even fifty people can die in a mass shooting, and nothing changes. If there's going to be change, then the truth has to be set indelibly at the feet of those in power. Like Franz did when he became the executioner. The case against them needs to be overwhelming. And it needs to be built in secret."

As he began typing, a fleeting pang of guilt overcame him, like he felt in the dream, before his exhaustion, rage, and grief twisted and wrung it from his consciousness.

"No. They won't change," he said. "They forced me to come here. They fired me and cut me off. They want me to disappear. What makes you think they wouldn't do worse? I'm right where I need to be."

"It might take three hundred people to start. Maybe four hundred," James said aloud, rubbing his hands together, reminiscent of the early days in his career. Long days in a small cubicle in Palo Alto. Singularly focused on tasks he was assigned. Coding, testing, optimizing. Repeating, over and over again.

James spent hours furiously building lists of mental health-triggering terms, many similar to what captivated Sara. He integrated the terms Stiller King used in his videos and what his followers said in their comments. The glow of the laptop screen cast long shadows on the wall behind him, changing shape as he would crack his knuckles or stretch out his arms.

Using programming scripts he'd written for Sara's briefing, he downloaded thousands of comments matching his searches. Separating usernames from the comments they posted resulted in two thousand unique names. Individuals venting, whining, or suffering, seeking help, guidance, connection, validation—or just an audience. Many needing real help but instead finding themselves in the peripheries—or the full gravitational vortex—of algorithmically manipulated social media, search engines, and discussion sites.

Just after four in the morning, James stood from the table to use the bathroom. As he lifted his body with both hands on the arms to rise out of the distinctively non-ergonomic chair, his hips and kidneys ached from the vice-like position they'd been locked in for hours. As he began to walk, his shoulders curved and chest bowed forward, molded by his body's position at the table, too low for his height. Making no effort to stretch, straighten, or adjust, he relieved himself and returned to continue working.

One of his programming scripts returned a username meeting the criteria for engaging with or writing harmful content.

"You've been busy, *MissMiniMitchell*," James said while pulling the aluminum cover off the can of mixed nuts—the same kind that had been replenished several times during his stay.

Stiller King and *MissMiniMitchell* followed each other on several social media apps.

"So they either know each other, or they are both well known," James said. "Music industry? Parents know each other?"

Although James was not personally active on social media, he assumed the user was female. She commented on many of Stiller's videos, always using a repeating pattern of emojis.

"Younger in age. She's talking in emoji code because she's a digital native. Born after 1997," he said, typing with one hand while tipping the remaining contents of the mixed nuts can into his mouth.

James revisited Stiller's profile, scrolling through the comments on the last video he posted before his suicide.

There, a comment from *MissMiniMitchell.*

*"Looks like a dream SK. Funny no one tells you about the Blvd of broken ones #fml #crashburn"*

Stiller "liked" the comment but did not respond to her.

He continued to search for her posts and comments. MissMiniMitchell often appeared to be replying to videos containing professional sports highlights.

*"Must be nice to have a career that doesn't end before it starts. Some ain't so lucky."*

*"Everyone celebrates the wins. But no one talks about the ppl left behind."*

*"Yo, what's it like to have everything handed to you nothing taken away. #crashburn"*

Comments also appeared on videos highlighting dramatic plays and comebacks involving the Seattle Seahawks, specifically when the team's star quarterback, Ryan Mitchell, was part of the play or victory.

The star quarterback had finished his 18th season with the Seahawks, signing a contract extension for another two years, seemingly defying age—even after a concussion the previous season had caused him to miss the first three games.

*Holy shit*, James suspected. *MissMiniMitchell is Ryan Mitchell's daughter. Kimberly. Kimberly Mitchell is going to be my first test.*

Using black-market websites and transferring twenty euros in cryptocurrency, James purchased the usernames and passwords for Kimberly Mitchell's email address and social media accounts.

James installed software on his laptop to trick apps into believing he was accessing her accounts from Seattle rather than from Salzburg.

As was typical for most young users, Kimberly had no security features in place to protect her accounts from hackers and had not set up warnings to alert her if any unusual activity was detected.

In less than an hour, James was logged into the first site as *MissMiniMitchell.*

Pausing momentarily, James was folded back into the experience of seeing inside Sara's social media accounts for the first time. Messages she exchanged with friends the previous summer. Cute things. Vulgar things. The things everyone says when they believe they're alone in a room with a friend. Photos and viral videos she received of babies just born or ex-boyfriends who'd let their health go. A side of Sara's presence on social media that made him smile, feel nostalgic. Because she was gone.

Kimberly Mitchell, on the other hand, was alive. Maybe she was depressed. Maybe she was just pining for attention. But she was alive. And he knew nothing about her. She could be out with friends. She could be lying on the couch, scrolling through another app. She could be logged into the same app he was staring at, right now. James Wohlmuth, a lost and desperate man, rummaging through a young woman's closet, nightstand, or medicine cabinet—at the moment she walked through the door.

James's concave body bowed closer to the table, as he felt the remaining fragments of his morality and soul drip from his fingertips and onto the keyboard and trackpad.

*They didn't care that it was my wife, Sara,* he reasoned. *I can't care that it's Kimberly Mitchell.*

He continued rummaging. Her Security and Preferences page indicated she set no limitations on sharing her personal data with third parties. Including EchoWave.

Data from every click, post, view, comment, share, like, and scroll. Collected, stored, manipulated, and sold. The time she spent on every social media app, video-sharing site, and search engine. Images that caused her to pause. Videos she replayed over and over again. When she slept, walked, showered, and lounged. Where and how fast she drove. To her actual location—different from the location showing on her parents' screens—spoofed by a GPS scrambling app installed by her ex-boyfriend.

In other words, the truth.

The truth, set free by Kimberly clicking 'I accept' each time she agreed to the incomprehensible, undecipherable terms and conditions each service required. Free to know her better than any friend, family member, minister, or confidant. Free to know her better than she knew herself. Free to target, persuade, and manipulate her however they pleased.

With no one in the background to tell her it's time to take a break. To make sure she returned home by eleven. Demand he use a condom. Ask how she's really doing. Or intervene when she's showing signs of anxiety and depression.

*That's right,* James thought. *We know all of that, too.*

Her search history gave James a view into topics she found interesting. It also gave the app a direct line to what she was interested in at the moment she clicked Enter. Also freely shared to EchoWave and other apps.

*Fashion. Depression. Competitive soccer. Coping with failure. Concussions. Natural cramping remedies. Hopelessness. Celebrity kids. Weight loss.*

Kimberly was already searching for, and watching, darker and more alarming videos each time she logged in.

His hands began to shake as they touched the keyboard, the last reflex of a decent man's natural instinct to do the right thing, no matter what the cost. Fighting to emerge from the place death, betrayal, abandonment, and history had dragged him.

In the search bar, James began entering new combinations of words and phrases. Phrases used by Sara, Stiller, and others who commented on their activity. Each time he entered a search term, he scrolled through the results, clicking and viewing several videos before entering the next term.

None of his searches contained overly dark or violent language. He entered words and phrases Sara used prior to being inundated with content that triggered her into self-harm. Words and phrases he knew would captivate Kimberly's eyes, dreams, heart, and soul. Leading her like a trail of breadcrumbs down the only path the app cared about: the path that leads to more viewing and scrolling.

After entering and documenting thirty search terms on Kimberly's account, James clicked on "Erase Search History." Although the data had already been sent to EchoWave, he wanted to cover his tracks and make sure she wouldn't see the terms he entered.

James logged out of the first app and into another app using the same username and hacked password.

After several hours of logging in and out of apps and sites she used, he returned to the first video-sharing site and clicked on the search bar.

Before finishing and allowing the awareness of his activity to glide over his hardened consciousness like a glacier on a mountain, James pressed Enter after entering three characters into the search bar:

~ S ~

# 25

James dressed and left the hotel into the crisp morning air below a sky that was free of fault or blemish. Walking through the old town, he noticed the young man and his mother he'd seen a few nights prior, walking toward the famous Hohensalzburg fortress.

As he approached, he could hear the boy speaking in protest with his mother.

"Why are we to depart our home so early?" Franz Joseph asked Anna Maria as they walked under the dim remnants of the street lanterns. "I am not bound to the schoolhouse for some time."

"Today, your schooling shall take place underneath an open sky, my son," Anna Maria responded. "Today, you will learn about justice by witnessing its absence. So, one day you might stand for its omnipresence."

Franz Joseph appeared perplexed by his mother's words but seemed to take pleasure in the opportunity to miss school, skipping by her side in his sturdy boots, tweed knickers, beige blouse, and overcoat.

The bell rang seven o'clock, just as the mother and son rounded the corner of the eastern foothill of the Hohensalzburg. A lively harmony of bells emerged from Nonnberg Abbey above.

James slowed his pace slightly as the boy turned around and caught a glimpse of the stranger. He continued to follow them as they turned up the gravel path toward an abbey just below the fortress. As he ascended the path behind him, a number of nuns appeared, reciting aloud their morning prayer and meditation.

"Let us go Its ways under the guidance of the gospel so that we can look at Him who has called us into His kingdom...Let us go Its ways under the *guidance of the gospel so that we can look at Him who has called us into His kingdom..."*

*After they passed, James could hear the boy again beginning to question their destination.*

*"Pray, mother, for what cause did we have to ascend to the Sisters' Abbey so early in the morning?" Franz asked.*

*"This is where we shall kneel and pray in vigil until the clock strikes noon."*

*"And for what cause will we appeal so earnestly?"*

*"As I have spoken earlier, my son, we will pray for justice to prevail over a terrible injustice that is soon to occur."*

*James followed them inside the soaring sanctuary, as mother and son walked tepidly to the furthest, darkest corner, a reflex from carrying the Wohlmuth name on their backs everywhere they traveled. And the second-class social status that accompanied executioner family names, which generally required them to enter a church last. That is, if they were welcomed at all.*

*Anna Maria did not take a chair or a pew, choosing instead to kneel on the stone floor, praying and crossing, praying and crossing, while Franz sat in a chilly corner. He passed the time flipping through his mother's Bible and poetry book. He gazed at the soot-covered frescoes, brass bells, and other emblems and symbols adorning the holy space, added at different times in its five-hundred-year existence.*

*As the morning carried on, more women joined the vigil—young and old, some with children, some needing aid to enter the chapel after the exhausting traipse up the steep and uneven incline from the old town below.*

*At regular intervals, one of the Sisters would ascend the circular stairs to the pulpit and recite the Abbey's prayer:*

*"God is present everywhere, we believe,*
*and the eyes of the Lord look at good and evil in every place.*
*Therefore, let us always think of the words of the Prophet:*
*Serve the Lord in fear.*
*Sing the Psalms in wisdom.*
*Before the face of the angels, I want to sing you psalms."*

*Underneath the words of each prayer recital, women could be heard humming and sobbing. They rocked back and forth, clenching their fists and squeezing their eyes, hoping to manifest a concentration of repentance dense and powerful enough to alter the intended course of the very Church and God whose earthly representatives, the day before, had sealed the young maid's fate.*

*Mid-morning, Franz saw from the corner of his eye, his Aunt Eve walk into the entrance of the sanctuary, scanning back and forth for her sister and nephew. Franz ran to her, attempting to limit the clip-clop of his boots on the floor—off tempo to the chants and hymns taking place. He grabbed the hand of his Aunt Eve and escorted her toward his mother.*

*As the bells sounded eleven times, the women departed the sanctuary and scattered down the hill toward the outskirts of town.*

*Crowds had already begun lining the street as a horse-drawn cart carrying a young woman, no more than sixteen years of age, passed by. The cart was flanked by two guards wearing black hoods and accompanied by a more senior looking official.*

*James followed the procession as it made its way south of the old town, continuing down narrow gravel roads lined by Salzburgers. Women wept, and men spat, each releasing the hormones necessary to cope with or offer approval for whatever was about to take place.*

*Some time later, the procession reached Neukommgasse 26. The executioner's house.*

*James stood at the edge of a crowd gathering around a platform in a field next to the house.*

*The guards removed the girl from the cart and placed her in a chair on the small platform. They bound her hands behind her back and feet to the front legs of the chair, standing guard as the crowd cheered like mountain runoff over boulders.*

*When she was secured, the front door to the house opened. An obese, wiry-haired man with a crow's nest beard emerged, carrying a long, polished blade of steel. He staggered down the two steps to the ground, appearing drunk to the point of near blindness.*

*The raucous crowd parted briefly as he swung his legs in front of each other toward the gallows. After making his way up the stairs to the platform, he* used his sleeves to remove the sweat from his brow and catch his breath as the officer read aloud the Prince Archbishop's death sentence.

James slowly worked his way close to Anna Maria and Franz, standing just behind them.

As the officer recited charges of sorcery, orchestrated and rehearsed, a documented confession, and witch-like behavior after having been observed for over a year, sixteen-year-old Maria Pauer was then ordered to be executed by beheading, followed by burning at the stake; on this the sixth day of October, seventeen hundred and fifty, the year of our Lord.

"Dear Mother, I assumed Father was going to save this girl," Franz Joseph whispered loudly.

Anna Maria could only squeeze Franz Joseph's hand.

"Your father's efforts fell on deaf ears, son. This is why we prayed with the sisters this morning."

"Executioner Georg Pinkl," the officer exclaimed from the top of the podium. "You are hereby ordered to carry out the execution of Maria Pauer!"

Georg limped toward Maria, carrying his blade and a black hood, and asked her if she held any last wishes before he covered her head.

"I desire no concealment or cover. Let the world witness me."

"So, it shall be. The witch's final wish is accorded."

James watched Anna Maria squeeze Franz's hand to the point it appeared like the fatty, marbled muscle of a lazy ox, white and beet red. Under her tongue, she murmured, "She has not renounced her faith. Dear God, Thou must spare this poor maid. She was baptized; she remains as Your child."

Franz looked up to his mother, tears streaming down her cheeks. He scanned the horde of onlookers, women from the church a short time ago now scattered throughout. Their presence separated; their fear, collective. Their fear, their strength in separated presence. Their strength of will now dispersed; their fear returned to unity.

Anna Maria repeated, looking down at the blades of grass in the field, "She hath not forsaken her faith! Why persist here, O Dear Lord Almighty? For she is no witch!"

James looked around the crowd, seeing Eve glance at her sister, wide-eyed, *holding back the urge to warn her to close her mouth, for fear authorities were interspersed among them, without daring to shout her name.*

James heard other women in the crowd murmuring similarly, *"She is no witch. She is no witch. She is no..."*

"How could the authorities arrest all these women, even if they heard them clearly among all the other chanting and taunting?" James thought.

*The crowd began swaying and chanting.*

*Away with her head! Dispatch this witch! Complete your duty, scharfrichter!*

*"SHE HATH NOT FORSAKEN HER FAITH!"* Anna Maria screamed in one final, desperate show of protest.

Young Maria's face gazed peacefully at the Untersberg, remorse, resolve, and insanity intertwined, as Georg lifted his arms, clutching the long, heavy blade, up and over his right shoulder, a mass of energy having left the surface of the sun eight minutes prior, landing, concentrating and bouncing off the polished steel, pointing to and momentarily searing Franz's retina, causing him to raise his hand to his eye, just as the blunt side of the blade fell swiftly, striking the condemned's frail neck, bloody vertebrae exposed but not severed, the executioner now swearing and cursing in vain to the Lord, examining the blade for error but knowing it was his own, ordering his apprentice to lift the condemned's limp body back into position, as he turned the sword around, swinging again, meeting the neck an inch higher from the point of the initial strike, still not fully severing the soul and consciousness from the body, cursing and spitting and swinging again, his third attempt powered by every animal instinct that had ever migrated from the Sahara, into Mesopotamia, and finally Europa, the blade now at an angle more suited to a sun dial, as Maria's life and memory blinked during its fall to the grass below, landing with the wallop of a large stone, and coming to a halt after rebelliously shaking, back and forth, no.

The baritone of cheers offsets an alto harmony of sobbing, while soprano solos of sparrows in the nearby trees filled in the choir, all preaching their sermon to the pulpit.

A short time later, only the clarinet sound of crows and the click-clack percussion of Maria's body, burning at the stake, could be heard.

James opened his eyes wearily to the click-clack percussion of a horse and carriage, along with the intense daylight of midday, passing through the wide-open window of his room.

# 26

The knock-knock at the door of the hotel room sounded on schedule, as it had each morning of his stay.

"*Bitte? Haushaltshilfe,*" the housekeeper said, sending her voice through the crack after opening the door.

"I'm sorry. I just woke up," James said, staring out the window, listening to pedestrians, horses, and carriages. "Can you come back—"

"Ah yes, but Mr. Wohlmuth, it is nearly twelve o'clock, and we see you checking out of your room this morning."

"I'm sorry?" James replied, leaping too quickly out of bed and walking toward the door.

"If you need some additional time to pack and prepare, Mr. Wohlmuth, I am certain the front desk can make an arrangement."

"Yes, please. I will need to make an arrangement," James responded.

The return flight booked by EchoWave was scheduled to depart Munich the following afternoon. He was originally scheduled to check out from the room, board the train to Munich, stay in a hotel for one night, and fly to Seattle the following day.

"Mr. Wohlmuth, I certainly hope you caught up on your sleep last night. We have barely seen you in the last several days of your time here. Did you enjoy your stay in Salzburg?"

"I—It—Yes. Although my flight plans have changed. I need to finish something here before I leave. Would it be possible to extend my stay two more nights? I know my employer paid in advance. I can pay for the additional nights on my own."

Handing his credit card to the front desk manager, he secured the additional two nights.

"And Mr. Wohlmuth, since you are paying for the room, why not enjoy breakfast in the dining room tomorrow morning? It is, after all, included in the rate."

The vivid images of Maria Pauer's execution clung to James's consciousness, feeling less like a dream and more like a terrible memory. Stepping out of the hotel, he followed the same route to the executioner's house.

In his dream, the air was tinged with the smell of smoke rising from the chimneys of homes and establishments. Now, the air was odorless. The sky crisp and clear. In his dream, a rickety horse-drawn cart pulled an innocent young woman out of town toward her demise. Now, polished horse-drawn carriages carried smiling tourists, taking photos and videos with their mobile devices. In his dream, men and women lined the street to the executioner's house, donned in simple clothing, shouting, crying, spitting, and begging. Now, cars and bicycles rushed past banks, shops, and restaurants, into and out of town.

James walked back and forth around the now grassy, manicured area where the gallows had been constructed for Maria Pauer's execution, next to the house where the drunken executioner, Georg Pinkl, emerged to carry out the Prince Archbishop's death sentence.

Sitting on the grass, he watched as mothers pushed strollers carrying newborns, and elderly couples held hands, walking along the concrete pathway in front of the house, connecting neighborhoods built since the last inhabitants occupied the house more than two hundred and fifty years ago.

Air that once smelled of blood and death had been kneaded by time into normalcy. The distant echoes of all the condemned souls' final pleas and screams, long since faded, sodded, and paved over.

Just a short time ago, in the old town of Salzburg, James loaded a cart, albeit of the digital kind. His also contained an innocent person, Kimberly Mitchell. Pulling it down the gravel streets, amidst all the onlookers, through the smoke-tinged air, to the place he now found himself. He knew the end of her existence was approaching. But he didn't know exactly when.

Just as the sun began to wane, James walked along the *Nontallerstrasse* toward his hotel.

Over centuries, the road evolved into a busy street lined with quaint cafés, coffee shops, and apartment buildings, mixed with an occasional business. And tombstone companies, close in proximity to cemeteries originally placed on the city's outskirts.

As he walked, James's attention was diverted by a young man driving a forklift across the gravel-covered yard of one of the tombstone companies.

Thick, raw granite slabs used to make tombstones were stacked on heavy-duty scaffolding, waiting patiently to be cut and shaped into a permanent memorial of someone's temporary existence.

James paused to watch the vehicle raise its forks to the highest level of scaffolding in the yard, fifteen feet from the ground. The forks entered a pallet of three stacked slabs of uncut gray granite. The man briefly pulled the load back from the scaffolding before changing gears into drive. In an instant, the machine backfired, jolting forward as the entire pallet fell, shattering the slabs and damaging the shelves as the load came crashing down to the ground.

James froze as the owner stormed from the workshop, shouting violently at the operator and the damage he caused.

Taking a moment to catch his breath, the operator calmly reached for the ignition key, turned off the engine, and exited the forklift, walking briskly toward the street before hurling the keys through the air.

As he passed James at the entrance, his face showed an angry smirk of satisfied rebellion. The young man pulled a vape pen from his front pocket, inhaled a deep puff from the device, and allowed his head to pass through the large plume of exhaled aerosol as he walked up the street to the next bus stop.

James stood in witness, still frozen.

The owner walked toward James and the street, continuing to shout polysyllabic German obscenities, before turning to search for the keys, now buried in foliage at the edge of the yard.

"*Entschuldigung*," James said to the man with meek hesitance. "Do you speak English?"

"*Ein bisschen. Was?* What is it? Do you need something?"

"I think I saw where the keys landed," James motioned, as if playing charades, using an ignition gesture for the vehicle and a directional motion for their path through the sky.

"*Ja, ja,* young man. I speak at least that much English, okay. So, where?"

The owner followed James to the area, dense with vines and bushes. Although the violent crash and ensuing scene cleared his mind for a moment, like a windshield wiper in the fog, he wasn't exactly sure where they landed. After all, light refracts in the fog.

James tried to retrace the trajectory as the men dropped to their hands and knees, clearing leaves and dirt. To no avail.

"Maybe they landed a little further over here," James said, motioning with his hands.

"I'll never understand," the owner said, his scratchy voice releasing years of pent-up frustration. "*Mein Vater*—my father—watched the SS march right up the *Nontallerstrasse*. He kept the business going, not knowing if any future existed for his children. Gravesites were simple markers and pits. I learned this trade after the war. Carved my own father's headstone, with precision. I have carved hundreds, thousands, more since then. Find me any man these days who does work to last a lifetime."

"Yes, that is rare. We haven't looked here yet," James replied.

"Well, *Scheisse*, leave it," the owner said, brushing the dirt from his hands and knees. "I realize I didn't get your name."

"Wohlmuth. My name is James Wohlmuth."

"Wohlmuth? Really?" he responded in his heavy accent. "But you must know you have an Austrian—"

"Yes, I have an Austrian name. I learned the story of the executioner last week," James replied.

"*Natürlich*, and the house he used for—"

"Yes, I'm aware of the house over there. In fact, I was returning to my hotel after walking there earlier."

"History," the owner said. "We think we've learned everything. We've learned nothing. My father used to say, '*Jemandem den Schlüssel zu etwas geben.*'"

"What does that mean?" James asked.

"In English, this would translate not so good. But I guess it means, 'I give you the knowledge, so you can solve the problem.'"

James nodded, trying to find a place to store the reference in his murky mind.

"But for your effort, *bitte*. The least I can do is offer you a beer."

The owner asked no questions of James but seemed to welcome his company. They sat on the patio of the house that served as an office and looked out at the mess of broken stone on the ground—and a forklift with no key.

James learned how a makeshift mass grave was discovered in the 1960s, just two doors down, while the foundation for a new auto repair business was being excavated. Dozens of condemned bodies, not worthy of headstones, buried one by one. Covered in lime, covered in soil, and forgotten.

The owner described how residents of houses around the executioner's property would hear the click-clack of hooves in the middle of the night, some believing the condemned continue to be brought by cart from the old town to the executioner's house, awaiting their demise —even though there hadn't been a public execution on the property for over two hundred fifty years.

"But no one has occupied the house since the year 2000. The year my grandson was born," the owner exhaled. "And the year my son informed me he would not follow in my footsteps as a stonemason."

"So now you do this work on your own?" James asked.

"Unfortunately, yes. Meaning the dead will now have to wait," the owner said, raising his stein. "At least until I find someone else to operate the forklift."

*Sure, the dead have to wait,* James considered. *But what about those whose demise is predictable? Or planned or programmed? How many of them will there be?*

"I'm sorry I couldn't be more helpful in finding your keys," James said, placing the empty stein on the small table between the chairs where they sat. "I need to get back to my hotel. I have some unfinished business before I return to the States."

"A man with work ethic. A rare sight. *Prost.* Please, you are welcome here anytime. And next time, no apologies."

James walked to the exit of the yard, his murky mind now soaked with a daze of beer and a desire to sleep, battling with the adrenaline induced by the amount of work he had ahead of him.

Turning onto the main road, with its cafés and flower shops, James felt the urge to stop, turn around, and take in one more glance of the Untersberg from the vantage point of what was once the far end of town. It glowed purple from the light of the sunset, refracting off its towering walls.

Against its reflection, he caught a glimmer of silver in one of the tree branches.

The keys.

For all the effort James and the owner made, scouring the ground, gutters, and bushes, the keys had been hanging from—and camouflaged by—a tree branch. He shook the trunk, jarring the keys loose to the ground.

James returned to the office: the sign on the door showing *Geschlossen.* Closed. After a few knocks, the stonemason appeared and unlocked the door.

"Your keys! Hanging in a tree the entire time," James said, in a tone more relaxed than the time they'd known each other warranted. "Now the dead no longer have to wait."

"Well, they do until I find someone else to operate the lift," the owner responded.

# 27

Walking the familiar route to his hotel, James stopped briefly at a kebab restaurant, ordering a döner wrap similar to the one he enjoyed after changing the SIM card in his phone the previous weekend. The intense smell of the meat and spices was one of the last remaining connections he felt to Seattle, as the remainder of his well-structured, ambitious, fortunate life became displaced by the totality of the previous five weeks.

Slightly more light passed through his hotel room when he returned, as spring began to nudge winter out of the way. James placed the white plastic bag—with its foil-wrapped meal, box of crinkle-cut French fries, and Fanta soda—on the table next to the open laptop. After using the bathroom for the first time since he left, he ate and looked at the status of the programming scripts he started almost twelve hours prior.

Hundreds of usernames appeared on the spreadsheet he used to track potential candidates for manipulation—far more than he expected.

He opened another account, then another. The process became mechanical: hack in, input the search terms and sequences on a few social media or video-sharing apps, erase the history, leave the <S>, log out. Names blurred together—faces he would never see, lives he was quietly nudging from whatever emotional season they were in toward the coldest, darkest day of winter.

The human connections fate dropped at James's feet that day—a polite front desk clerk offering to extend his stay, the sight of mothers pushing their newborns in strollers along a path on a crisp afternoon, or the opportunity to help an old man find lost keys in exchange for a beer and conversation—were no longer enough to steer him from his trajectory.

Fifty accounts became a hundred. A hundred became two. The numbers no longer mattered. What mattered was the act itself—the methodical sowing of seeds that would grow into something he believed was necessary.

As the night wore on, lines of code on the screen began to waver. The letters twisted into unfamiliar lines and shapes, like the calligraphy drawn when pens were made from quills.

*James's mind drifted as the chair beneath him began to feel different— harder, more rough-hewn in its texture. The branches of the tree providing the lumber that would become the chair began to regrow, lifting him from the room. Before he could fully disengage from his work, he found himself standing in a dense forest of evergreen trees, south of Salzburg, along the Salzach River.*

*Franz began walking, waving to James to follow. The air was crisp, carrying the earthy scent of pine needles and damp soil. The bends and wisps of the tall trees morphed into persistent, repeating whispers. Like those of a weary mother as she rocked her infant. Shh shh shh shh.*

*Franz, now a young adult, moved with purpose, his boots crunching on the forest floor. A gaggle of owls warned each other of the two-legged intruders passing by on the forest floor below.*

*As they descended the last ridge, the forest gave way to the mist-covered valley of Bad Hofgastein. A thin veil of fog clung to the banks of the river, its waters glistening under the morning light.*

*Franz paused at the edge of a pasture, the silhouette of a farmhouse visible ahead. An old man worked near the barn, his movements slow but deliberate. Franz turned to James, raising a hand to signal him to keep a safe distance.*

*"Hans Wohlmuth? The executioner?" Franz called out.*

*The old man straightened, leaning on his pitchfork. "My services are no longer for hire," he replied. "As you can see, I'm as frail as a dried cornstalk swaying in the winter wind."*

*"I did not journey here to hire your services, Herr Wohlmuth."*

"Then make your business be known."

"I am your grandson, Franz Joseph Wohlmuth. From Salzburg."

Hans narrowed his eyes.

"You must be mistaken. I have no kin in Salzburg."

"Your firstborn son—my father—is dead," Franz replied.

"Again, you must be mistaken. I have two sons. Each of them carries on the executioner trade of our family in Tyrol. I have no other."

"My name is Franz Joseph Wohlmuth. The only son of Samuel Wohlmuth. He chose a different path."

The man looked straight at the boy and squinted slightly.

"In my eyes and the eyes of his family, the man to which you refer has been dead for eighteen years. For refusing to carry on the family trade. Therefore, it would be impossible for him to have a son. And therefore, again, impossible for me to have a grandson, from Salzburg."

Franz stood looking at the man, without removing his gaze, waiting for the elder man to blink. He finally did.

"How did the life of this man you are referring to come to an end?"

"My father drowned."

The man then spat at a pile of manure next to his feet.

"I could only have assumed as much. A weak man from the moment of his entry into this world. Carry on with your journey, pilgrim. I have no further business with you."

Franz glanced over the man's shoulder and noticed a sickle leaning against the barn. He set his rucksack down and walked toward it. The old man stood with his brutally leathery and calloused hands over the end of his pitchfork, waiting for Franz's next move.

He grasped the sickle's worn handle, feeling its weight. Gently, he ran his thumb along the blade's edge, testing its sharpness. Satisfied, he walked toward a small pen beside the barn where a large swine rooted in the mud.

Opening the gate, Franz stepped inside. The swine looked up, oblivious to any threat. With deliberate steps, he positioned himself beside the animal. He raised the sickle high above his shoulders, the morning sun glinting off the blade.

In one swift, powerful motion, he brought the blade down. It sliced cleanly *through the swine's thick neck, the force driving it deep into the mud. The animal let out a brief, sharp squeal before collapsing. Blood pooled around Franz's boots, seeping into the soil.*

*Franz, expressionless, turned to the old man, eyes open but calm, and wiped his mouth with his sleeve, waiting for a response, as James stood in witness, frozen.*

*"My name is Hans Wohlmuth. You, pilgrim, are now indebted to me for one swine," Franz's grandfather said.*

*"I will repay the debt I have just incurred to you, old man, as well as whatever you feel is the debt owed to the Wohlmuth name by my father. I will do so by working in service to you as you train me to carry on the family legacy—as an executioner."*

*Franz stood in front of his grandfather, the blood of the swine beginning to dry into a deep red wine color on the blade. Hans wondered if the boy had energy left to make a clean cut on his own neck, as he certainly possessed the rage. From the stare and volume of air he appeared to bring into his lungs with each massive breath, the old man concluded, "Yes, he could."*

*"So it shall be," he said with an aged, bitter laugh. "The wish of the young Wohlmuth from the city is accorded. You seem to believe you possess some skill in ending life on command. But what you have not yet learned, young Wohlmuth. Cutting down a beast may build the man. But cutting down a man, I can assure you, most certainly builds a beast."*

# 28

"Wohlmuth. What brings you here this morning?" the stonemason asked, standing in front of the damaged scaffolding where the granite slabs had fallen the previous afternoon.

"My apologies. Would you remind me of your name again?" James asked.

"Steiner. Wilhelm Steiner," the owner responded, caught off guard by the man with such a strong work ethic missing a fundamental detail.

"I see the forklift remains as it was when I left," James observed, kicking himself over the blip of absentmindedness.

"*Ja*. My son says he will try to come in the next days. But, as you may recall, he has his own life and stonemasonry, south near Villach. I am no longer his priority."

"Maybe I can help you."

"Help me? Help me with what?"

"With operating the forklift. And cleaning up this mess."

The old man paused and gazed at James with intense skepticism. Although he'd consumed six steins of beer to James's two, he couldn't recall hearing the young man from Seattle stating his ability to operate industrial machinery.

"I am not in need of another mishap, Wohlmuth. But *danke*."

"Please, I insist. Yesterday—I was tired. Jet lag. May I see the keys? It's a three-stage mast, right? The kid hadn't engaged the hydraulic tilt mechanism to stabilize the load. That's why the slabs fell over."

Wilhelm stood, arms crossed, glancing at the scaffolding, the shattered slabs, and the forklift, which had exactly the features James described.

He slowly removed the keys from his pocket and placed them in James's hand. James gripped them quickly and placed his hands in his pockets, concealing the tremors that had begun days ago.

After climbing into the operator's chair and securing the four-point harness, James inserted the key into the ignition. Before turning it to start, he placed both hands on the steering wheel and took a deep breath, summoning his neck and arms to relax as he scanned the pedals, levers, and controls of the machine.

"Wohlmuth, if you're jet-lagged, this is not—"

The ignition fired, bringing the machine to life. As it warmed up, James lowered the forks to the ground before looking over his shoulders in both directions. Engaging the drive to reverse, the machine emitted the familiar beep! beep! warning as it crawled slowly backward, clearing itself from the fallen granite slabs.

James moved the machine into drive and made one tight loop around the yard, helping to reduce the tension he could see in the old man's face and shoulders. After completing the turn, James returned to the spot of the mishap, placed the forks, with precision, under the empty pallet, straightened the machine in front of the scaffolding, and raised it to the top shelf.

Wilhelm could do nothing but move the toothpick positioned halfway out of his mouth from one side to the other, using nothing but his tongue and jaw.

James parked the forklift next to the house and walked to the old man.

"Your keys."

"*Na ja, Scheisse,*" the old man said in his scratchy voice. "An ambitious, humble American. Not a combination I ever expected to meet."

"How long do you think it will take you to find a forklift operator?" James asked, dusting his hands on his pants, his ears ringing, and his vision narrowed like a pair of binoculars in a movie scene.

"If the last one was any indication—weeks, months," Wilhelm said.

"No one wants this work. And it's impossible to get rid of the bad ones in this country, unless they walk out, as you saw yesterday."

James nodded, maintaining the persuasive eye contact EchoWave's media trainers had drilled into him for months.

"Why? You looking for work?"

"For a while, while I finish a project. And a place to sleep. Pay me under the table while you look for the next guy, and you can fire me whenever you want. Save you some money."

Wilhelm remained perplexed at how James pulled off the stunt. A man from Seattle, working for a technology company? Austrian-named key finder and forklift operator? Appearing at the yard out of the clear blue sky?

Although tired and unshaven, he showed glimmers of refinement, intelligence, and work ethic. Not an American Superman, by any stretch. But a man to do the job for the moment.

James didn't blink. Nor did he notice he hadn't blinked, making him appear all the more persuasive.

"Start tomorrow," the old man relented. "There's a guest cottage behind the house my son used to use before he moved. No guests. Don't expect breakfast. One mistake, I'll bury you under the auto repair shop where your other Wohlmuth left his condemned."

# 29

The gauze rolled out of its plastic core onto the floor of the small guest house. James was attempting to cut a strip from the roll to wrap two fingers he'd injured earlier, cut on the edge of a block of granite that had fallen from the large saw used to cut tombstones into shape.

Similar to his absence of reaction to the slicing of his fingers, James simply watched the white fabric lie on the floor before gathering it up and trying again.

Wilhelm began to wonder if his guest and under-the-table worker was actually an American Superman. James slept infrequently and was never seen eating or drinking. Unlike the vaping twenty-something who walked off the job, heaving the keys into the bushes, and leaving a pile of broken granite, James faithfully heeded each of the old man's requests and never argued. On the contrary, he frequently volunteered to clean the cutting and polishing machines. Never hesitating to lift and discard fallen chunks of granite as they were being cut into their final shape: arch, cross, star, monolith, or otherwise.

Nearly every day, the boss, or '*die chef*', as James called him, had to order him away from working.

"I'm certainly glad you are not here legally, Wohlmuth," the stonemason said. "Austria caps the work week at thirty-eight hours. I'd be arrested if they knew how many more you put in."

When pried away from the gyroscope of waiting, James walked to the executioner's house and settled in the grass, now turning emerald green from the longer days and frequent rain. He observed as mothers pushed their infants in strollers, elderly couples walked hand in hand, and young children rode their bikes between neighborhoods and the houses of friends, unaware of the amount of blood that had been spilled right beneath their feet.

James spent most evenings inside the tiny guesthouse. If Wilhelm were awake, he could see the glow of a computer screen illuminating the small windows. Casting faint light on the flower boxes, their contents now fully in bloom.

After patching up his fingers, James wondered aloud how he was going to enter the evening's search terms with one of them attached to its neighbor. James set his elbow on the small kitchen table, using the space between his thumb and index finger to rest his forehead. He'd already begun the content manipulation sequence on over ten thousand users and had revisited and updated the terms on over five thousand. The EchoWave algorithms were performing as expected, but he'd seen no news indicating anyone else had descended into self-harm the way his wife had.

"Michael, Vik. Those assholes were probably right, Sara. Maybe your death had nothing to do with my algorithms. Maybe it was just me. Too busy pitching EchoWave's value proposition to customers and investors. Too busy to see you—the real you—on your path of suffering."

Bulbous raindrops began to fall intermittently on the roof, sounding like a pen tapping impatiently on a desk, waiting for its master to quit thinking and start working.

"I had one job in the world, love. And that was to protect you. Through health, sickness, and everything in between. And I failed," James said.

James glanced down at his bandaged fingers, blood now soaking through, and let out a large sigh.

"Do I just go home, Sara? Start over?"

He stared out the window at the LED light fixed above the shop's garage door, becoming transfixed by the passing drops.

*His mind registered each drop moving more slowly, morphing into streaks of white, like a camera with the shutter left open. James blinked slowly and turned to see Franz Joseph Wohlmuth, now a grown man, sitting across from him at the small table in his tiny cottage, drawing in thin black ink flowing from his quill. With each dip of the pen, the image came into shape. An outline of Franz, standing deftly in the gallows, his sword held high above his head. You could see the weight and the force with which the blade would fall from the sky. When it was time. Just in front of him, kneeling on the ground, was the condemned soul. Hood covering the head. Hands tied behind the back. Maybe a killer. Maybe a petty thief. Didn't matter. They were an example to be made. As much as a threat to be eliminated.*

*Franz looked up from his work and for the first time, said, "I don't know them, James. But at the end, just before the sword falls, I know everything. Just like you."*

*"You knew what I didn't, Franz. The sword without the pen is just a killing tool. The pen and the sword need each other to make change. My briefing needs a sword, or else they will bury it."*

*Franz nodded.*

*"So write."*

James pulled a pen and a pad of paper from his backpack and began to draw in large letters on the cover:

*With Just a Flick of the Thumb. You Become Numb.*

As he drew the lines, he watched Franz continue to dip his pen and write.

*Although we seem to find ourselves on the cusp of having our eyes opened—to date—I bear witness only to a sliver of light being allowed to penetrate the area of our minds containing reconciliation and forgiveness. Until fully opened, the cruelties of the role in which I—and the unsightly others, wallowing on the edges—were bequeathed. I will forever be haunted.*

James opened the cover of the notepad and began to allow his agony, guilt, rage, and sorrow flow through the pen, as the rain fell more steadily on the roof.

*This is the way I designed it. I wanted this. We all wanted this. I made it faster than human thought. Even human consciousness. You can't keep up anymore. No one can.*

In between dips of the quill into the ink, the image of Franz peered at James's opening salvo, nodding in satisfaction. He continued in his own diary:

*My eyes now fully opened—looking God full in the face—toward those who have the power to decide justice on a whim—never fully allowing the populous to understand rule, process, or punishment. Whether it be worthy of a man's death and torture—punishment worthy of hard labor—or punishment worthy of a man walking free. We will forever be blind—until we are eternally allowed to see.*

James continued, letters connecting within the words and the words flowing together:

*Everything is just distraction and engagement. Feel good? Stay put. I'll make you feel better. Feel bad? Don't worry, this will only sting for a moment. Feeling worse? It's okay, you're not alone. So is everyone else. See them? Right there, above and below you. Don't turn away just yet. I have something else for you.*

James watched as the vision of Franz pulled out a new piece of parchment and set it on the table. In large, ornate cursive text, with ink pouring onto the page, more red than black, he wrote:

*In which all the included, and by me,*
*Franz Joseph Wohlmuth, Salzburg-appointed Executioner,*
*"EXECUTIONS" of the "DELINQUENTS"*
*by the High Priest, the Prince Archbishop, so ordered, beginning*
*January, Seventeen Hundred Sixty-One,*
*the Year of our LORD—*

After drawing ornate lines and swirls of ink around his declaration, Franz penned the first entry in his executioner's diary:

*No. 1. Jeremiah Hügel Twenty April 1761. By order of the Prince Archbishop and said Courts of Salzburg, I have duly executed Herr Hügel with the blade. Earned wage as Wasserträger, in Straubing aus Payrn. Charged and duly convicted of theft. Aged forty-eight. Never married. Prior to placement of hood, quiet. Behaved in manner indicating little discord or aware. Then branded with letter "S." To great applause of many bystanders.*

The rain continued to fall with greater intensity, as James tried to keep up, copying the spirit of Franz's declaration, which he would return to. Instead, he turned a new page in the notebook:

*Number 1—Sara Hauser-Wohlmuth. Twenty-three February, this year. Daughter. Wife. Friend. Project manager. Age 34 years. Married to James Wohlmuth seven years. Suffered three miscarriages. Inundated with content around anxiety, depression, miscarriage, peace, and freedom from worry. Triggered by frequent commenting on parenting forums and group pages on the two largest social networks. And husband's departure for business trip.*

# 30

James sat outside a café in the old town one afternoon in spring. The underbelly of the cobblestone pavement had finally begun to warm, hindered for months by winter's shadow. Nearby, street vendors showed an extra spring in their step, handing bread, cheese, and wurst to customers without their fingers freezing. As the cool April breezes and sudden rain showers waned, outdoor tables and chairs began to fill with patrons willing to enjoy coffee or a slice of cake outside longer than twenty minutes before retreating indoors.

He used his spoon to lift the remaining frothy milk from the bottom of the coffee cup, then turned it and let the froth slowly fall.

A table jostled as a tourist attempted to stand, their knee striking beneath it, spilling glasses and bottles forward. It brought James's attention back to his pad of paper, the single entry of Sara Hauser-Wohlmuth having been retraced by his pen so many times that the letters appeared as solid black lines, resembling information redacted from a top-secret government document.

The sounds of the streets and the surrounding conversation were allowed passage into his brain as he overheard two women from America sitting at the table next to him in Salzburg for a conference. They were reviewing printouts of a draft presentation that one of them was to deliver the following day. Drinking cappuccinos, they shared a slice of traditional Austrian *Topfenstrudel* and ice cream.

James grinned at the opportunity to glimpse the world he left behind.

One of the women picked up her device from the table.

"Ugh, these notifications. Let me switch on DND."

Her colleague nodded, pushing her glasses up the bridge of her nose. "Tell me about it. I've had to seriously cut down on my scrolling. It was messing with my evenings. Like yesterday, I looked up things to do after the conference, and the next day my feed was flooded with ads for luggage. Even though Mark just got me a new suitcase for Christmas."

"Right? It's like they know exactly what to push at you. Once you show any interest, it's relentless," the first woman replied, shaking her head.

"I still use that app sometimes. I've quit most of the others. It got too overwhelming."

It was never in James's nature to interject in a conversation, but hearing the two women talk about social media, rather than staying locked in its vortex, caught his attention.

""Digital detox", as soon as I land back in the States," one woman said, raising her cappuccino cup.

"Agreed. Digital—and pastry—detox. One month," the other said as they toasted in agreement.

James allowed the muscles in his face to lift a subtle smile. One side of his face coy and calculating, knowing they would never keep their 'digital detox' commitment. The other side more sentimental, as he reflected on Sara and her friends sitting together at coffee shops around Seattle, setting aside work for a few minutes simply to enjoy each other's company. As these women were.

A moment later, his smartphone vibrated in double pulses, moving the device slightly closer to him. A notification from a news tracking app appeared on the screen. He set the spoon from his coffee on the saucer next to the cup, lifted his device, touched the alert, and felt his heart stop in his chest.

### Daughter of NFL Quarterback Ryan Mitchell Found Dead in Apparent Suicide

# 31

Nervously rushing out of the old town, James stopped at the baroque chapel fountain, cupped his hands in the fountain's cool water, and splashed his face.

Once. Twice. Three times over.

The sting of the icy droplets against his skin jolted him back from the blur of shock that had overtaken him at the café. He looked up at the church, the sun's reflection off its façade warming his face and body. And yet, there was no sanctuary to be found here. Nor would he dare walk through its doors seeking absolution. Not yet.

As he leaned back down into the basin, drinking from his hands, he heard chatter over his shoulder, as three college-aged men held empty bottles, waiting for him to step aside from the fountain. Students, speaking German. He wondered if there were any language he understood anymore, as the world continued to spin, even as his had stopped.

Muttering, "*Es tut mehr sehr leid,*" he stepped aside and continued walking, his apology sounding chiseled, unnatural. And foreign.

The cobblestones beneath his feet appeared hard and gray, as they did in winter, but he could look in no other direction. Everything was down. Every car passing him and every person he encountered seemed to exude blame and abhorrence.

Continuing to the stonemason's yard and the relative safety of the cottage he was loaned, James was unsure if he was running away from the headline or toward the consequence of his work.

By the time James arrived, the evening sun had begun its descent, casting long, purple shadows across the granite slabs. The sound of his boots on the gravel path leading to the guesthouse seemed louder than usual, as if each step was accusing him of the same crime.

He spotted Wilhelm through the window in the office, but didn't acknowledge or greet him. Once inside, he locked the door behind him, leaning his back against it for some backbone. The cottage felt colder than it should have. Smaller than its already tiny frame, as if it had absorbed the weight of what he'd done.

James moved to the table, where his open notebook and pen sat, untouched since the night before. The sight of it—the empty page waiting for him—mocked his earlier resolve. He had set out to change the system, to force the world to confront the dangers he knew too well. But Kimberly Mitchell's death was not a statistic, or a theory. It was a life. A life extinguished.

He sat heavily, the chair creaking under his weight, and placed his hands on the table. The bandages around his injured fingers were stained red, but he didn't care. He picked up the pen and stared at the open notebook. His grip tightened as he began to write.

*Number 2—Kimberly Mitchell. Twenty-first May, this year. Daughter of Ryan and Elizabeth Mitchell. Age 17 years. High school senior, athlete, and aspiring artist. Engaged extensively with content related to despair and hopelessness. Search terms entered on her accounts included: "coping with failure," "feeling invisible," "life after loss," "escaping pain," and "overcoming darkness." Mother found a library of more than 3,000 videos her daughter had bookmarked, liked, saved, or tagged as a favorite. Algorithmic manipulation led her to a curated feed of videos and posts amplifying her distress. No intervention occurred. Family and friends unaware of the depth of her struggle.*

He dropped the pen, staring at the stark black ink against the page, and rested his head in his hands. The silence of the cottage was deafening, interrupted only by the occasional sound of an aircraft flying overhead, making its final descent, or initial climb, out of Salzburg.

Closing the notebook, James walked to the bed to lie down. Now he knew there would be more. Many more. Now he knew his job going forward was to walk the cart of the condemned. From the house of the Prince Archbishop to the executioner's house. Over and over again.

# 32

Franz wiped the quill on a towel and placed a cork in the clay pot of ink. Next to him, under the dim light of a single candle, sat the diary, growing in thickness, now bound between two thin wood plank covers, covered in a sheet of pigskin. The latest entry read:

> Number 181. I executed the man Wolfgang Helmbacher, who was in custody of the Prince Archbishop of Salzburg, charged with the crimes of theft and assault. A native of Tyrol, his profession was that of a farmhand. Age thirty-three years, he was not married at the time of his execution at the edge of my sword. A single stroke, without incident. I also severed three of his fingers. Along with his head, the three fingers were nailed to the stake. Per the orders of His Holiness, the body was burned, and the ashes were used to make yellow paint. June 7, 1786.

Sitting in the workshop behind his house at Neukommgasse 26, James watched Franz, having grown older, remain steadfast in his routine and his duty. The sun wouldn't rise for hours, yet he continued to work, focused and free of distraction.

Franz placed the blade he'd acquired from his grandfather, Hanz Wohlmuth, in a vice on the table. The blade James saw behind the glass in the museum.

The year of the blade's manufacture had been inscribed at its base: 1663. By the time it was placed into Franz's hands by his grandfather, it had already met the flesh of the condemned for over one hundred years.

Franz steadied a chisel over the shiny, slightly curved surface, as wide as two leather belts placed side by side. He stood and, with a large wooden mallet, struck the top of the chisel, creating a slight indentation. He removed the chisel and checked the mark, blowing away the tiny shards of metal. He continued. A strike of the mallet, check, puff. Strike, check, puff. Over and over again.

Through the slats of the wooden walls, the light of dawn seeped in, brighter and sharper than it should have been, illuminating each particle of dust suspended in the air. Slowly, after dozens of strikes of the chisel, a word began to form:

## JUSTICA

Each time the mallet descended from above to strike the chisel's handle, Franz thought of his mother, Anna Maria, and the wrongs she could not right. He thought of his father, Samuel Wohlmuth, and the bravery he showed in forging his own path, serving in the name of justice with dignity—even amidst corruption. And he thought of each execution order he had received thus far, building a body of proof against a six-hundred-year-old system where guilt and innocence were seldom determined by solid evidence or due process—a system where fear and control were deemed acceptable sacrifices to maintain order.

When the word was complete, he used a towel to check his work. With precision and his steady hand, he knew each strike into the blade would last for centuries.

James watched as Franz continued hammering the metal, inscribing tiny letters across the blade that began to form a poem: "Whoever finds it will find it and will fail," warning the blade and the flesh that meets it—once they connect, there is no escaping death.

Hammering, hour after hour, without standing to nourish or relieve himself, he continued pounding letters, one strike at a time, to the next line of the poem. "Who dies He will be killed," reminding anyone who meets his sword that the fate of their eternal existence has been sealed and cannot change. For by being ordered by the Prince Archbishop, their demise was ordered by God.

Late in the morning, Franz's hands, now blistered and bloody, pounded the last line—"I hope and will die." Contemplating each time the sword swung around his body, praying for mercy for the brutality he'd willfully, willingly engaged in the name of some future justice and order that had not yet been foretold. Knowing he, too, would meet death one day, whether by the edge of a blade, condemned for his own "wrongdoing", or a disease that climbed inside him, or from the shards of a shattered heart.

When finished, he stood from the place he was working, rolling his neck, trying to massage his shoulders while gazing out the window. His hands and eyes exhausted from the hours he'd spent toiling over every minor detail, wanting to ensure, whatever the outcome, his words would stand the test of time. The message would be clear. They would serve as wisdom and a warning for the ages. He would be heard. He would be proven right.

It was essential for society to look deep within its collective soul and determine how much longer it would permit the secrecy and dishonesty of those intent on remaining unaccountable

# 33

"I don't know what to make of the conversation I overheard," Chris Phelps said to his college friend, Nate Bennett, both sitting at a small table in the dive bar they used to frequent in college.

After graduating from the University of Washington, Chris joined Microsoft at just the right time, cashed out his stock options, and, a decade later, retired and opened Code&Craft on the East Side of Seattle. Nate started his career in law enforcement, eventually rising through the ranks in the cybercrime division of the FBI's Seattle field office. While their economic trajectories diverged greatly, they remained close friends.

"It was two senior executives. Sitting at the far end of my bar. The conversation wasn't the normal startup technobabble drivel I hear every time I work the floor," Chris said as the second round of IPAs was placed in front of them.

"You've owned Code&Craft for what, eight years? Why don't you just hire some bartenders?" Nate asked.

"I have. I do. But they don't like to work much. They call in sick. Or quit. Don't show up. Don't give notice. Right about the time happy hour starts."

"Of course, Gen Xers," Nate said, peering at the young cocktail server as she walked back to the bar. The nature of his investigative work—with the explosion of corporate network breaches, organized computer fraud, and identity theft—left him skeptical of everything. Resentful of most things.

"Anyway, the conversation stood out in my mind because of a woman, Sara Hauser," Chris continued. "On the last Thursday of the month, for the previous two years, she brought her work team to the lounge for dinner. Like clockwork, except for December."

"Yea?" Nate asked, nudging Chris along.

"In February, she and her team didn't show. Unusual, as they'd become so predictable. We always had a private room ready. And we couldn't get in touch with her afterward."

Nate scanned the various televisions in the bar, team flags from Seattle and Washington State draped nearby, his focus wandering.

"A few weeks later, two guys sitting at the bar were having a heated debate about a woman, Sara, and another executive at their company. Someone claiming their algorithms contributed to—or caused—her death."

"I've always wondered why people tell secrets sitting at bars," Nate replied, taking another sip and not taking his eyes off one of the screens. "Always louder and uninhibited as the night drags on. Killer algorithms, huh?"

"Nate, listen—The woman who hosted her team every month was named Sara Hauser. One of our managers learned her married name is Sara Hauser-Wohlmuth. She died the day she was supposed to host her dinner at my lounge."

"Chris, it's been a really long day."

"I didn't know Sara that well, but the guy sitting at the bar that night mentioned another person in their conversation—Wohlmuth. I put the connection in the back of my mind. Until last week, when I saw the news about Ryan Mitchell's daughter."

"The Seahawks quarterback?" Nate asked.

"Yes. Seahawks—the Seattle—really, my friend?" Chris asked.

"I pay little attention to American football, you know that."

"Mitchell and his wife found their seventeen-year-old daughter, Kimberly, in their house. Dead from an apparent suicide. Why?"

"Why did she commit suicide? Off the top of my head?" Nate replied with a tinge of frustration in his tone. "Let's see. Because the rate of adolescent mental health issues has reached epidemic levels? Most go unchecked because it requires parents to actually sit down and listen to their kids? Kids feel hopeless and resort to bad things? Should I go on?"

"I get that," Chris said. "And then the day before yesterday? The attorney in his early thirties—accused of taking payoffs from the contracting firm that dug the tunnel under the city—jumped from thirty stories onto 3rd Avenue during rush hour."

"Yes, that one I'm aware of," Nate responded, growing impatient with the conversation and his wealthy, lounge-owning friend reciting the local news. "He was being indicted on a dozen federal charges. Embezzlement and mail fraud. And probably would have gone to prison for a very long time. Why are you surprised the guy snapped?"

"Not when you put it like that," Chris conceded. "But he was a family man. He was adamant about his innocence—holding his wife and kids in front of the press after his arraignment."

"You know, Chris, it just occurred to me. The bureau really should start recruiting lounge owners as investigators. And as behavioral therapists. And human lie detectors."

Chris stared blankly at his friend.

"I've got to get home, my wife has me doing a thing," Nate said as he stood and pulled his wallet from his pocket. "What do you want me to do about this?"

"I have no idea, Nate. Could there be a connection between these suicides and the conversation I overheard?"

"Doubtful," Nate responded, skeptical and resentful about taking on any new headaches at a time when work headaches were as common as stolen passwords. "Three separate, unrelated suicides. In Seattle. There will probably be three more next week you don't hear about."

Chris turned to the window before looking back at his old friend's face. Discouraged by the layers of callus, accumulated over Nate's empathy, while he sold twenty-two-dollar absinthe cocktails to overpaid tech workers.

Nate glanced at the receipt and pulled a few twenties from his wallet.

"Two beers and an order of tater tots. Thirty bucks. Fucking Seattle," Nate said.

"I've got this, buddy, don't worry about it."

"Thanks, Chris. Listen, I'll do a bit of digging and tell you what I find when I see you this weekend. Okay?"

"I appreciate it. It's just that woman, Sara. Makes no sense. She was always so confident, so put together."

"Your customer, who you barely knew, clearly put on a very different face at work and in your bar than the one she wore at home. But I'll look into it for you. By the way—who was the executive?"

"The executive?" Chris asked.

"The guy you overheard talking about Sara Hauser-Wohlmuth at your bar."

"Two guys, not one. Michael Valeno, CEO of EchoWave. A Code&Craft regular. And the other guy I don't know. About our age. I assume another top exec at the company."

"EchoWave? I think my wife has one of those in our kitchen."

"No, man, it's a high-tech co—"

"Yes, Chris, I know who they are. Their headquarters campus is less than a mile from your lounge."

# 34

James sat at the workbench in Wilhelm's shop, his chisel posed against the rough granite of a new headstone. The air was thick with powdery dust from material removed from the front of the slab. Names and inscriptions. Entire lives that occurred in the dash between two dates: birth and death.

Each time James was given a stone to complete, he continued to work until it was finished, focused and free of distraction, even if the sun had set hours ago. Most tombstones were carved by machine. A design entered into a computer, and the granite slab set on a plate. Violent sounds and sprays of lubricant blur the intention and the outcome. Moments later, a surface emerged, engraved and polished, with precision.

Wilhelm had considered moving to such a system in his waning years. After James's arrival, he could continue his tradition of engraving the old-fashioned way, for the time being, with its mistakes and imperfections. Like life.

A vibration emitted from the phone in James's back pocket. For a moment, it interrupted his attention, but not his work.

*The dead are patient,* James thought. *But they still deserve our attention.*

The grooves in the stone deepened, forming the outline of a name. He didn't know the person—Wilhelm rarely discussed the lives behind the names they carved. But James found himself imagining them anyway. A life lived, joys, and failures, all reduced to indentations and memories.

James gave one final puff of air against the surface and wiped it with his polishing cloth. He stood up from his stool, rolling his neck, trying to massage his shoulders while gazing out the window across the yard. Wilhelm pulled into the yard in his small van. After wiping his brow with his towel, James pulled out his phone to read the notification.

## Third Suicide in as Many Weeks Prompts Emergency Mayfair Town Hall

James clenched the phone tightly, his hand shaking. Glancing around the workshop, his gaze landed on Wilhelm as he emerged from the van, who acknowledged him with a slight wave. The old man stretched out his back, tired and arthritic from decades of lifting the proof of lives lived, before looking up into the warmth of the sun and the silver silhouette of the Untersburg in the distance. A man entirely unburdened by his life's work.

James yearned to feel the same. The alerts were relentless now, each headline another name, another life to add to the diary, another soul twisted and severed by the algorithms he had designed and the content they exposed them to.

He entered his cottage, stripped off his clothes, and walked to the shower. The warm water cleansed him of the dust of the name and dates he'd just engraved. But it couldn't wash off the guilt and the grief.

Emerging from the shower, his body was sore. He could barely open his hands from holding the hammer, chisel, and pen. After drying himself off, he walked into the small kitchen area and sat in front of the diary, growing thicker by the day with diary entries, drawings, and verses he remembered from his time with Franz.

"What if they ignore the diary?" he said as the water in the bottom of the shower turned from translucent gray to crystal clear. "Even if it contains two hundred sixty-two names? Or twenty-six thousand? What if we're all beyond paying attention to what is killing us?"

—

After a dinner of Reuben sandwiches, kettle chips, and tall lagers on the terrace at the Queen Anne Ale House, Julie Frager and her boy-friend, Adam, walked her golden retriever, Max, along the side streets before returning to their apartment. The sunset blazed with hues of bitter orange and deep purple, altering the color of the homes and pavement on the hill above the Puget Sound.

Spring was in motion, with children playing on trampolines wedged in the small yards, while cheers from the goal, just scored, carried through the air from the nearby soccer pitch.

"Come on, Max," she urged as the dog pulled her in the opposite direction of Adam, who had stopped momentarily.

"Are you coming?" she asked.

"Take a look over there," Adam said, nodding toward a cluster of unmarked black SUVs parked in front of a house. A group of men and women in jackets bearing the FBI emblem were moving up and down the stairs of the small craftsman carrying banker's boxes and reams of papers.

"Hang on to Max for a minute, will you?" Julie asked Adam.

She walked across the street, her body releasing the surge of adrena-line that emerged every time she smelled a potential story—an instinct she'd had since she was ten years old.

Olive Madelin stood with her arms crossed on the two concrete strips of pavement serving as the driveway to her detached garage behind the house.

"What's going on here?" Julie asked Olive gingerly.

"For the life of me, I have no idea. It's not as though this couple hasn't been through enough."

"Who lives here? Is it that family—" Julie asked, attempting a jour-nalistic trick to coerce another party to finish the sentence, or move the conversation into another direction.

Olive, having dealt with real estate vultures since her husband passed, wasn't having it.

"And you are?"

Julie paused.

"I'm Julie Frager, ma'am. I was with the Wall Street Chronicle for years—" she said, attempting to prevent Olive from resisting her questions.

"—until they went corporate and stopped covering the important local stories around here. Now I'm on my own."

Olive looked at Julie up and down, trying to gauge her intention.

"Progress has done more harm than good to this town, if you ask me," Olive said as one of the FBI agents tripped on a paver in front of the house, dropping and spilling one of the boxes of James's work.

"This house belongs to James and Sara Wohlmuth," Olive relented. "Well, just James now, I suppose. His wife passed away almost four months ago. And he hasn't been here for nearly three."

Julie's stomach turned. She remembered the text James had sent her months ago, just before he disappeared. And the story she pitched to her editors after the EchoWave conference, which was met with a hard pass. Ultimately, the decision led her to quit and set out on her own.

"Adam?" Julie shouted.

Adam raised his arms, just as Max nearly pulled his out of its socket, having spotted a tabby cat heading down the alley.

"Go on ahead. I'll be home in a bit."

Adam looked back after being forced into a nutcracker-like pace, Max having already made the decision to leave.

# 35

*"I've freed many lost souls from the injustices of this world. But it has come with a price," Franz said as he'd finished penning what would be the final entry in his diary. The Executioner's Diary—*

> *Number 262. September 12, 1817 I executed Antoni Tändl with the sword from life to death. Branded him with "S." After cutting off his right hand, burned his head and body to dust, I then dumped the ashes in the Salzach water as so ordered by Your High Princely Grace.*

The weather was pleasant, and the stars shone brightly. Franz had set up a small writing table outside the house on Neukommgasse 26 house next to a fire. He wiped the quill clean and placed the cork into the clay ink pot, before extinguishing the lamp that lit the surface where he wrote.

When it was dark, he leaned back into his seat and looked up to the sky.

"Did you ever experience joy, Franz, during your sixty years of keeping the diary?" James asked Franz.

"I believe there are a few memories of the decent or calming sort," Franz responded.

"Any you can recall off hand?" James asked.

"Oh, it must have been a score ago. One day I walked into an establishment owned by Anna Schoiberin, a seamstress. She was with child. The previous day's work had resulted in a long tear in my hosen. And my wife's hands were far too frail to repair the garment. As executioners are of the dishonorable class, I was required to seek permission to enter, which the seamstress granted willfully. And as well with kindness, she obliged to fix my garment. It was of very rare treatment she bestowed. Although upon my return in the following days, the seamstress of exceptional skill and grace was sitting at her table, weeping terribly."

"Why was she crying?" James asked.

"Her child was to enter the world in just a matter of weeks. And Samuel Mohr, a mercenary soldier, and the child's father, had abandoned Anna and his paternal obligations. The Prince Archbishop commanded any child born without a father could not be baptized in the church. Such an action likely condemning the child for life as another of the dishonorable class. Like me."

James sat, staring at the fire as he listened to Franz's tale, each flame spelling out the names of people in his diary. The people hiding behind their usernames.

"The boy was born eleven December, seventeen ninety-two, at twelve noon. Christened Joseph Mohr. And with I, Franz Joseph Wohlmuth, listed in the baptismal as the godfather. Ensuring the young man would have at least a chance of life with prosperity and recognition."

James considered the gravity of Franz's willingness to step in as the child's godfather, in comparison to optimizing the performance of a social media ad. It made him feel nauseous.

"I was unaware you were married," James said.

"Ah yes, after having been trained by my grandfather in the executioner's trade, I returned to Salzburg and took the hand of executioner Georg Pinkl's widow. And then, I took his role."

"I was here, Franz. At this house. The day Pinkl executed Maria Pauer. I saw him. But he was much older. Wasn't his wife as well?"

"Yes. In fact, she was thirty years my senior at the time of our union."

Franz paused and stared into the fire.

"By marrying her, I could ensure no children would be born of us. I could ensure the line of executioner Wohlmuths ended—with me."

# 36

"Sir, we believe Agent Bennett could be onto something. We believe Wohlmuth could be leaving a mark."

"A mark?" replied Steve Murphy, Special Agent in charge of the FBI's Seattle office, waiting as six cybercrime analysts and three other agents readied their notes for the meeting.

"A mark. A breadcrumb. A clue."

The agents and their boss sat quietly in the room, waiting for the next breadcrumb of data to be fed to them.

"Let me explain, sir. About fifty thousand people take their own lives in the United States every year."

"Are you—are you kidding me? Fifty thousand a year?" Peter Henries, one of Steve's deputies asked.

"Well, no, I'm not kidding you. And the number continues to rise. I believe we'd briefed you on this already."

"You may have briefed us. But hearing it in this context—that's unbelievable," Steve replied.

"I know. Tragic. There's some regionality, seasonality. Other attributes. But it averages about one hundred thirty-six people per day— one every ten minutes. Tends to be about six men to every four women. This is all historical data, which is part of the problem."

"A problem bigger than fifty thousand Americans killing themselves each year?" Steve quipped.

"The stats I just gave you are from last year, sir. To verify Agent Bennett's claim, we need to follow the path of the one hundred thirty-six who will be taking their lives tomorrow—and the next day, and so on."

"So, what does this have to do with James Wohlmuth?"

"We have reason to believe, sir, that in at least some of these cases, he could be digitally manipulating people into self-harm."

"You mean, like, cyberbullying?"

"He doesn't communicate or interact with them. At all actually. That would be the definition of cyberbullying. Someone needs to know they are being cyberbullied for it to be classified as cyberbullying."

"You're going to need to pretend, for a minute, that I didn't get a Master's in criminal justice from Michigan and a Medal of Excellence as I rose up the ranks in this Bureau over the last twenty years. You're saying he's manipulating them, but not bullying them. You're saying they're alive today, but they might not be tomorrow. You're saying they wouldn't have killed themselves if he wasn't doing what he's doing?"

"That's the tricky part. Most of the individuals we've found with this 'mark' probably would have gone through with it anyway. He's just—"

"He's just what?" Steve exclaimed, slamming his pen onto his pad, his impatience increasing by the second. "Say it!"

"He may be digitally manipulating them to do it *faster*."

Steve rose from the chair at the head of the large conference table and walked to the wide span of thirty-second-story windows, boasting an unobstructed view of the Puget Sound. For a moment, the seemingly simple things taking place on the other side of the glass had his attention. The great Seattle Ferris wheel, spinning, loading, and unloading tour groups, kids on field trips, and kids skipping school. Ferries that appeared small from this vantage point, but took him and his SUV to and from Seattle and Bainbridge each day.

He cupped his fingertips in a prayer over his nose and cheeks and pulled them down over his chin, letting out a sigh as everyone else in the room awaited his response.

"Now—why would he do that?"

"We're not one hundred percent certain, sir. But we think it could be revenge."

Steve turned around and leaned on the air vent below the window, just high enough to provide a comfortable stance for a minute or two.

"Revenge? Revenge on what? Who?"

"Well, his wife took her own life in February of this year. She suffered a miscarriage three days before her suicide. And she'd had two prior miscarriages. A short time later—a few weeks—Wohlmuth left the country. Our sources tell us sometime between his wife's death and his leaving the country, he was terminated by EchoWave."

"Well, isn't that just a shitty thing to do," Steve stated as he walked back to the head of the conference room table, sat down, and took another sip out of a trademark white Starbucks cup.

"And, I should add, why you guys should feel lucky you took government instead of private sector jobs."

The men and women sitting at the conference room table knew they could be earning much more lucrative pay and stock options packages outside the Bureau. It was just a matter of time before each of them took the bait.

"Ruthless start-ups. Go on." Steve smiled coyly while taking another sip of his coffee.

Another analyst weighed in.

"This is a hypothetical, sir. He could be searching online for individuals who are displaying at-risk behavior through their posts and comments. That activity is prevalent. We can narrow it down to tens of thousands of individuals per day."

"Tens of thousands of individuals per day in these United States publicly and consistently tell the world their life sucks on social media?"

"On search engines, social media, and in online forums, yes sir. In fact, the number is exponentially higher, but it's a start," the analyst continued.

"Let's say he hacks into these accounts as the actual user and creates certain combinations of search terms. Based on what he knows about how his own algorithms work, he could be manipulating the kind of content these people see no matter what app, site, or social media platform they are using. He could be manipulating content that is likely to further push them into self-harm."

"I don't believe any of you, for one damn minute, that this is possible. You are wasting my time. Anything else?" Steve said as he stood up, closed his portfolio, and started walking toward the door.

"With all due respect, sir," one courageous but nervous female analyst said. "This is already happening. Today. Whether you keep us on this assignment or not."

"Explain," he said, returning to the table but remaining standing.

"Well, sir, it's part of these companies' business models. Depressive content is good for visibility and engagement. When someone posts that their life sucks or they want to end it, in most cases, that signals to the algorithms in these social platforms, or search engines, to actively promote similar content."

"And?"

"Well, sir, there have been extensive studies on how these algorithms work. Individuals spend a lot of time on these platforms each day, as you know—"

"Yes, my daughter can confirm that," Steve responded.

"I'm sure, although I don't know your daughter's age," the analyst continued. "But in one study, sir, test accounts were created to simulate the scrolling behavior of normal thirteen-year-olds. If the test accounts searched for mental health videos, the algorithms then delivered a tenfold increase in content related to mental health. And when that happened, by the end of the first hour, almost twenty percent of the videos contained 'mentally harmful' content. By the sixth hour, it increased to almost half the content."

"Jesus Christ," Steve responded, not so much sitting down as deflating into the chair. "Okay. So, can one of you explain to me what this company EchoWave does?"

"EchoWave collects a huge amount of data from social media sites and search engines, sir," the first analyst chimed in again. "EchoWave isn't a social media site. They take whatever data people allow to be shared from other social media apps and sites, combine it and analyze it, and use it to build profiles on everyone. Probably including, uh, you, sir."

Another analyst added, "And even if you don't allow sharing, the apps send them anonymous user data, and EchoWave uses it to *guess* who you are."

"Why?" Steve asked, not looking up from a text message he was sending to his wife.

"Well, sir, they claim it improves user experience. What it actually does is make advertising more effective. But what we really think they're doing, with some of their users, anyway, is more overt behavior modification and content targeting."

"Users, modification, targeting, go on," Steve mumbled as he hit Send on the message to his wife, instructing her to block all their daughter's social media accounts on her smartphone as soon as she arrived home from school.

"Yes, sir, *behavior modification.* Which, amazingly, is perfectly legal in the United States. What Wohlmuth might be trying to tell us is that there are aspects of the system that are working, let's say, too well. This would violate at least the spirit of a number of different privacy laws."

"Wait a second. Slow down. You think Wohlmuth is trying to... communicate with us?"

"It's not out of the question, sir."

"How does he access their accounts to make this happen?"

"Again. Hypothetical. After he finds users searching and posting publicly about certain topics, he finds individuals who aren't using enhanced security on their social media accounts. Or they are using the same password across multiple accounts."

Steve re-opened his folio and made a few notes on the yellow pad in front of him.

"We don't know how he's finding these less secure accounts yet, sir. But when he does, he could then buy their login data and passwords on the dark web, paying in cryptocurrency, which would be really challenging for us to detect without more access. And, of course, a warrant."

A more senior agent at the table raised her hand.

"Steve, this is a highly skilled engineer who invented a lot of the core technology at EchoWave. He's listed as primary inventor on eighteen patents EchoWave owns."

"Speaking of warrants, where is this Wohlmuth now?" Steve asked, glancing at the analyst.

"He hasn't reentered the United States, sir."

"Where did he fly when he left?"

"Originally, he flew from Seattle to Munich. He then took a train to Salzburg. Stayed in a four-star Gasthaus hotel for about ten days."

"And then?" Steve prodded.

"About nine days into his trip, he started using his US ATM card to withdraw slightly less than the maximum daily amount of cash allowed by his bank," the agent responded, looking at a printed report.

"How much cash?"

"About $75,000 total, sir."

Yet another agent interjected. "He used his credit cards in and around Salzburg for several weeks, sir. But on the day his visa expired, he stopped. No further withdrawals. No further credit card usage. No further use of his cell phone."

"Cell phone too, huh?" Steve asked, looking around the room.

"Yes, sir. In fact, he stopped using his US cell phone about three days into his trip."

"How the hell did we not know this?" Steve exclaimed, removing his glasses and setting them momentarily on the yellow pad of personal notes.

Steve's second-in-command saw the conversation turning into an interrogation of his own team.

"Steve, sir, with all due respect, how would they have? Wohlmuth hadn't broken any laws. He didn't generate any red flags with his bank. He made all the withdrawals and expenditures while his tourist visa was active. We had no reason to be watching this guy."

"Oh, this is wonderful," Steve responded. "Let me ask all you geniuses something. If Agent Bennett hadn't brought this issue to your attention, considering you just spent the resources of six cyber person- nel and four weeks of Bureau resources, by the look of your faces, and your overall wardrobe and hygienic disarray, when do you think this would have been brought to your attention?"

"Sir, have you ever heard the phrase, 'the number of possible chess moves equates to the number of grains of sand on Earth?'" one of the analysts asked.

"No, what the hell is that supposed to mean?"

"Sir, with the number of variables at play here and the complexity of these systems, I believe if Bennett's friend hadn't overheard this conversation in the bar—this likely would have never come to our attention."

Silence. Steve tapping his pen impatiently on his closed folio.

"Okay, write it up, and let's figure out who to talk to at EchoWave. Maybe you guys are overdramatizing this, and it's actually nothing. Maybe you're not."

Steve stood and walked out, with three of his immediate reports following behind.

Peter remained in the room, his job to pick up the pieces and create a plan for the conversation that had just taken place.

"By the way, I wasn't able to interject at the beginning of this meet- ing. What is the 'mark' you believe he's leaving?"

"We're still early on this, sir, and we're trying to build some math around how to scale this. It's a fairly tedious process thus far."

"Go on," Peter stated.

"There are a number of instances where the day after a death, most of the search histories on the social media, search engines, and forums are cleared out, but on these, one search is left."

"How long do I have to wait before you tell me what he's doing?" Peter demanded.

"He leaves an 'S', sir. The letter 'S'. It's how we're tracking this pattern. Empty searches, with the exception of a search for the letter 'S'."

"Why the letter 'S'?" Peter asked.

"Three possibilities, sir. First, it's his wife's first initial. 'S', Sara. Second, where he traveled. 'S', Salzburg. And third, sir—" the man said, looking at a disheveled analyst in the group.

"And third?" Peter repeated.

"Forget the third, sir."

"No, please, tell me. You all have put on a commanding performance here today—"

"I hold no stock in this, sir. It comes from a guy on our team who's a Dungeons & Dragons, Middle Ages history buff."

"Go ahead."

"Hundreds of years ago, the letter 'S' was branded, like as in *burned*, into the skin of nearly every criminal who was ever executed in Salzburg."

"And how many times has this 'S' shown up in the data you're tracking?"

"As of yesterday, sir?" The analyst paused.

"As of yesterday—two hundred fifteen times."

# 37

"Julie, it's Nate."

"Yes, from the screen of my phone, I can see when the FBI is calling," Julie Frager responded, a touch of friendly sarcasm in her voice.

"I may have something for you. Something I'm not sure the Bureau is going to be able to fully flush out."

"I'm listening."

"There's a company on the East Side of Seattle called EchoWave, recently went public," Nate said.

"Of course. I know them."

"I figured you would; they're in the tech space."

"No, I mean I *know them*, know them. I was working on a story on EchoWave months ago. Before my editor scuttled it."

"Why did it get—" he asked. "Never mind that, tell me later. We believe one of their key executives could be harboring information about some kind of online behavior manipulation."

"James Wohlmuth—I know."

"What? How the hell could you know about this?"

"Because you're on the thirty-second story of an office tower looking at a screen, and I'm on the ground. Where your vehicles are. The vehicles that cleared his out his basement."

"We need to meet. Now," Nate responded.

"Alright. Where and when?"

"Storyville in the Market. One hour."

Julie ascended the stairs to the top floor of the triangular-shaped building, windows overlooking the famous red neon "Public Market" sign and clock.

She ordered and waited for her latte, which required several minutes to prepare, even though there were no other customers. She glanced at Nate, sitting against the window in the farthest corner, focusing his contemplative stare in the distance toward Vancouver Island or Alaska. Anywhere he could imagine a different conflict. Sensing, tracking, and apprehending king salmon with a line and hook. Rather than former tech-execs turned elusive behavioral manipulators and possibly murders.

She gingerly walked toward him with her bag and latte, the design of a swan poured into the deep chestnut froth.

"Let me see your phone. And your smartwatch. And your laptop and tablet."

She handed him the pile of devices, which he placed into an unassuming canvas laptop bag lined with material that prevented electronic or audible eavesdropping. Julie rolled her eyes as Nate waited, taking a sip from his drink and scratching his eyebrow with his free hand.

"Tell me what you know," he started.

After taking the first sip of her third latte of the day, she gently set the cup down in its saucer.

"One of their founders and, I believe, the inventor of much of their core technology is James Wohlmuth. I grilled him on privacy during their annual conference in front of a big audience. Late February. Before the company went public. The CEO, Michael Valeno, cut me off before James could answer my question."

"Okay," he responded.

"His wife killed herself later that day—suicide. James discovered her when he arrived home from the airport."

"I know," he muttered.

"He sent me a text. A few weeks later. Pretty early in the morning. Concerns about some unintended and possibly dangerous aspects of the company's algorithms he thought would make an important story.

It wasn't much more than that. I responded that I was interested in talking but needed a day or two to run it by editorial."

"And then?"

She paused and nodded before speaking.

"It took editorial about three hours to come back with a pass. In fact, it wasn't just a pass. It was an oddly hard pass. No explanation other than I was needed on another story—one that turned out to be far less interesting. Employees at a high-tech computer networking company over in Woodinville were using sledgehammers to smash their own perfectly useful products outside of their warehouse to make fake insurance claims."

"Of course, startups," Nate scoffed.

"I told him the story wasn't going to happen. Never heard back from him."

"So, a former founder of a company about to go public and make its founders millions, tells you he has a story and then disappears," Nate said.

"Wait, you said former founder?"

"Yea, we know a thing or two also. Apparently, they sent him on some kind of forced sabbatical. Outside of the United States. We think possibly Austria. Salzburg. After he arrived, they terminated him. No warning."

"James never mentioned to me where he was."

"Now I'm off the record, and you're on background."

"Of course," she said, taking another sip.

"There are a number of suicides we're investigating," he said.

"Suicides? Why suicides?"

"We have evidence to suggest James Wohlmuth is seeking some kind of revenge for being fired, losing his wife. Real shit. We believe he may be hacking into social media accounts with minimal security protection, and essentially juicing the EchoWave algorithm to inundate his targets with content that manipulates them into depression and, ultimately, self-harm."

"Jesus," she responded, another burst of adrenaline that in any other setting would have caused her to immediately pick up her phone and hit the record button. "You mean, like suicide? Like his wife?"

"Yea, you get it," Nate said, tapping his mug on the sturdy wood-plank tables.

"It's early. He's not officially a suspect. He's not in the country. We don't know yet precisely what charges we'd bring forward for a grand jury. Can't charge him, can't arrest him. Secondly, traditional surveillance isn't working. His phone was disconnected. They shut off his computer, but he's clearly using something to make all this happen. And, sadly, it appears as though the only law he's broken so far, which isn't even our law, is that he's overstayed his tourist visa in Austria by a few months."

"Nate, from what I learned at their conference last year, what you are describing doesn't surprise me at all. But I don't understand. How do you know he was personally involved in these activities if you're unable to surveil him?"

"I can't tell you that. But I can tell you there's a pattern to his activities and he's leaving some breadcrumbs. Which means he's fallen into some deep psychosis or he's trying to communicate with someone. Or something else entirely."

Julie nodded.

"I do have one other thing," Julie responded.

"Okay?" he nodded.

"I actually didn't take myself off the story. I kept digging on my own time. Every single filing and public record I could get my hands on. And through that, I discovered the Chairman of my paper quietly made an investment in EchoWave through a secretive family office in Chicago that happens to be run by a man named Dieter Hauser."

Nate shrugged.

"Okay. Who's Dieter Hauser?"

"The father of Sara Hauser-Wohlmuth, the now deceased wife of James Wohlmuth."

# 38

As the tombstone bearing the name Franz Joseph Wohlmuth was being prepared for carriage to the cemetery, a representative from Salzburg inspected the granite block, which James had been carving for the last several hours.

"It appears may have mistaken the correct year of birth on executioner Wohlmuth's tombstone," the man said to James. "You carved the year seventeen hundred thirty-nine."

"Yes, this is what the church recorded as his birth year," James responded.

"If that were to be correct, it would make Herr Wohlmuth aged eighty-five years at the time of his death."

"Yes. And for nearly sixty years the executioner endured the screams, the blood, the agony, and the nightmares on the orders of the Prince Archbishops."

"How in the world could a man endure his namesake's arduous duty for this many passings of the sun. This many Easters and Christmases. Across the rein of three Prince Archbishops?"

"I don't know how he did it. But from this day forward, he is free to rest."

A layer of mist curled around the tombstones in the cemetery, just south of Salzburg, standing guard. Softening the edges of a world that had seen so much suffering. The distant chime of church bells echoed against the surrounding forest, a requiem for a man finally freed from his burden. The small procession of four men and three nuns walked behind the carriage carrying Franz Joseph Wohlmuth, to a plot prepared next to his mother, his father, and his wife, Johannes, widow of the second-to-last executioner of Salzburg.

\* \* \*

Upon learning of Wohlmuth's passing, now thirty-one-year-old Joseph Mohr traveled by horse to his godfather's resting place, to pay his respects. James sat on a bench nearby, staring up at the purple reflection of the Untersburg.

Mohr had completed seminary and spent many days writing poetry, his life forever altered by the executioner standing in at his baptism.

"Herr Wohlmuth, my mother passed on to the heavens not more than ten years into my life. Had it not been for your grace in the absence of my father, I would most certainly not have been allowed to enter the seminary, or spend my days writing prose. For the gift you gave me, I am eternally grateful."

The young priest then removed a small piece of parchment from the pocket of his overcoat.

"On Christmas Eve, several years prior," Joseph continued, "I walked to the home of a friend in Oberndorf. In my possession was a poem I'd penned earlier in the year. I was in need of a carol for the Christmas Eve midnight Mass. As the church choir master and organist, I asked my friend for his aid in setting the poem to music."

Joseph began to read the poem aloud.

"Silent night! Holy night!
All is calm, all is bright
Round yon virgin mother and child!
Holy infant, so tender and mild,
Sleep in heavenly peace!
Sleep in heavenly peace!"

As tears began streaming down James's cheeks, Joseph set the parchment of his original copy of the song, 'Stille Nacht, heilige Nacht,' which began as a poem, under a small rock in front of Wohlmuth's final resting place.

"Thank you, godfather, for allowing me to give this gift to the world."

# 39

"If this pattern is true, Michael, and James is leaving this 'S' mark with greater and greater frequency—well—"

"Continue, Rob?" Michael responded.

"I think there's a real possibility that someone I care about—or people we're close to—could be next."

"Rob, with all due respect. You're making it sound like he can simply flip a switch and set someone on a trajectory of self-harm. If that's, in fact, what he's trying to do, we have enough resources now to be able to address this problem. Which, Vik, I'm still not convinced is a real problem."

Michael, Vik, and Rob Cook, James and Vik's college advisor and company board member, were huddled in Michael's office. Outside the floor-to-ceiling windows, landscapers were mowing the grass and tending to the Trumpet Lillies next to the pond.

"I believe it is, in fact, a real problem, Michael," Vik responded.

EchoWave began trading on the public markets two months ago with substantial fanfare, and the value of the company skyrocketing to over twenty-six billion dollars, solidifying its position in the tech and AI industry.

"Okay, Vik. So, you believe it's a real problem. Continue to walk us through what you have."

"James is not hacking into EchoWave. That's the first issue. He's hacking into the accounts of individuals, using methods many people here could figure out. He's finding people with public social media and short video-sharing accounts. He searches hashtags to find people showing certain emotional or behavioral warning signs. He then logs into their accounts and enters sequences of terms in the search bar."

"How does he do that, exactly?" Michael asked.

"He's probably buying their usernames and passwords off the dark web, paying with crypto, so the transactions can't be traced," Rob said.

"It can't be that easy," Michael continued.

"Knowing James, he probably hacked into your accounts, too, Michael" Rob mumbled.

Michael picked up his phone from the table and began typing. "Continue."

"He watches videos and clicks hashtags. He covers his tracks and leaves an 'S.' Probably repeats this process every couple of weeks. Some people bite, so to speak, and descend into depression or self-harm. Most don't. But enough do."

"Remind me what the 'S' is for?" Rob asked.

"'Sara', Rob. His wife?"

"Holy shit, are you f—" Rob responded.

"Calm down, Rob," Michael interrupted, still typing on his phone.

"What makes this so difficult to track is that he's using what he knows about core EchoWave technology—that he designed and coded —to initiate the process. James covered a lot of this in his brief—" Vik said.

Michael interrupted. "Yes, but—"

"That's right," Rob recalled. "James wrote a briefing on this right after he came back to the office. Why don't we start by reverse engineering his briefing?"

Vik gazed at Michael, knowing the team had shelved their work a week after the meeting Michael called. Michael looked at Vik, knowing he demanded Vik remove the most incisive and effective elements of the briefing prior to presenting it to those in the room.

"Where is James's briefing?" Rob asked.

"Which vers—" Vik responded.

"Why can't we just modify the algorithm?" Michael interrupted.

"You're kidding, right?" Vik asked, his anger becoming apparent.

"Watch yourself, kid," Rob said, raising his hand slightly and glancing at Michael.

"Michael, the big concern isn't James or what he knows, or what he's able to do manually from wherever the hell he's hiding."

"Okay, then, in your opinion, what is the big concern?"

"The concern is the sheer scale of what we're dealing with here. The volume of data and the number of sources—is enormous. We're just not ready."

"We have far greater resources after the IPO to deal with this, Vik, I'm—"

"What James understands that you don't, Michael, I'm sorry. There are literally trillions of combinations of search terms, clicks, and engagement patterns that can lead someone to self-harm. The terms that initiate the process don't even have to be that negative, dark, or violent."

Michael gazed out the window at the Trumpet Lillies next to the pond. His mind drifted to a thought of sitting on a bench at the Chelsea Physic Gardens in central London, within walking distance of the townhouse he was planning to purchase after the board allowed him to sell some of his equity in the company.

"Michael, listen to me. After James left, I ran one test scenario where the taste of bitter fruit could eventually lead someone to be inundated with dangerous videos, posts, and ads."

"You haven't heard from James at all?" Michael said, slowly returning his attention to the discussion.

"You told me I'd be fired and charged with corporate espionage if I attempted to contact him."

Rob shifted in his seat and glanced around the room before locking in on Michael with a skeptical look.

"But you know what, Mike?" Vik responded, emboldened by Rob's presence. "I did. I did anyway. I tried to contact him even before the public offering. He didn't respond. He took his brain and his briefing and he vanished under the guise of PTSD or dissociative disorder, or whatever the company line was."

"Listen, Vik—you piece of—" Michael interrupted, knowing he couldn't use his fully loaded magazine of threats and hubris in front of a board member, whom he now regretted inviting to the meeting.

"Enough," Rob stopped the discussion with his hand slapping the table.

Both men were seething, prepared to use different weapons to spar in a battle that would lead nowhere.

"Michael, we're a public company now, with a market value of over twenty-six point two billion dollars. I sit on EchoWave's board of directors. You're its CEO and also sit on its board. When did you first know about this briefing?"

"There's just no proof that EchoWave's technology is harming people, Rob!"

"There's no proof? There's no proof because there's nobody who can audit what these algorithms do prior to a company raising money or going public. There's no regulation on this tech—and you know it," Rob said emphatically. "All the investors needed to see were the revenue and profit margin numbers going up each month after you joined the company."

"I see your point. We'll look into it," Michael responded, in a manner Vik had previously not witnessed.

Rob stood, zipped his fleece, and placed both arms through the rings in his backpack before knocking a couple of times on the solid ebony table.

"I have a class to teach in an hour. I'll be late if I don't head over the bridge now," he continued. "Guys, this news gives me significant cause for concern that I need a day or two to fully process. At a minimum, we need to convene a task force to revisit James's briefing once you guys get back from Munich next week."

"I agree with you, Rob," Michael said. "Vik and I are going to review materials for the EU privacy hearings before we head to Munich on Saturday. We'll address this as soon as we're back."

"Good enough for you, Vik?" Rob asked.

Vik could barely nod but motioned gently.

Rob glanced out the window at the workers tending the Trumpet Lillies. His hippie, laid-back personality made him chuckle at the tokens of pomp and symbolism on display these days at companies flush with cash and overflowing with ambition.

While walking, Rob turned back to Vik.

"Quick question, Vik. Have you tried to link the 'S' mark to people who you could later assume had met their own demise?"

Vik glanced at Michael and then down at the table.

"Yes. We have been quietly building a list."

"And? How many people are on that list?"

Vik paused, tapping his pen on the stack of papers in front of him.

"As of yesterday—the list contains two hundred sixty-one names."

# 40

"What the hell are you doing here?" James exclaimed as he walked from the sidewalk onto the stonemason's yard towards his cottage.

"James," Vik said as he spun around quickly. "Holy shit, man, you scared me. It's good to see you."

Vik's body caved forward in an attempt to embrace his old partner and college roommate.

James extended his hands, resisting Vik's approach.

"Okay, I get it," Vik relented. "I—Michael and I were in Munich with some of the team. Addressing some privacy issues with European Union regulators. Total bullshit, you know. But—remember in Orlando? I gave you my cord case to charge your laptop. You were going to give it back to me the next day at the office. But then—"

"Sara," James nodded, turning his gaze toward the canal near the executioner's house, from where he'd just returned.

"Yes, Sara," Vik replied. "When we landed in Germany last weekend, a notification appeared on my phone. The GPS tracker I'd folded into the pocket of my cable case. I'd completely forgotten about it. Thought I'd left it somewhere in the convention center."

James looked at Vik, squinting one eye in the sunlight.

"As you can see, I decided to take a different career path."

"The team doesn't know I'm here, okay? They all flew back to Seattle yesterday. I rented a car and drove to the location showing on my phone. I thought you might be here, but I didn't know what I'd—"

"How are Beth and the kids?" James interrupted.

"They're good," Vik replied, welcoming the diffusion in the tension. "Beth is stressed out about getting Lilly into that school, and from the never-ending kitchen remodel that's—it doesn't matter. At all, actually."

Vik spoke while trying to relearn James's face and appearance. No longer polished and neat, James had allowed his wavy brown hair to grow out several inches and was carrying a couple weeks' worth of facial hair, growing down his neck and above his cheekbones. His upper body was broader and stronger, and his improved posture made him appear taller in his already long frame.

"James, I came here to tell you the FBI is looking for you. They want to talk to you about the algorithms and a few suspicious de—."

"The algorithms," James interrupted. "The algorithms that got me fired. The algorithms that took Sara from me. My entire life from me? Are those the algorithms you're talking about?"

"James, yes. I know. There's nothing I can do or say about that now. But more than that, I just wanted to tell you I'm sorry. In person."

"Thank you, Vik, for coming to tell me in person."

A long pause extended the distance between them, even as they remained in place. Similar to the meeting in Vik's office the year prior when James presented his briefing.

"What is this place? A tombstone company? Why—"

"This is where I live, Vik. This is what I do now. I carve the memories of people into stone. So, they won't be forgotten. I even learned to drive a forklift—by watching online videos."

"I think you should come home, James. With me. Right now. We can figure this out together. I can help—"

"You know, Vik, it's funny you showed up today. There's a project I finished recently I think you'd be interested in," James said, wiping the sweat from the palms of his hands on the front of his untucked shirt as he began walking toward his tiny guest shed.

"Come on," James waved with a slight upward cheer. "I have cold beer. Austrian beer that's cheaper than bottled water in the States. Let's make it worth the trip you made to pick up your cable case."

"You know I didn't come here for my case," Vik responded, nervous that the man he was following had somehow escaped the orbit of the only path either of them had known since they were eighteen.

James opened the door to the simple, minimal space furnished with a bed, a table, and two chairs. A small L-shaped kitchen counter flanked by bar stools led to the bathroom and a back exit.

A packed duffel bag and backpack sat at the foot of the bed. A large scrapbook sat at the center of the table, bursting with printouts and clippings. Its wooden cover had been branded with a single letter: a large German medieval Fraktur "S". Four holes drilled through the long edge held the book together with brown twine.

"James, there are so many people who have been gutted by your disappearance, including me. And your team. You were supposed to be here for two weeks and come home. Not vanish in Austria so you could make a scrapbook," Vik said, attempting to ease the palpable tension. And the guilt he felt seeing his friend and colleague living in a tiny guest cottage on the grounds of a tombstone company, compared to the Mercer Island waterfront home he purchased after EchoWave went public.

James pulled two bottles of Stiegl beer from the refrigerator and set them on the table with glasses.

"I didn't entirely vanish, Vik, I think you probably know that. Anyway, Prost," James said after sitting down, looking into Vik's eyes, slightly raising his glass.

"Prost," Vik said as he touched the top of James's glass and took a sip. He set the beer down and turned the binder toward him. "So, what is this?"

James pulled the book closer and used a finger to trace the "S" embossed on its cover.

"You know what I came to realize over the last year, Vik? Every one of us. Our whole company. That whole industry. We're the *Unehrlicher Beruf*."

"What does that mean, exactly?"

"It's an old German phrase. It translates to the 'dishonest profession'."

"James, maybe I—"

"See, Vik, back in the 1700s, Salzburg was like its own country, governed by a Prince Archbishop. He was both religious leader and lawmaker. Essentially, the people of Salzburg paid their taxes and offered their confessions to the same office, the same person. The Prince Archbishop changed the laws whenever he wanted, mostly in secret. Rebellion, of any kind, was not tolerated. Any crime could result in brutal torture or a death sentence. Can you believe that? Usually by beheading. Usually in front of a crowd of people. Usually at that house, right over there."

Vik did not take his gaze off the binder or his beer, even as James pointed out the window in the direction of the executioner's house.

"Does any of this sound familiar, Vik?"

"James, we didn't really take any classes—"

James scoffed and nodded with an eerie smile out of one side of his mouth.

"User agreements, Vik. Terms and conditions. The data we collect. The algorithms we use. Everyone clicks '*I accept*' when they sign up for accounts on social media apps, video sites, and search engines. They have no idea what they're agreeing to. They have no idea what the rules are. And have no idea how we're going to use the troves of information they give us—to keep their attention, manipulate them. Or kill them."

Vik's eyes shifted nervously as the color started to flush from his face.

"You know what it took to finally change the system? To put an end to torture and public executions in Salzburg?"

"No. What did it take, James?"

"The executioner, Vik. The man responsible for torturing and beheading the people of Salzburg on the Prince Archbishop's orders. He was also the one who helped to end the barbarism."

"I'm not following you, James."

"A man named Franz Joseph Wohlmuth. Yea, Wohlmuth. He was the last ever executioner appointed by the Prince Archbishop of Salzburg. Franz was loyal. Franz followed orders. But through his own tragedy, Franz realized the system of justice and order here was, in fact, completely broken."

"How did you find out about this guy?"

"I'll get to that in a minute. So, he started keeping a diary of his work. Every night after he tortured or beheaded someone, some who were completely innocent, he secretly documented the terrible details of two hundred sixty-two executions that he performed. After his death, the diary became public. The diary helped end the practice of torture and public executions in Salzburg. And for that matter, it helped bring down the whole system."

"So, what, you think all this research about a bad system and a killer with a conscience from three hundred years ago is going to convince our company—our public company—and our industry to see the error of our ways? You spent a year here doing this? Carving tombstones and learning about some dude named Wohlmuth?"

James remained calm, allowing Vik to vent.

"Do you have any idea how much money is at stake here, James? All the shares you donated to a holistic, hippie mental health nonprofit instead of building your life. You foolishly donated all your equity in EchoWave to some hippie-holistic mental health nonprofit, instead of coming home to Seattle, getting help, and moving on with your life. None of this shit is going to bring Sara back, James. And how do you think Michael is going to respond? Or the investors?"

"This isn't research, Vik. You see, Franz Joseph Wohlmuth detailed two hundred sixty-two executions he performed in order to expose the injustices and brutality of the system."

"The book in front of you, the one I've been working on over the last year, details two hundred sixty-two suicides. Of Americans. Suicides that are directly attributable to EchoWave's technology and platform. This book is proof."

James slowly pulled open the cover.

"Beginning with Sara Hauser-Wohlmuth."

Vik's hands began to shake. He pushed the beer aside, his face fully flushed, staring for a moment at the photo of his good friend's deceased wife.

"It was actually fairly straightforward, Vik. I created fake social media profiles. Found people experiencing depression, anxiety—any trigger like behavior. People falsely accused. Lost teens. People going through divorce. Couples with difficulty conceiving. If they were gun owners, all the better. I bought passwords for their social media accounts off the dark web. Used search terms and combinations I'd detailed a year ago. All I needed to do was nudge the process along a bit. It was the sterile testing lab you promised me. Before you had me fired."

"James, I didn't have you fired. I would never—Michael—"

"I know," James continued.

Vik entered the same trance James found himself in a year earlier.

"Two hundred sixty-two people killed themselves, James! And you 'nudged them'? James, these are people, not simulations in a research lab!"

"I've spent a lot of time thinking about that, Vik," James responded with unwavering calm. "Last year, fifty thousand people in the United States took their own lives. Hundreds, even thousands of those, can be attributed to some amount of online influence. Michael, the Prince Archbishop of EchoWave, knows everything about the damage it causes, and yet we keep doing it."

"Michael is not the Prince Archbishop, James. Nor is EchoWave or any company that uses algorithms to persuade or manipulate people. We don't purposefully harm people. But James, you—"

"Some of those fifty thousand were triggered, unknowingly, by being exposed to the technologies we invented. Their families and friends never knew. But we did. I tried to show you one example. You, that piece of shit, Michael, and the whole search engine and social media industry, tried to bury what we all know. Our technology is killing people. For money. I buried my wife. EchoWave buried my brief."

"You're—you're going to go to jail, James," Vik said, at a loss to reason with what had already taken place, irreversible no matter what words left his mouth.

"I know that, and—"

Vik vaulted from his chair in a split-second attempt to run to the back door and out of the guest house, his knees striking underneath the table, spilling the glasses and bottles forward and into the diary, while James, his arms still folded, quickly turned and extended his leg, a reflex from one of the thick table legs hitting his knee, his foot extending in front of Vik's intended path, causing him to lose his balance and trip, the left temple above Vik's eye abruptly meeting the corner of the kitchen countertop, piercing his skin, flipping him over violently and unconsciously, as he fell to the floor, the back of his skull cracking against the stone floor with a short, urgent breath of exhalation, followed by a desperate, immediate attempt to inhale again, the last reflexes of a body having already processed its fate and demise in the previous one and a half seconds.

"Oh, no, Vik! What have you done?" James shouted, first glancing at the diary and then immediately turning to the dripping beer pooling and mixing with the blood emerging out of Vik's temple and cranium.

The air filled with a metallic tang of blood, James had never experienced before, mingling with the sharp yeastiness of the spilled beer, creating a nauseating cocktail that clung to James's senses as he stared at Vik's lifeless body.

As James's heartbeat slowed and he regained composure, he sat on the beer and blood-soaked floor. Wanting to fully understand the passing of a soul from this life to whatever else was out there, in a way he was never able to with Sara.

# 41

Twenty-two microphones and name plaques were placed around the deep, richly polished mahogany dais where the Senate Judiciary Committee would meet, inside the United States Capitol building in Washington, D.C.

James, scheduled to testify, would not be present in the committee room. A secure closed-circuit video link had been set up in a small room within the Criminal Justice Center in Vienna, Austria. Staffers at the Capitol placed a massive, flat-panel screen on the witness table facing the committee, enabling them to see James and his attorneys, four thousand four hundred miles away.

After the senators entered and were seated, James was led into the holding room, carrying softbound copies of his testimony, the original, unedited briefing he'd researched and written one year prior, and a copy of his Executioner's Diary.

When the video feed commenced, the committee chair, Senator Maria Santoro, from the State of Washington, sounded the gavel and commenced the hearing by reading from her prepared remarks.

"Today, the Senate Judiciary Committee will continue to explore an issue that is top of mind for most American families. For thirty years, Section 230 of the United States Commercial Code has remained largely unchanged. This has allowed big technology companies to grow into one of the most profitable industries in the history of capitalism. But this law was written before social media and online video companies developed their complex targeting and behavioral algorithms. And it allows these companies to operate without fear of liability for unsafe practices."

Santoro paused and raised her head to the screen.

"James Wohlmuth, we appreciate you appearing to testify, even as you await sentencing in Austria. These are extraordinary circumstances that reach to the heart of who America is as a society."

In the front of the gallery, parents, spouses, and family members of those who had taken their lives sat solemnly, with large photos of their loved ones on their laps. At the very end of the first row sat Sara's mother, Patricia, holding a photo of her daughter.

"I now recognize the leading member, Senator Henry Wallace of Nevada."

"Thank you, chairwoman. Each time this committee meets, regardless of which party is in power, we fundamentally agree—there seems to be some 'black box' that dictates what we're exposed to these days on social media, video-sharing sites, and in our search results. Whatever is happening, there is evidence to suggest these services are harmful to children, increase the political divide between us, and provide safe harbor for misinformation and fake news."

He looked over the top of his glasses for approval.

"We have previously resolved that many of these companies should be reined in, regulated, or broken up, or, as we've been told, 'the worst is yet to come.' But nothing has changed. I yield back to the chair."

"Thank you, senator, we are in agreement," Santoro continued. "Yesterday, we heard from CEOs of the big social networks, and I think we gained some insights on your points in advance of Mr. Wohlmuth's testimony. Without further delay, I will call today's witness, James Wohlmuth, the former co-founder and head of research and development for EchoWave Corporation, based in Bellevue, Washington. Thank you for joining us, Mr. Wohlmuth."

A senator from South Carolina interjected.

"Would the chair yield for one minute?"

"Yes, for one minute. The gentleman from South Carolina is recognized."

"For the record, I can think of no reason why we allow the testimony of this man. He is a cold-blooded killer of two hundred sixty-two American citizens. And yet he sits comfortably in some room among the hills that are still alive."

It was a statement made purely for an evening TV soundbite.

"With all due respect to the gentleman from South Carolina, Mr. Wohlmuth has not been charged with any crime in the United States," Santoro remarked.

"He has not been charged with a crime because there is no law on the books, yet, to charge him. But he has been charged with murder in Austria. Furthermore, he is guilty in the eyes of God, and I believe, will be punished accordingly."

"Your statement has been entered in the record, senator. Please, Mr. Wohlmuth, continue."

"Chair Santoro, Ranking Member Larson, distinguished Members of the Committee: My name is James Wohlmuth. Allow me to begin by stating I am presenting this testimony of my own free will and understand my testimony can be used against me in charges that may be brought against me by a number of States in the future."

James cleared his throat, already dry from the recycled air in the windowless government holding room. He slowly took a sip of water from a small plastic cup before detailing both his academic and business credentials.

"I have prepared my statements, which I will make fully, and then take any of your questions. As the senator from South Carolina correctly noted, I have been charged with second-degree murder in the Republic of Austria. And as the senator also correctly noted, I have documented the tragic deaths of two hundred sixty-two Americans who ended their lives with varying degrees of observation and influence that I am solely responsible for."

There was a visible change in the expressions of the gallery, which James could not see, mirrored by several senators on the dais. "But I am also here today to testify that I believe I am personally responsible for tens of thousands of additional deaths. And not just Americans, but citizens of many other countries," James said.

The collective gasp sounded like a high-powered vacuum hose, immediately removing the breathable air from the Committee room, as well as the room in which he was speaking. Both his attorneys immediately placed their hands over his microphone, facing James.

*This was not written in your remarks, James!*

Senator Santoro slammed the gavel three times on the round wooden plate.

"Order, please. The witness will be allowed to continue his remarks."

James pushed the hands of his attorneys away and mouthed, *Please, I would like to finish.*

"For some time, I believed the only death I was ultimately responsible for was of my beloved wife, Sara Hauser-Wohlmuth. I believe if I had been more attentive to her, as she fell into depression, she would be alive today. But I wasn't. I was working with my team to perfect a technology I now believe is systematically leading at-risk individuals to contemplate, and ultimately, initiate, self-harm, including suicide."

There was no sound from the gallery or the committee.

"I believe I have the proof in my exhibits and my testimony that implicates me and many co-conspirators, including my former employer EchoWave, the company's senior executives, including Michael Valeno, as well as executives at other companies in this industry.

"After Sara's passing, my next-door neighbor, who unfortunately passed away late last year, told me she had also suffered three miscarriages in her life, as my wife did. Free of digital influences and algorithms, society encouraged her to turn outward, seek help and support, mourn and cry, with family and among community. She believed by doing so she ended up living a fulfilling, happy, and healthy life."

James paused.

"This is not what is happening today. Today, we're encouraged to present the best versions of ourselves online. If that version is not perfect, we use apps, filters, and AI to further manufacture the lie. When hard times come, as they do for every human, we're conditioned to continue using these powerful platforms. We search and scroll for content that makes us feel pleasure, escape, and detachment. Content that makes us feel more comfortable in our isolation. Content that makes us feel more accepted—and acceptable—in our sorrow. Why? Because human nature dictates that the more jarring and negative the content is, the more likely we are to consume it. Human nature, algorithmically enhanced, has created one of the most powerful and profitable industries in the history of mankind. And who reaps the benefit while millions suffer? Executives and shareholders in these companies."

As he continued, he could see the differences in each senator's expression, between those who were aware of the industry and its practices. And those who had no clue.

"Delivering digital darkness, senators, has a very bright future ahead of it. Unless, of course, this committee, this body, and this government is willing to change the law, construct rigid regulatory frameworks these companies must abide by, and rein in the opaqueness of the technologies and algorithms they use to promote more and more usage and exposure to ads, no matter what the cost."

He was feeling a surge of adrenaline and took a breath to slow down.

"This phenomenon is really just ten to fifteen years old, but it is a public health crisis of the highest order. The human brain isn't prepared for what these platforms are delivering. And the mental health community isn't prepared for the aftermath. Nor do these apps have the proper tools or the scale to help the tens, even hundreds of thousands of Americans who find themselves in their grip."

James cleared his throat and took a sip of water.

"Last year, I presented EchoWave's roadmap at a conference in Orlando. Later that night, I returned home, expecting to embrace my wife. Instead, I found her lifeless in our bedroom. The strongest woman I ever knew. She never stood a chance. That's how dangerous these technologies were. Twelve months ago. And under the right circumstances, none of you stand a chance against them, either."

"This is absurd. I move to dismiss this witness immediately," said another senator loudly.

"The motion is denied. The witness will be heard," the chair responded.

James paused for dramatic effect he didn't know he possessed.

"The members of the Committee each should have two documents. One is the briefing I wrote on bereavement leave after my wife, Sara Hauser-Wohlmuth, took her own life. In it, I meticulously retrace her online behavior and how it was influenced by social media, search engines, and discussion forums, all of which leverage algorithms that I had a critical role in developing. Algorithms that I developed for an entirely different purpose.

"The second document is the *Executioner's Diary*, for which I apologize in advance for both its title and for the detailed and horrific nature of its contents.

"I returned to my offices at EchoWave after two weeks of bereavement leave. During that time, I meticulously documented and objectively concluded with precision and without question that my wife was, in fact, triggered into suicide after being inundated by harmful and negative content. Content which was recommended to those networks by EchoWave's algorithms.

"As a result of my findings, my company forced me to take an overseas sabbatical. I learned much later this was simply a plot to remove me from the process of making our algorithms better at detecting mental health crises and triggers. To discredit me if I ever attempted to come forward. And finally, to fire me for the categorically false accusation of violating my company's non-disclosure policy. As I have previously stated, and as the senator pointed out, I am one of the co-founders of EchoWave. I stood to make millions of dollars from the company's success after its IPO.

"Early in my time in Salzburg, a chance encounter with a restaurant proprietor revealed to me a man who lived and worked there over two hundred and sixty-three years ago. His name was Franz Joseph Wohlmuth. He was the last appointed executioner of Salzburg. He felt at a loss for injustices he witnessed in the system, so to speak, and felt helpless to make change in the face of very powerful forces.

"At his core, Franz Wohlmuth was a smart, thoughtful, good man who realized change would only come by exposing what he knew about the barbaric nature of his trade to the public. The pen was only effective through the story of the sword.

"A year ago, I saw myself as a smart, thoughtful, good man. My wife's demise and learning the story of Franz Wohlmuth made me realize change would only come by exposing the barbaric nature of this industry to the public. It is my hope that my pen will be effective through the story of the sword.

"Franz documented in detail two hundred sixty-two executions that were carried out under the orders of an opaque, inconsistent system of justice. About as opaque as all of these companies are with the technology that has the power to alter human behavior.

"Franz Wohlmuth's *Executioner's Diary* became the catalyst for change. It is my hope, once and for all, that this body and the regulatory agencies in both North America and the European Union will use my document, my *Executioner's Diary*, as a baseline for transparency, so that the American public can understand how these technologies are being used.

"With the exception of only one company—EchoWave, the company I co-founded—I do not wish for these companies to cease to exist or be driven out of business. Their ability to connect, inform, and build community is unprecedented in human history. The opaqueness of the algorithms they use to alter our behavior, isolate us, and misinform us is also unprecedented in human history.

"These documents, including my initial briefing, the supporting data that accompanied it, as well as the *Executioner's Diary* I compiled in Austria, should be vetted by experts in a number of disciplines, far outside the reach and checkbooks of industry interests. If and when they are, I believe they can serve as a catalyst for real change. If we as a society have the courage to examine, act on it, and enforce those policy decisions and actions, regardless of the economic cost.

"What if, senator, we, me, the industry, are just getting started? Because that's what's happening. The people you heard from yesterday, and everyone who works for them, are just getting started.

"I am here today to testify to you, members of the committee, that you simply cannot outsmart the executives representing the companies you have brought in front of you. All the time and effort spent in these hearings, which, might I remind you, have been taking place for a decade, has resulted in exactly zero positive impact on this life-or-death issue.

"And to the families of the two hundred sixty-two Americans who took their own lives under my supervision and influence, I do not ask for your forgiveness. I do not ask for sympathy. I do not ask for leniency. I fully assumed I would follow in my wife's footsteps as a casualty of what I created in the name of commerce. Your sons, daughters, sisters and brothers, friends, and loved ones followed the same path that thousands of others who remain nameless to me followed. For these two hundred sixty-two, my hope is that they are never forgotten and that their loss saves the lives of thousands of others."

James laid down the pages before him, took a sip of water, and looked down the camera.

"Kimberly Mitchell, age eighteen, Seattle, Washington.

Justin Taylor, age thirty-four, Las Vegas, Nevada.

Nicole Allen, age twenty-six, Westlake, Ohio.

Chase Richardson, age eighteen, Tiburon, California.

Heather Lopez, age twenty-two, Sioux Falls, SD."

"Did this man memorize the entire list of two hundred and sixty-two people in his diary?" one senator whispered to the senator sitting next to her.

"I think he did," the senator responded.

"Mr. Wohlmuth," the senator from South Carolina interrupted as the gavel fell again, "with all due respect, we're going to be here all damn day."

"The senator will refrain from interrupting the witness!"

"Would you prefer I not read aloud the next name?" James responded. "A name that happens to be a teenager from the state you represent?"

The senator stared deeply into the camera.

"Emma Clark: age nineteen, Union, South Carolina, which I believe is your hometown, senator."

"How dare you! Emma Clark was the daughter of an upstanding member of our community and a long-time patron of my political career. You're lucky you're not in this room, boy."

"I understand that, sir," James whispered into the microphone. "But she deserves to be memorialized. Because before she took her own life, she was searching online for ways to escape from a father who was molesting her."

The senator engaged in the sidebar conversation leaned over again to her colleague. "I think we let him finish reading the list out loud."

"Agreed. That was the evening lead on CNN."

James continued down the list as the gallery, the media, the congressional aides, and most of the senators in the room sobbed or openly wept.

After twenty minutes of reciting names, ages, and hometowns from all across the country, he came to the end of his memorized list.

"Laila Aziz, age nineteen, Basking Ridge, New Jersey.

Dylan Moore, age seventeen, Chippewa Falls, Wisconsin."

James lifted the photo he'd brought in of his wife.

"—and, finally, like everyone else in this Diary who left us too soon, my beloved wife, Sara Hauser-Wohlmuth, age thirty-four, Seattle, Washington."

The room was filled with sobbing legislators, witnesses, and media.

"Senators, I believe, with every fiber of my being, that if I had not recreated the *Executioner's Diary*—if I had not tracked, documented, and in many cases, yes, influenced the tragic final chapters of these individuals lives', each of whom was already under the spell of forces far more powerful than families, friends, churches, communities, and their governments, you would continue to call hearings, year after year, at the behest of your increasingly desperate constituencies."

He continued.

"However, you would be making absolutely no progress. And the mental health, self-harm, and suicide crises would continue, with some responsibility for those being triggered falling squarely on social media and search engine companies we celebrate as the bastions of innovation and entrepreneurship in the United States."

James paused for the last time.

"As I conclude my remarks, I wish to offer loving and lasting memory for all of those who should still be with us today. It is my deepest hope that my testimony and this Diary will be the catalyst for real change. Change in the business practices of these companies and how their platforms are designed. Change to adequately arm and inform the public around the dangers of these services so they can be used safely for all their benefits. And change to how mental health is diagnosed and treated in this country. It is time to end the stigma, end the finger-pointing, and put real resources behind this crisis that is largely of our own doing."

"I love you, now and forever, Sara Hauser-Wohlmuth."

# 42

*The Sara Hauser-Wohlmuth Digital Transparency Act* narrowly passed both houses of Congress and was signed into law several months later.

Sara's mother, Patricia, her two sisters, several friends, and members of digital rights advocacy organizations, were gathered in the Map Room of the White House, symbolizing the charting of a path forward.

After the signing of the bill, the President stood and turned to Patricia, placing the pen in her hand while whispering in her ear.

"I'm so sorry for the loss of your daughter. Please accept this memento in her memory. In our digital-first world, may we never forget the power of the pen."

After pausing for a moment, the President turned toward the group of reporters, "I believe we have time for a few questions. Julie Frager, please, what is your question?"

"Thank you," Julie began, clearing her throat, suddenly dry given the opportunity to directly question the most powerful person in the world.

She regained her composure and continued.

"In the vast complexity of computer systems and networks of American and foreign governments and law enforcement, what information tied directly to my identity are you collecting, processing, storing, and sharing—specifically?"

"Ms. Frager, while this bill is comprehensive, and while I wouldn't want to—," the President began before glancing at the Press Secretary a few feet away.

"Julie, the President believes your question deserves a more detailed answer," the Press Secretary quickly interjected. "Why don't we continue this conversation at the conclusion of the signing ceremony and keep the focus on the Sara Hauser-Wohlmuth Digital Transparency Act and the lives it will save?"

The law included sweeping new requirements for social media and search engine companies. Any algorithms used to influence users based on their activity would be prominently disclosed. New disclosures would allow users to easily click on maps that showed how and to which companies their personal information traveled, enabling them to turn on or off the flow of sharing to any or all external companies with one click. Social networks were required to add optional daily and weekly usage timers to the top bars of their apps.

Similarly to how many modern car companies now have systems to detect driver fatigue, social media apps would now be required to alert users if users began signaling heavy consumption of at-risk content, or were showing signs of mental health fatigue.

The legislation also imposed strict penalties for parents of children under the age of thirteen years, if their children were found to have installed or were using social media apps, similar to laws already in place in the European Union.

State governments were given funding to create networks of mental health providers, who could be accessed directly within social media apps. Oversight and compliance would occur through independent audits and strict regulatory oversight.

Upon enactment of the legislation, EchoWave immediately saw their market value plummet, and declared bankruptcy in the following months.

# 43

James sat in a holding cell at the Salzburg Justice Center, in a building now standing at the south end of the old town. The building where, for fifteen years, Samuel Wohlmuth fought for the dignity and rights of the accused. Including the rights of sixteen-year-old Maria Pauer, who spent the final year of her young life in a small basement, relentlessly interrogated and tortured until she finally, falsely confessed to witchcraft and was sentenced to public beheading and burning at the stake.

In a room that could have been just feet away from where the young girl slept and wept, James told prosecutors he had no idea Vik would show up at the tiny cottage on the grounds of the stonemason's that day. He had forgotten about the bag of cables Vik had casually thrown at him that morning in Orlando. But once he was in the cottage, James connected the reality of the diary to Vik.

"Maybe I had purposefully caused Vik Gruber to trip and hit his head," James said to the prosecutors, through his attorneys and a German translator. "After all, look at the document I was showing him right before his death. It was a diary of two hundred sixty-two suicides I tracked and may have influenced."

With the appearance of a confession and no request for leniency, James was charged with *Mord*—murder in the second degree.

Against the behest of his attorneys, James neither confessed nor did he testify on his own behalf. The trial was short, and a jury of eight *Geschworenen* handed down a guilty verdict on all charges, with a recommended sentence of life in prison. The three *Schöffengericht* judges concurred with the recommendation.

James Wohlmuth was sentenced to serve the rest of his life in a high-security prison outside Leoben, Austria.

* * *

After the trial concluded, James was transferred out of his temporary cell in Salzburg. An unmarked van and escort vehicles pulled away from the justice center and began their journey south, along the Salzach river toward Leoben. The same path, he realized, Franz walked to Bad Hofgastein to confront his grandfather. As the convoy passed through the modern tunnels cutting through the Alps, James looked out the window at the trees and the water and the birds Franz would have observed, which James only witnessed in dreams. He imagined the dense forests and the deep hills and valleys Franz must have navigated. On his journey to make change.

The van pulled up to the correctional facility without fanfare, entering through winding gates. The convoy stopped twice so that police mirrors and dogs could examine all sides of the van and its contents.

Today, the facility would be processing James Wohlmuth.

The Salzburg Executioner.

Two hours after his arrival, James was led to his cell. He sat his duffel bag of assigned clothes, toiletries, and footwear on the floor and took a moment to notice the walls and the ceiling: clean, white and textured. In a translucent paper envelope, James removed his original briefing, a bound photocopy of his Executioner's Diary, and a photo of his wife.

"*Wie geht's dir?*" James's cellmate asked as the door closed and locked behind him.

"*Alles gut, und sie?*" James responded, pleased the man appeared reasonable and nonviolent.

A few moments later the cellmate asked, in German, "So what are you in for?"

"I killed a man in Salzburg. Someone I knew and once trusted. But my real crime was allowing thousands more to die at the hands of a dangerous weapon I invented."

The inmate, staring at James for a moment as he slowly stood from a small stool in the cell, finally blinked.

"You can have the top bunk," the man replied.

"*Danke*. Maybe we switch every so often," James responded, as he glanced out the barred window toward the soccer field and basketball courts on the grounds outside.

"Every afternoon, even in winter. Two hours for football, assuming you play," the man said.

James nodded in approval, although he wished there was a softball diamond.


"I should clarify about the man in Austria. He tripped and hit his head on the corner of my counter, killing himself instantly."

"You took the fall for this guy's death?" the convict asked.

"I'm not sure if it was me that took the fall or—"

"Herr Wohlmuth," a warden exclaimed, standing outside the white door of the cell.

"Yes? I'm James Wohlmuth."

"A package for you," the warden said, setting the items on the slot in the door, waiting for James to walk up and accept them. He reached through the slot, just large enough to fit a tray of food, clean sheets, or other small objects.

"My first mail," James said to his cellmate, waving the letter.

James sat at the small table in the cell, bolted to the floor, and removed the contents of the envelope, each stamped with various red and black markings, approved by attorneys and prosecutors. Inside was a letter and several pages sent from Patricia Hauser, his mother-in-law.

The first was a news article from a tech industry website in Seattle. The headline read:

### Disgraced Tech CEO Found Dead in Apparent Suicide
*Ousted Chairman/CEO of EchoWave Faced Fifteen Counts of Conspiracy,*

*Fraud, and Perjury in Federal Court after Damning Congressional Testimony
and Nasdaq Delisting*
**By Julie Frager**

After reading the article twice, he thought back to his first text to Julie, and the night he received the termination documents in his email.

"It took Franz Joseph Wohlmuth two hundred sixty-two executions to initiate the course of change," he muttered out loud. "It took me two hundred sixty-three."

Before he read the other pages, he opened his Executioner's Diary, turned to the page just before the back cover, and inserted the article about Michael.

"The last one was for you, love."

The next page was a letter, handwritten by Patricia. James took the letter, the book, and the other pages, ascending the ladder to the top bunk. Once lying as comfortably as he could on a prison mattress, he read it.

*James—*

*Sara placed this letter and book in the mail on the day of her passing. I received them before the funeral, but didn't read the letter until after you flew back to Seattle. I thought about it for weeks, wondering when I should share them with you. By the time I'd decided to send them to you, you'd left for Salzburg.*

*It has taken me a long time to even think about recovering from the loss of my daughter. I will never fully. I can only imagine what this time has done to you. Whatever you think of me, always know: I raised my daughters to be brave-hearted, powerful, and determined.*

*Dieter came clean. His firm was the last investment in EchoWave prior to the company going public. They got their money. But I will never have my daughter back.*

*When your briefing finally went public, I realized it was greed that took my daughter from me. Not you.*

*Sara chose a good man, son. I'm proud of you. And I'm proud of her – for finding you.*

*Patricia*

James wiped away tears streaming down each side of his face. It was the first time he could remember crying since Sara's funeral. He laid the book and the letter from his mother-in-law on his chest, jolting somewhat as he looked at the next page, a letter written in Sara's handwriting. It read:

*My Mother—*

*Years ago, on a family trip we took to Europe for one of my birthdays, you gave me a book of poems. All were written by incredible European women. I always kept the book close at hand when I needed strength or a reminder of purpose.*

*You highlighted one poem in the book before giving it to me. Written by a young Swede, centuries ago. I have read it a thousand times. It always comforted me and gave me strength even as I decided to resign from my role in this world.*

*"To a Mighty Duchess*
*Your feminine nature, your power,*
*To command, praise, and write about,*
*Can delight the brave-hearted,*
*And dedicate themselves to your fame.*
*As wise as strong, and, above all,*
*In high virtues,*
*Provide protection to the valiant people*
*From the heart of a mother."*

*While you may never understand why, I want you to know: I am brave-hearted. I am powerful. I am determined. And I love you.*

*I was never royalty, mom. I took what I learned from you and daddy, and was never afraid to do what needed to be done to make a difference. I hope James knows that, too.*

*Always,*

*~ S ~*


Two hundred sixty-three years after Franz Joseph Wohlmuth began penning his diary to forever change how justice was delivered, James placed the book of poems and the letter from his beloved wife on his chest, next to his heart. He closed his eyes.

And fell asleep.

# Mental Health Resources

If you or someone you know is struggling, please reach out to a mental health
professional or one of the resources listed below for support.

**UNITED STATES OF AMERICA**
National Suicide Prevention Lifeline
Phone: 988
Website: 988lifeline.org
**Crisis Text Line**
Text: Text HELLO to 741741
Website: crisistextline.org
**National Alliance on Mental Illness (NAMI)**
Phone: 1-800-950-NAMI (6264)
Website: nami.org

**CANADA**
**Canada Suicide Prevention Service**
Phone: 1-833-456-4566 (toll-free)
Text: 45645 (available 4 pm–12 am ET)
Website: crisisservicescanada.ca
**Kids Help Phone**
Phone/Text: 1-800-668-6868 or text CONNECT to 686868
Website: kidshelpphone.ca
**Mental Health Helplines**
Hope for Wellness Helpline: 1-866-585-0445

Website: mhww.ca

## EUROPEAN UNION AND UNITED KINGDOM
*Please note that resources vary by country. Below are some key resources for select European countries.*

**United Kingdom**
Samaritans
Phone: 116 123 (free to call)
Website: samaritans.org

**Austria**
Telefonseelsorge Österreich
Phone: 142 (available 24/7)
Website: telefonseelsorge.at

**France**
SOS Suicide
Phone: 01 45 39 40 00
Website: sos-suicide.org

**Germany**
Telefonseelsorge
Phone: 0800-1110111 or 0800-1110222
Website: telefonseelsorge.de

**Italy**
Telefono Amico
Phone: 199 284 284
Website: telefonoamico.it

**Netherlands**
113 Suicide Prevention
Phone: 113
Website: 113.nl

**Spain**
Teléfono de la Esperanza
Phone: 914 590 055
Website: telefonodelaesperanza.org

**Switzerland**
Dargebotene Hand (The Outstretched Hand)
Phone: 143 (available 24/7)
Website: dargebotene-hand.ch

**Other resources in the European Union**
**International Association for Suicide Prevention (IASP)**
Website: iasp.info/resources/Crisis_Centres/
**World Health Organization (WHO) Mental Health**
Website: who.int/health-topics/mental-health
**European Alliance Against Depression (EAAD)**
Website: eaad.eu

# Acknowledgements

This work would not have been possible without the support and countless hours of feedback, guidance and encouragement from many people, including Debbie Liebold, who helped immensely with the early drafts; Glenn Hauser, whose lifelong friendship and words helped me overcome imposter syndrome in my transition from entrepreneur to writer; and Bryan Phillips and Scott Murphy, always encouraging and advocating for me.

To Julie Walton, for the honest, raw feedback offered at almost every step of the process. And for your candor, ensuring the more difficult topics were conveyed accurately, with grace and empathy.

To Delilah Necrason, who has served as my Renaissance generalist and right-hand for the last few years. Always stepping up, cracking the whip, and finding answers, even when it isn't easy.

To Jill McMahon, LPC, for the friendship, encouragement, and coaching that appeared, often eerily, at the moment it was most needed. And for your expertise, ensuring this work put mental health awareness front and center.

To my proofreader, Vanessa Macfarlane, the very definition of grace under pressure, and my editor, Zoe Fishman.

To my intellectual and emotional stimulus partners: James Owen, John Cook, Matt Crenshaw, Jason Moriber, Steve Hane, Ralph Fascitelli, and Georg Blanckenstein. My life is far richer, far more interesting, with each of you in it.

And, of course, my deepest, eternal gratitude to my family.

# About the Author

Prior to becoming a full-time novelist, observer, and technology skeptic, L.A. spent his career as a technology entrepreneur, CEO, and investor, having founded more than ten software and services companies. Most of the companies were focused on the areas of social media, big data, and artificial intelligence.

During his tech and business career, L.A. has been featured in Inc. Magazine, Forbes, PR Week, Seattle Business Journal, Denver Business Journal, The Seattle Times, and other publications where entrepreneurs like to see their names when building companies.

L.A. grew up in Littleton, Colorado, at a time when tumbleweeds would occasionally roll up in the driveway and Habitrails could be tunneled through drifts of snow.

He lives in Salzburg, Austria.

The Salzburg Executioner (2024) is his first novel.